So Great a Man

The Ploughboy

Robert Scott

with

Lucy Skoulding

First published 2018
Published by GB Publishing.org

Copyright © 2018 Robert Scott and Lucy Skoulding
All rights reserved
ISBN: 978-1-912031-82-5 (hardback)
978-1-912031-91-7 (paperback)
978-1-912031-90-0 (eBook)
978-1-912031-89-4 (Kindle)

Cover Design © 2018 Articulate Creative Design
Illustrations by Julia Von Behren, Robert Scott and Articulate Creative Design

CBP

GB Publishing.org
www.gbpublishing.co.uk

1791-1817

In the beginning...

The story spans more than 200 years in the life of a family; its ups and downs, from rags to riches, and back to rags. In this case it takes place over more than 3 generations, and has been set back in time.

The idea for this story came from family history research. There was indeed a little ploughboy who ran away from picking up stones in furrows on a large Border's estate to find a better life in England. He never did reach London or amass great wealth. His name was Robert Scott.

This book is dedicated to that little ploughboy and his courage in escaping servitude.

Rest in Peace.

Robert Scott is a nom de plume for a now retired member of the medical profession. His great-grandfather was that ploughboy whose real escape was 40 years later than that of our first hero.

Lucy Skoulding is a graduate in English of the University of Warwick., She works as an editor, author and freelance journalist

CONTENTS

ILLUSTRATIONS

The Plough Boy

A flaxen-headed cow-boy,
As simple as may be,
And next a merry plough-boy,
I whistle o'er the lea;
But now a saucy footman,
I strut in worsted lace,
And soon I'll be a butler,
And wag my jolly face.

When steward I'm promoted,
I'll snip a tradesman's bill,
My master's coffers empty,
My coffers for to fill.
When lolling in my chariot,
So great a man I'll be
You'll forget the little plough-boy
That whistled o'er the lea.

I'll buy votes at elections,
But when I've made the pelf,
I'll stand poll for the parliament,
And then vote in myself.
Whatever's good for me, sir,
I never will oppose,
When all my ayes are sold off,
Why then I'll sell my noes.

I'll joke harangue and paragraph,
With speeches charm the ear,
And when I'm tired on my legs,
Then I'll sit down a peer.
In courts or city honour,
So great a man I'll be
You'll forget the little ploughboy,
That whistled o'er the lea.

List of Characters

Iain, 2nd Earl of Brackenholm A well liked progressive farmer, keen to improve yields and look after his workers. Lives well and likes hunting. A man of his times.

Countess of Brackenholm Runs the household well and has greater social ambitions than her husband. Spoils her only child, a son.

John, 3rd Earl of Brackenholm A spoiled wastrel, not interested in the land unlike his father. Likes gambling and is always looking for more money. He never marries.

Mr Muir Tutor to the future 3rd Earl

Robert Neal Senior, ploughman to the Earl of Brackenholm husband of

Annie Neal Robert's wife and mother of his four children.

William Neal Son of Robert, a ploughboy who escapes his life of servitude.

Mr Robertson Church of Scotland Minister at Brackenholm

Elizabeth Robertson His wife

Mrs McPherson Brackenholm's midwife

Mr Dunbar The 3rd Earl's stonemason and builder

Jeremiah Barnes A bargee

The Sergeant A lock keeper

Joseph The Corporal, another bargee

Billy Bow A wizard with playing cards and a prestidigitator

William Neal His namesake, a London banker

Annabel Neal Wife of William the banker, a martinet

Brampton Coachman to William Neal the banker.

Reid Butler to William Neal the banker

Charlotte Neal Daughter of William and Annabel Neal

Mary her lady's maid

Jonathan Neal Son of William and Annabel Neal

Young Reid Footman then Butler to William and Charlotte

Mrs Fenwick A landlady

George Fenwick, A printer, husband of Mrs Fenwick
John Trevelyan A non-conformist Minister
The Sergeant and his men Wounded British soldiers

The Neal Family Tree

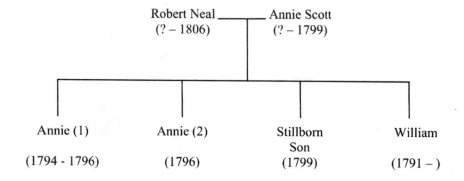

Robert Neal ———— Annie Scott
(? – 1806)   (? – 1799)

Annie (1)   Annie (2)   Stillborn   William
                                  Son
(1794 - 1796)   (1796)   (1799)   (1791 –)

PART 1 – THE PLOUGHBOY

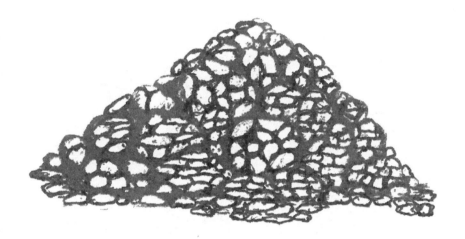

1

'Courage is rightly esteemed the first of human qualities... because it is the quality which guarantees all others'
Sir Winston Churchill

It was a raw December day in Nottingham in the Year of our Lord 1894. The wind was blowing from the north and the skies were thick and dark with the prospect of a heavy snowfall before morning. Would there be a white Christmas? Robert Neal hoped so as he stepped into the hallway of his house. There was a coal fire blazing away and the room was quite warm. As he removed his coat, hat and gloves, one of the maidservants, a pretty young girl called Rosie, stepped forward, made a bob, and said 'I'll take those for you sir. Welcome home'. Then she turned away and went through a door towards the rear of the house carrying his clothes with her. There, she hung them to dry and air ready for early the next morning when her employer would be leaving for work. She hoped the coachman would be up early too. If it snowed, he would need more time to drive his master to work so the horses would not slip on the road. The harnesses would be stiff in the cold and harder to buckle up. She must also make sure that there was at least one blanket, warmed in front of another fire in the servant's quarters, to wrap round her master. It would never do if he caught cold as he had very important work to do in the city each day, and she intended to look after him properly.

As was his habit, Robert stepped towards the fire to rub his hands in front of the glowing embers and looked up to the large portrait above the mantelshelf. This picture did not hang on a hook, but was firmly screwed to the wall in a show of permanency. As he did each morning and evening when he left his house or came home, he bowed his head ever so slightly towards the old gentleman pictured there and whispered to himself, "thank you grandfather for all you have given me. God bless you".

The portrait was quite old and had become somewhat discoloured by the smoke from the fire below where it hung. It was possible to make out a handsome man in his late sixties wearing the smart dark green coat he always wore. He had wondered why his grandfather chose to wear this colour for a long time before finally daring to ask about it. His grandfather's reply had simply been 'it's a very long story' and he smiled slightly as he said it.

There was a smile on his face below brilliant blue eyes with the hint of creases at their corners. Here was a man who had done well for himself. But why his grandfather had agreed to sit to have his portrait painted by one of the most expensive and fashionable artists of the day in London was intriguing. It was quite unlike the man who had always been careful with his money. His wife had passed away some years before, so it could not have been painted to please her. Perhaps a new lady had come into his life whom he wished to impress. It was a mystery, although the family could speculate as to why. Robert had the portrait and intended to keep it. It was his most treasured possession, despite the fact that here were many other fine things in his home. Perhaps there were too many, but that was the way of Victorian Britain and he always wanted to please his wife, who he loved dearly, when she suggested purchases to enhance their home.

He made his way through a door leading off the hallway into his study. There was another fire here to keep him warm, with a comfortable armchair to sink into and relax after his day's work. As he looked around at all the books lining the shelves he let his eyes close. He was too tired to read at the moment, and so he fell into a gentle sleep before he would have to get up and dress for dinner. As he dozed off, he wondered what had his grandfather done to have made so much money?

2

The Ploughboy

You forget the little ploughboy who whistled o'er the lea...
so great a man, so great a man, so great a man I'll be.

The ruts in the dirt track were filled with ice, making walking to the bothy at the end even more difficult than normal. At least it was slightly easier than after the rains, when the track turned to a clinging clay mud. It was cold and the harsh northern wind suggested it would get colder than usual on this March Sunday. Robert Neal sat outside and sheltered in the lee of the wind. He was a big man with muscles made firm from work in the field as a ploughman to the Earls of Brackenholm in the Scottish Borders, just as his father and grandfather had been before him. He believed it was God's Will that he held this lowly station in life. His 3-year-old son, William, sat on his lap. Robert pulled him closer to his chest and did his best to wrap him in the meagre clothing he had to keep him warm. It was better than nothing, but both man and boy shivered and kept their vigil. Neither knew how long they would have to wait, so wait they did.

Earlier in the day William had walked with his mother, Annie, and his father into the village they called home to attend divine service at the Kirk. They did this every Sunday, or the Sabbath as they called that day. It was expected. His lordship had made it known for many years that he expected his estate workers to attend the Kirk every Sabbath, just as he and his family did whenever they were in residence in their big house at Brackenholm. His lordship was always the last to arrive. He required his workers and their families to stand as he entered, and touch their hands to their foreheads as a mark of respect as he walked past each row of pews right to the front where he and any guests who were staying with him always sat.

As he sat down, a tall thin man standing at the front and wearing a long black Geneva robe nodded his head ever so slightly to the last member of his congregation to arrive. He waited until that man gave a slight nod of his head in return. That was the sign that he could start the service and call the people to worship God. He raised his right hand and spoke in a firm voice so that everyone could hear.

9

William was always confused as to why the Minister referred to God as our Father. What did they mean and why did everyone have to say them? His father sat next to him and his mother on the other side. But he knew he had to keep silent inside. It would be another few years before he would understand the significance of the Minister's words.

On that Sabbath the service followed its usual form. At one stage the man in the black robe spoke 'Hear the Word of the Lord'. Yet his Lordship had not spoken and had listened to every word the man in black had said. He had spoken for precisely 30 minutes, the amount of time that his Lordship had stipulated a decent sermon should last. 'Not too short so that my people understand the message, but not too long to keep me from my home and my day of rest.'

Towards the end of the sermon, Annie broke the golden rule that all must remain silent while the Minister explained the Word of God, and whispered in her husband's ear 'I think it's time.'

Robert knew exactly what she meant. The wait for his next child and his wife's pregnancy had come to an end. He found her hand and gave it a gentle squeeze of support so Annie knew that Robert understood what was going to happen later that day.

After the congregation left the Kirk at the end of the service, Robert looked for and found one of the important ladies of their small community, Mrs McPherson. This was the woman who knew about childbirth and helped her fellow villagers bring their children into the world. In former times, she might have been called a witch, and in later times would be called a midwife. No matter what her name, she was the person Robert needed now.

'Annie's started and needs your help please' was all Robert had to say.

'I'll get my things and be along shortly. You take her home and lie her down and make sure there is the best fire you can make going in the hearth just as when your little Willie was born' she instructed.

So, Robert found his wife and son, and the family walked carefully back to their meagre home. Robert placed his wife down gently on the dry straw he had been saving for this day. He told Willie to stay with his mother while he gathered the dry sticks and wood that would be needed to start the fire. He found the flint and steel so carefully stored in a little leather pouch that when rubbed together would make that vital spark to ignite the dry materials he had so lovingly kept for this day.

After a few strikes of steel on flint the sparks worked, and his fire began to catch. Soon he had a good blaze in the hearth, and slowly the single room that was their home began to get warmer. He placed the small amount of straw he had on the hard earth floor. It was not much, but it was better than nothing.

It was just as well, because Mrs McPherson arrived soon afterwards carrying a bag of her things.

'Right Robert Neal, this is a woman's work, so out you both go and you are not to come back until I call for you.'

So Robert and his son left the warmth of their bothy and sat outside until they were allowed back.

* * *

Mrs McPherson set to work. She asked Annie if her waters had broken yet, but they had not. This meant that she would be there for quite some time so the two women sat and talked together. Their chatter was interrupted from time to time by Annie's cries of pain as her contractions became more frequent, until with a sudden great sigh her waters burst onto the straw bed her husband Robert had so carefully prepared for her. Then, as the cries of pain became more frequent, Mrs McPherson saw what was happening and gave words of encouragement until the top of a little head appeared in the birth canal. It would not be long now she hoped, as she uttered the time-honoured midwife's words to her patients to push hard with each contraction.

The cries became louder and more frequent until, quite suddenly, they stopped as the new arrival came into the world. A smacked bottom later, different sounds filled the small room that made up the family's house to signal the first cries of the newborn infant.

* * *

As they sat and shivered outside, cries of pain came at increasingly frequent intervals from inside. With each cry, Robert gave his son a hug which helped him relieve his own pain as his wife cried out during her time in labour. Suddenly the cries of pain stopped and there came a much sharper cry, that of a baby.

Soon afterwards Mrs McPherson found the menfolk and said. 'You are a lucky man Robert Neal. You have a fine baby daughter and your wife is fine too. What will you call the new bairn?'

Robert thought for a moment and decided he would call her Annie after his wife so he just mumbled a reply 'Annie.'

11

When they entered the bothy they found both of the Annies. The older Annie was asleep after her exertions giving birth while the younger Annie lay wrapped up also sleeping in her mother's arm.

Robert gave up a silent prayer of thanks for their safe deliverance as he showed his son the new addition to their little family.

* * *

During the months of spring and summer the little family prospered as well as they could in such harsh surroundings. Robert worked in the fields for the Earl for long hours each day and in the small patch of land beside his home, where, thanks to his master's generosity, he was able to grow some food to supplement their staple diet of oats and porridge.

The Earl was the second man to hold that title. His family had owned land in the Borders for more years than anyone could remember. More had come into their possession following the 1745 rising. His father had been granted the earldom in recognition of the support he had given to the English during those turbulent times. That was of little concern to Robert now. He had his work, his home, his wife and his growing family. That was what mattered as he laboured in the fields to provide for them, just as his ancestors had. 'We are the ploughmen to the Earl' his father had taught him, and 'that is our station in life. It's God's Will for us.'

* * *

The Earl had also been well taught by his father and the senior men employed on the estate, that their wealth and easy lifestyle was bought on the backs of their workers and he should never forget that. He understood the cycles of nature and the way the seasons changed. There would be good years and bad. Sometimes harvests could be gathered early while others could be delayed by summer rains. He wished he could predict what each year would bring but that lay far into the future. He was a landsman through and through, and that was his station in life.

He had also learned to give back to his estate workers something to help them through the winter when times could be so hard. After the harvest had been gathered in and stored in his barns, his workers were granted the right of gleaning. They could go to a field and gather up any straw that had been missed by the reapers and any ears of corn or oats for their own use. In practice about 5 per cent of the crop was collected by gleaning. It was better

12

his workers had this little benefit than the rooks and crows that nested noisily around the fields and were all too ready to accept this bounty.

The Earl was also a clever man who understood human nature. He was aware that if he allowed one family to always glean the same field, they would be tempted to be less careful with his harvest and leave more of the crop behind. He made sure that none of his workers were ever given the same field to glean for more than one year together. He hoped this would keep them on their toes.

He also knew that families in the village may choose to help each other, so that the poorer were helped by the richer, although in these hard times such terms were relative. If the families chose to share, thought the Earl, that was up to them. He had other things on his mind. He liked to fox hunt and was Master of his very own pack of hounds. He liked to ride around his estate to see what was happening. He liked to read about how he could improve his land, and frequently put forward suggestions for better ways of working to his Steward and senior people.

He was an enlightened and progressive man of his times. He wished his son showed more interest in the estate, but he was young and there was plenty of time yet to teach him Nature's ways.

3

The months passed since the arrival of little Annie. The late summer harvest turned into autumn gold as the leaves turned colour and fell to the ground. There was no ploughing. That was a spring job, so Robert was sent to help repair fences and rebuild walls. Gradually the days grew shorter, and the time for work between sunrise and sunset grew less. The days were colder, and snow could fall at any time. Fortunately, this year there was no snow on the ground as the four members of the Neal family made their way to the Kirk for the Christmas Day service.

The Minister, Mr Robertson, welcomed them all as usual. On this day, his sermon went on and on and exceeded the 30 minutes the Earl required. As Mr Robertson continued to preach, the Kirk became colder as the day wore on. His congregation shivered, until as if by some miracle, just like Jesus' birth, the final blessing was given when all could leave.

Robert Neal's family were cold too. During the service, little Annie had been whimpering softly into her mother's bosom. She had become colder than the family had realised.

* * *

Normally little Annie was a very placid child. However, in the few days from Christmas to Hogmanay she was slightly restless and a bit off colour. Neither of her parents were worried and thought it was just one of those things that happened during childhood.

Hogmanay was a special day at the estate. The Earl gave his workers an extra day off. In truth, the ground was often so hard and frozen real work was difficult. On this day, all workers and their families were required to attend the Great House, but naturally at the servant's entrance rather than the front entrance for the 'quality' as members of the local gentry were known.

At the servant's door, the Earl had arranged for each family to receive a parcel of meat. He knew this was a great luxury for them, although he ate meat and often meat aplenty for most days of the week.

Annie Neal planned to use this meat to make a big bowl of stew. She knew it would feed her family for nearly a week and little Annie would have the nourishing stew liquid to sustain her. But why was little Annie refusing this food, and why did she have a slight cough that was getting worse until she coughed for most of her waking hours? She had started to develop a fever too, and then her neck started to swell. She became desperately ill. Despite the cuddles close to both father and mother, and her father's prayers for her recovery, she died on the Feast of the Epiphany. Diphtheria had taken her life.

All her father would say was 'it's God's Will for us' or 'it's our station in life.' He knew he should grieve, but in those times death in childhood was a frequent occurrence and he had his work to do so he could feed his little family. His daughter was wrapped in a cloth and buried in a pauper's grave in the cemetery next to the Kirk.

Mother Annie grieved inwardly for her loss, but remained silent. She dare not raise the matter with her husband Robert. His answer was always the same 'it's God's Will.' She also knew she was just pregnant again, so perhaps the Almighty had a healthier daughter in His infinite wisdom for her.

* * *

Winter turned into spring, then summer. As the seasons changed so Annie Neal's belly got bigger until by July she was ready to give birth. It was hot this year, and this was making her so much more tired than the times when she had carried William or Annie. She rested as best she could until her time came, the contractions started, and another call was made for Mrs McPherson. Once again, the men were sent outside, and at least at this time of year it was not cold, and any wind that blew relieved, rather than exacerbated the weather conditions.

On this occasion, Annie's cries of labour pains lasted for less time than before. As often happens with the second and subsequent births, labour is shorter and so it proved here, until, at last the cry of a new born baby taking its first breath was heard.

All was not well. Mrs McPherson did not understand the massive changes that occur when a baby takes its first breath; its lungs expand, the heart changes position slightly, and an embryonic blood vessel called the ductus arteriosus rotates to shut off the former, embryonic, blood flow pathway. She did know however that a baby should have a healthy pink skin colour soon after its arrival into the world. This baby had a bluish colour, something she had not seen in all her years as a midwife, and she was worried. Like all good practitioners of the medical arts she did not let her worries show to Annie the mother or Robert the father.

When she saw Robert, she said 'you have another baby daughter. Your wife is very tired despite it being a quicker birth than before. By the way, your new daughter's skin has a slightly darker colour. I think it's because the birth was quite quick and it should pass within a few days.'

So Robert rushed in to find his wife and new baby daughter closely followed by little William. He had already decided that he would call her Annie too out of love for his wife and the little daughter he had lost so tragically earlier that fateful year.

But new little Annie's colour did not change and if anything it had got slightly darker than when she was born. She was not feeding well from her mother's breasts despite there being ample milk, so much so that mother Annie had to express the excess to relieve her own discomfort from the engorged appendages on her chest. When little Annie tried to suckle she could only do so for a very short time, and became bluer in colour during these natural exertions.

* * *

Robert knew in his soul that something was wrong with his new daughter. His prayers for her were not being answered and she seemed to be weaker by the day. He knew what he must do and with a heavy heart made his way the servant's door of the Minister Mr Robertson. He knocked loudly on the door and with a heavy heart waited for a reply. To his surprise the door was opened by Mr Robertson's wife, Elizabeth. Robert removed his cap and knuckled his forehead to show his respect for one of his betters.

He asked 'is the Minister in please ma'am?'

'No' was the reply 'but can I help you? Do come in and tell me what my husband can do for you.'

So Robert went into the house and stood still on the stone floor. He was wringing his cap in his hand partly in despair, partly in nervousness, and partly in fear. With a hushed and hesitant voice he explained 'it's my little new bairn Annie. She's not well and I think she'll pass to God's Kingdom soon. I need to have her baptised please as I could not live with the thought that her soul will be damned to hell if I fail in my duty as a father to her.'

'You poor man. To think that might happen to your family. I'll tell the Minister as soon as he comes home. I know he will want to help you' said Elizabeth.

Then Robert left to go back to the fields where he hoped his absence had not been missed.

* * *

He was in luck. On this day, a Friday, his absence had not been missed, and shortly after he had left the Minister's house Mr Robertson returned home. He had been out riding with the Earl who had been discussing the arrangements he had in mind for the Harvest Festival service in September. Mr Robertson owed his living to the Earl's patronage, so everything the Earl wanted he knew he had to agree, unless there was a strong theological argument he could muster against the man. He never succeeded as the Earl had not only read and knew his Bible, but was a sensible, practical man of the soil, who rarely, if ever, would ask for something he had not thought through, unless it was something his wife had demanded. And there could be the difficulty.

Mr Robertson's horse, a mare, trotted up the drive to her master's front door where he dismounted and stroked her nose while he waited for his groom. She whinnied back in pleasure at her master's touch. When the groom arrived to take her back to the stables, she tossed her head once in anger at the intrusion, then dutifully followed him to the stables where she would be unsaddled, wiped down, then l`given a bundle of hay as a reward for her day's work.

Meanwhile Mr Robertson opened his front door and entered his hallway only to find his wife waiting for him. She had heard the clop of the mare's hooves on the driveway as she carried her master home. Robert Neal's business was important because it involved a child's immortal soul and she knew her husband would want to ensure its salvation.

The Minister would never forget her words. 'Husband, I fear for the soul of a little girl. Her father Robert Neal, one of the Earl's ploughmen, has been to see me not an hour ago. His new bairn is not well and he thinks she may die before she can be baptised into God's kingdom. What can you do?'

If his wife feared for the soul of a little girl, devout Christian that she was, then this was an important and possibly urgent matter. He would have to think of a solution to this problem without delay.

While it was possible under the rules of his Church, for a minister to baptise a sick child at home, this was not his way. He believed that the only place for a baptism to be valid was when it took place under the consecrated hallows of a Kirk. He disliked the thought of trudging down a track to a dirty bothy to carry out God's Will. Then he knew he had the answer.

He replied 'Elizabeth my dear, thank you for telling me that. I agree that no child should slip into eternity without being baptised. We must arrange for this as soon as possible. Today is Friday and it is quite late, and tomorrow Neal will be working in the Earl's fields. I think I should arrange the baptism for our next Sabbath. I'll send our groom to tell them that is what will happen. They can come to my Kirk early when we can finalise the arrangements. Now I think we should pray for the wee lass.'

And so they both sank to their knees to pray for Annie. It was only much later that their servant was sent to give that message to Robert and his family.

Their groom was not pleased at being given yet another job, but he valued his position and had no alternative than to follow his master's instructions. He arrived at the Neal's bothy just as Robert had returned from the fields and dusk was falling. His message was simple and short 'the Minister says if you will come early to the Kirk on the next Sabbath he will see you and baptise your bairn during the Service'. With that, he turned on his heels and walked back down the long lane back to the village. It would be dark before he reached his room over the stable. He was not pleased. He could have been sent at least 2 hours earlier than he was. He wondered why the Minister thought prayer was more important than action, but then he had never been trained as a Minister of Religion in the traditions of Calvin and Knox.

Robert and Annie took in that news with both shock at the bluntness of the message, pleasure that the Minister had heeded their call for an early baptism and fear for their daughter's life. They knew that they had to obey. That was their station in life. They were little more than serfs, although that had been abolished years before. Theirs was a life of servitude to the Earl, and they knew their place as their forebears had done for generations past.

* * *

The Sabbath came. Little Annie seemed weaker not stronger despite the Robertson's prayers. So the Neal's arrived early at the door of the Kirk as Mr Robertson had asked. He and his wife were waiting at the door. His first question was 'and so, Robert Neal, what will you call this new bairn of yours'. The answer was Annie. His second question was 'and who are the godparents?' The reply set him back 'we have none'. 'You need one godfather and two godmothers as you are presenting a girl to be baptised', insisted the Minister who was beginning to get quite irate at this particular problem. He was even more surprised when the next person to speak was his dear wife 'husband, I will stand as one of the godmothers'. Then 'if I remember the teaching of the Church correctly, in exceptional circumstances the parents can also be godparents. Is that not so?'

By now Mr Robertson had caught a glance of little Annie wrapped up in her mother's shawl. She did look blue and he feared for her life. He did not want to have his conscience troubled that he had refused to baptise an infant who then died soon afterwards. Neither did he want to fall foul of the laws of the Kirk but special circumstances are special circumstances and, if necessary, he would call on the Earl to support his decision. After all, the Earl's word was law in these parts. He paused, held his right hand up as if in benediction, and said 'in the Name of the Father I declare that these are special circumstances and that I will baptise this child into God's Kingdom during today's service. Amen.'

When the time came for the baptism there were 5 people around the font: Mr and Mrs Robertson, Robert and Annie Neal, and little Annie. The Minister spoke those time-honoured words 'I baptise thee Annie in the name of the Father, the Son and the Holy Ghost' while sprinkling water on the girl's forehead as he invoked the blessing of the Trinity. Normally when he baptised infants there was a lusty, healthy cry at the first sprinkle of liquid, but not this time. Little Annie's eyes were closed and she made not a sound. Mr Robertson knew then that he had made the right decision about her baptism and speculated how many days it might be before he had to bury her.

He had hoped his prayers would save her, but he knew in his heart of hearts that God would want to take this little girl to Himself very soon.

And so, only ten days later Robert Neal made that long, lonely despairing walk back to request that his daughter received a Christian burial. It was 'God's Will' that another daughter had been taken from him. He did not understand why. If post-mortem examinations had existed, they would have found that little Annie had a large ventriculo-septal defect, a hole in her heart, that made her survival impossible. (However, it was to take more than 40 years for the founding father of pathology, Rudolf Virchov, to establish the principles of systematic autopsies with microscopy when the cause of her death might have been determined).

* * *

After little Annie's burial the Neal family returned to their servitude. Robert worked in the fields, and his wife Annie grieved at her losses and tried to look after her two men as best she could. She thanked God that William was growing up as a fine strong boy who had boundless energy and would sometimes sneak away to watch his father ploughing a field. He admired his father's skill in ploughing a straight furrow and wondered how he managed to do that.

4

When he was seven years old, William should have started school to learn the three R's. The Scottish Government had passed an Act in 1696 requiring all landowners or heritors to establish schools for both boys and girls regardless of social status, while the Church of Scotland had to pay for and supervise the schools. There was no school in Brackenholm. The Earl would claim that he would open a school, and pay, but he had been unable to find a Dominie to teach the Children. Like so many agricultural communities he preferred to use child labour on his lands and in truth he had not tried very hard to find a schoolmaster.

When it came to his own son, that was a different matter. He employed a tutor, a young graduate from the University of Edinburgh, desperate for his first job, to provide education in his own house. This man could have been the Dominie, but it suited the Earl to not to employ him in this capacity. It saved money that he intended to spend elsewhere. He had been given little choice or his life would have become unbearable.

His son and heir had been born in 1786. The Earl and Countess had employed a nanny, and when she had served her purpose and formal teaching was required a tutor, Mr Muir, had been brought in.

Despite the tutors' efforts, the Earl's son, John, was a poor pupil. He was bright enough but lazy and took every opportunity to disrupt his lessons. He did not like being taken into the fields and barns of the estate by his father. He knew it would be all his one day, and he would find out what he had to know about the land when his time came to inherit it. Until then he would read the books he wanted, not those put before him to learn by rote.

By 1798 his education had come to a sorry pass. The Earl was exasperated that he did not want to learn about the estate, his tutor was exasperated by covering for his idleness, and the Countess was aware that her son, on whom she doted, was falling behind. She badgered the tutor, Mr Muir, and was making his life an even greater misery than John, the future third Earl.

Mr Muir decided he could not continue and sought to speak to the Earl 'Your Lordship' he started 'I am unable to continue in your employ. Your son does not want to learn and your wife keeps ordering me to teach this or that whether it is right for that lesson or nay. I am worn out, and intend to return to Edinburgh as soon as it is convenient for you'.

'Then go you must' replied the Earl, 'but what am I to do for my son's education?'

There was an answer that would teach him the error of his ways, but it would mean sending him away to school. 'May I suggest a way forward for your Lordship?'

The Earl nodded his head, so Mr Muir continued. 'There is an excellent school in Edinburgh called George Heriot's Hospital. It has been there for more than an hundred years, and you can pay for him to live at the school and attend the lessons there. The year starts in September after harvest time and pupils come home in June. If I had a son, I would want to send him there.'

Those final words, if I had a son I would want to send him there convinced the Earl that this is where his son John should go. 'What do we do to get him in?'

'With your permission your Lordship, I will write to the headmaster today and recommend that John becomes a pupil there. I am sure he will be admitted for later this year.'

'Do that for me' was his Lordship's instruction.

So Mr Muir wrote to the headmaster, extolling his pupil's virtues and how he would benefit from the best education in Scotland that Heriot's could provide. What he did not say to the Earl was that he, himself, had been a pupil at the school. It had been founded to educate orphans as was he, and had only recently taken in paying pupils, as the Earl would have to do for John. He was careful not to say too that the school policy did not spare the rod. Each master had a tawse on his desk and used it freely to instil order, discipline and work. That would really teach his former charge, John, a lesson.

After dinner that night the Earl indicated to his wife that he wished to talk to her on a matter of great importance. He said 'Mr Muir, our son's tutor, thinks that he has taught John all he can and that the time has come for him to go away to school in Edinburgh. He has recommended George Heriot's Hospital, right next to Greyfriars Kirk, as the finest educational establishment in Scotland, and I have agreed.'

At this, the Countess raged. 'How could you do that behind my back? I might agree that it is time for John to go away to school, but I want him to go to one of the best schools in England. Eton College or Harrow. Why Edinburgh?'

The Earl was furious with his wife. 'I have decided where John will go to school and he is going to Edinburgh, it's near enough, and that is final. After all, I will be paying for him, not you, so I get to decide, and decide I have. I want him in Scotland, not England, and will hear no more of this.'

21

At this, the Countess stormed out. How could her husband do this to her? She knew that he would not change his mind however she might cajole him.

The Earl could have offered Mr Muir the post of Dominie and asked him to start a school in the little village, as he knew he should. But his wife disliked the man. As a sop to her, he made sure Mr Muir went on his way, albeit with a good reference.

And so John, the future 3rd Earl was sent to school in Edinburgh. The estate coachman drove him in the best style he could over what passed as roads in those parts until, after several days, they reached Auld Reekie and the door to the school. The door was closed, so the coachman rapped on the door as loudly as he could. The door was open by a grizzled porter who demanded to know who they were.

'I have brought the future Earl of Brackenholm to begin his schooling here, so open the door and I can drive the coach in, to make it easier for me to unload his things'. His 'things' were four large heavy trunks.

'Nay we don't do that here' was the coarse reply. 'Put his things by the door and he can carry them in himself and ye can go.'

What a hard first lesson as John struggled under the heavy loads to the long low room he would share with 9 other boys. Why had his mother insisted on packing so much? Where was his own room like at home? He would never get one while a pupil at Heriot's. Mr Muir had made sure after he returned to Edinburgh, in a quiet conversation with the Headmaster, just what a spoiled rebel he could be and that he required firm discipline.

He got that in his first lesson for talking in class, two strokes of the tawse on each of his hands. It stung badly and left two red wheals across the palm making it hard to hold his pen. He was beaten again the next day for untidy writing. Why had his father sent him here? It was the first of many sore hands from the split ends of hard leather, until gradually he learned how to avoid trouble, to learn what he was taught and to behave in class. Over his five years at the school he also learned some other activities, which if he and his fellows had been found out, would have led to their expulsion after a very severe public caning in front of the whole school.

He was then sent, like many other rich young noblemen on the Grand Tour, returning home in December 1805, like the prodigal son he really was, having spent all of his father's money with little to show. He had found an interest in cards and the gaming tables and thought he knew how to control his losses. He had also made friends with other like-minded young men. He dreaded to think what might happen if his father found out about some of the things they did together.

5

Meanwhile at Brackenholm, as the summer of 1798 turned into autumn, Robert's wife Annie told him that she was with child again. She also told him 'it feels different this time, so it might be another son that I know you always wanted.'

Time passed into 1799, when Annie started in labour. Mrs McPherson was called again and Robert and William were sent outside to wait. Robert thought that Annie's cries were louder than on previous occasions, but kept this to himself. Labour was prolonged until they heard one last, desperate howl. There was no cry this time from a newborn, just silence.

A tired, blood spattered Mrs McPherson came out to meet the men. She explained 'Annie's had a real hard time. The bairn's head should come out first, but this time the feet came first. I'm sorry to have to tell you that it was a boy, but he never took his first breath and is dead.'

Robert with William beside him buried another child in a pauper's grave. Annie could not join them. She was unwell and in pain. She started to sweat, and although Robert kept wiping her forehead with a cold cloth, a fever started to burn in her body, that got worse and worse as Annie got weaker and weaker. Nine days after giving birth Annie died, as many other women both before and since have done, from childbirth fever.

Robert and William together buried her. 'It's God's Will and there are just the two of us now' explained Robert. You will have to come to the fields each day with me.

With these words William became a ploughboy, whose duty it was to follow in the furrow his father had created picking the stones from the soil. It was back breaking work for an eight-year-old. He had no choice. Sometimes he had to lead the plough horses over the rough ground too. He was tied to the land like his father, Robert. But as the months went by, he grew stronger.

Fathers expected their sons to follow in their footsteps and taught them their craft. Robert taught William to take a line from a feature on the far side of the field and plough towards that. This was his secret for an even furrow, and something he had been taught by his own father. He taught William how to groom the horses, to look at their shoes and when it was time to take them to the estate's smithy to be reshod. He taught him about the horse's harnesses and how to care for them to keep them supple for when his own time came and he would pass on the wisdom and skills of his lowly position to his own sons.

And every day that Robert ploughed, William picked up stones. It was drudgery of the worst kind, but that was his station in life.

The seasons came and went and a full year passed since his mother had passed away. The men looked after themselves as best they could. Perhaps Robert could have found another woman to look after his needs. He could not. He was a fiercely proud man and loyal to the memory of the only woman he had ever loved, Annie. He missed her and daily before he went to sleep said his own quiet prayers for the repose of her soul.

* * *

Robert and William continued to attend the Kirk each Sabbath as their duty required, and each Sabbath Mr Robertson the Minister spoke aloud and ended by saying 'This is the Word of the Lord'. Why then, thought William, does the Word change each week? He resolved to satisfy his curiosity and made his plan.

On that fateful Sabbath he put his plan into action. He deliberately left behind his scarf on the pew and made sure he and his father were the last to leave the Kirk. As they reached the door William said 'father, I have left my scarf behind, I had better fetch it or I will be cold in the fields as we work there next week.'

'Aye' was the reply 'you'd better fetch it.'

So William returned to the Kirk. It was not his scarf that he really wanted. He wanted to look at the 'Word of the Lord' from what Mr Robertson had called 'the Holy Bible'. The bible had not yet been returned to its place of safe keeping as William opened what he later found was called a page and found a jumble of squiggles on the page that he did not understand. He turned another page, then another and there were more jumbled squiggles. Just as he was about to close the bible, when he hoped nobody would find out what he had done a voice rang out 'William Neal what are you doing?'

Thank goodness it was not the Minister but his wife Elizabeth who had just at that moment returned to collect their precious bible.

Silence. What could William say? He had been caught in the act and would be in serious trouble now.

'Well William' asked his interrogator?

Silence.

'Were you looking at the bible?'

William wrung his hands and hung his head in shame. There could have been a little tear in his eye but he wiped that away and then nodded his head.

'Why William?'

A long pause 'Every Sabbath the Minister says this is the Word of the Lord, but it's different each time and I wanted to find out for myself.'

'Can you read?'

'What's reading?'

'Reading lets us know what each word says. Have you ever learned to read?'

A shake of the head.

'Would you like to learn to read the Word of our Lord?'

A pause, a gentle smile, followed by a nod of the head.

'Then William you will have to leave that to me. We shall say no more of what you have done. That will be our secret forever. I think you had better find your father now.'

So William left the Kirk and joined his father and held his hand more tightly than usual as they walked back down the rutted track to their little home.

There were other aspects of worship that William did not understand. Why did everyone sing so often and why did he have to learn the words and sing with them when he found that so difficult? Why did the elders call it 'The Lord's Supper' when there was no food on the table? Someday he hoped his father could explain what was happening. Meanwhile he had to keep a very big secret.

6

Mrs Elizabeth Robertson was a very clever woman. If the truth was known she was far cleverer than her husband the Minister, but as was the custom of the time, she had to keep her silence over many matters when she would have wanted to speak her mind. Her marriage vows had said obey her husband. Sometimes she could only do so with a very heavy heart.

She was a daughter of the Kirk. Her father was a Minister in Selkirk and had introduced her to her husband when he was a young Minister. Her father had said 'this young man has potential to go far. He would make you a good husband'. Being the dutiful daughter that she was, she had agreed to marry him. He had not gone far, only to Brackenholm.

As it was the Sabbath she knew she could not speak of what she had seen earlier that day in the Kirk. So she waited her moment which came much sooner than she had hoped.

Her husband the Minister happened to mention that Mr Muir would be leaving the Earl's employ and that John, the future 3rd Earl would be sent away to school in Edinburgh.

'What will happen to Mr Muir?' she asked.

'He will return to Edinburgh too I think.'

'But why has the Earl not asked him to stay and be the first Dominie at a school in the village. He knows that our Parliament passed an Act many years ago requiring him to do that, and he's done nothing about it. The children should be taught to read the Bible.'

'Well he's going to be sent away so he cannot be the Dominie.'

'That's a pity, if he cannot be the Dominie then I will be. I know I could teach the children their letters.'

'Well you can't. Teaching is a man's job. You do not have the time and anyway I do not think it is seemly for the wife of a Minister to work like that. I need you to look after my household.' And with that he left the room.

If he thought that would be the end of the matter, then he clearly did not understand his wife's determination to better the lives of the village children. She knew in her heart of hearts that education and the ability to read and write would help them better their lives and that would be to the greater glory of God.

As she prayed for the strength to carry out her plan, she knew what she must do. If there could not be a day school, and she could not be the Dominie she would establish a Sunday School. And so her plan began...

'Husband, did you notice in the Kirk last Sabbath the children had not heard about the subject of your preaching.'

'I wish the children knew more about the stories in the Bible.'

'If the children knew more about those wonderful stories in the Bible, they could appreciate your sermons better.'

So it went on for several weeks until one day Elizabeth announced to her husband that she knew what God's intention for her was. 'I believe that God has called me to establish a school for the village children on the Sabbath. I can teach them about his Word and the stories in the Bible. They will be better (that word again) Christians and I am sure together we can save more souls in this world ready for the next.'

These were very powerful words for the Minister. His work on earth was to prepare the souls of his flock for the glories of heaven above and so perhaps his wife was correct. A Sunday School would help to spread God's word. He could hardly refuse, but (and it definitely was a but) he knew the Earl would have to agree.

'My dear, I agree with that idea but I will have to ask his Lordship if we can do that.'

And so the Minister arranged to meet the Earl. Given there was no village school and no Dominie, his Lordship had little reason to refuse the request. A Sunday School would cost much less than a day school and he would not lose the child labour on his estate during the other six days of the week. As a result, Mrs Elizabeth Robertson achieved her aim to establish a school for the children on the Sabbath. Her prayers had been answered.

* * *

Where could she begin? There was nothing to help her achieve her real aim, the one she had carefully not mentioned, and that was to teach the village children not only about bible stories but to read and write, so that they could improve their lot in life. They should also read all of the bible, not just the few stories she might share with them. So she wrote to her parents.

Dear Father and Mother

The Minister and I pray that through God's good grace you are both well.

We have settled well into our new life here in Brackenholm, we have finished working on our house and I can now help my husband with his duties in our little parish.

We had hoped that our prayers for the blessing of children would have been answered. We will continue to pray for that miracle as we know you would like to have grandchildren to continue in the family tradition of Ministry.

He has preached many fine sermons on the Sabbath. Indeed, I heard the Earl himself congratulate him after one that only lasted for about a half of the hour, and that seems to be the pattern now.

Sadly there is no school for the children and they remain unlettered. The Earl has been unable to find the Dominie we need. Let us hope our prayers can be answered here too.

I have prayed that I might be able to help the village children know more about the miracles of Our Lord, and they have been answered. I shall start a school for the children on the Sabbath. I believe that this is the life that God has ordained for me here during my earthly existence.

Your loving daughter, Elizabeth.

Her father could read between the lines of this letter and concluded that her husband, the Minister, was failing in his duties in the marital bed and that his hoped for grandchildren on whom to dote in his old age would be a miracle. His daughter had organised her household as he knew she would and was now bored with life and the long sermons that her husband had been preaching. That man had become an ecclesiastical windbag, until the Earl in his wisdom had provided guidance – shorter sermons. Good for him. It was disappointing that there was no school for the children, the Law of 1696 was being flouted on the excuse that there was no Dominie. Elizabeth would have made a fine Dominie, but in this year of our Lord 1799 that was an impossibility.

The Sunday School was a brilliant ruse. Under cover of giving religious education Elizabeth was planning to teach the children to read and write. What a clever daughter he had. He would make sure her prayers were indeed answered.

A few weeks later a packhorse was led up to the door of Elizabeth's house, and several wooden crates were unloaded. She hid them in the stables after the groom had opened them. They contained slates and chalks and bibles. It was her miracle. Her father had understood her letter after all.

* * *

As the 19th century began so did Sunday School in Brackenholm. William was the first through the door into the little room for the classes, which were being held immediately following the service. He had persuaded his father to let him attend by explaining that he could walk home alone afterwards, so why didn't his father go home first and rest. That had done the trick.

Elizabeth had decided that her first lesson would be about the parable of the talents, in which she explained the importance of always doing your best wherever you had started in life and whatever you had. It would be your way to thank God for his many blessings. Do not hide away your skills like the man with the one talent, was her instruction. William never forgot her words for the rest of his days.

Gradually Elizabeth introduced the concept of the letters of the alphabet and how they had a different shape and sound and could be used together to make, first of all simple words, and then longer words. William was enthralled. He really was a very bright child, and when no-one was watching, he used a stick to draw out the letters he had learned in either the dust or mud of the lanes and fields around his father's bothy. He made sure that when he had finished he scuffed them out so he could keep his secret. He proved to be a very willing pupil and before many months had passed he was able to both read and write. And every Sunday he practised reading so well that before the end of that first year he could read parts of the Bible. He could not fully understand the meaning of all of the words, but Elizabeth could help with that, whenever she was not teaching the few other children in her class.

* * *

Another year went by. One day, to William's surprise, Mrs Robertson asked him to stay behind after her class. 'William I am so proud of you for learning to read and write. I have something for you' and with that she pulled out of the pocket in her skirt a book. 'I want you to have your own Bible and here it is. Read it every day of your life and think of both God and me.'

How could he forget her? She had given him a gift beyond price, the ability to read and write, and now his very own Bible. It was handsomely bound in leather and must have cost a fortune. He would never find out that this was one of the bibles Elizabeth's father had sent, nor that it was his penance for having her marry a man who had turned out to be unsuitable.

William opened his Bible. On the first page, Elizabeth had written in her beautiful, copper-plate handwriting 'this is God's Word for you.' William was nearly in tears with her generosity, then he turned to the next page where he found an elaborate design of curls framing the title Holy Bible and underneath *Printed by Thomas Guy, London.* What a man he must be to be able to print God's Word for him to read.

A few weeks later there was another surprise for William. During the Sunday School class, when the other children were practising their letters by chalking on slates Elizabeth sought out William who was sitting quietly in a corner on his own reading his own Bible. She had something in her hand.

'What are you reading William?' was her question.

'The Gospel according to St John,' was the reply.

'I have here another book for you to read. It's called *Robinson Crusoe* and it is the story of a man who lives on an island. You see there are many other books besides the bible for you to read. I have borrowed it from the Minister's collection of books, which is called a library, but I will have to put it back later today. You can read it here if you like.'

By this simple device, William was introduced to the world of books, and for the remainder of the time he attended Mrs Robertson's Sabbath classes he read the books she had chosen for him. He still picked up his Bible daily when he could sneak away for time on his own. As he read his world changed, but he was tied to the land and the Earl just like his father.

7

Another year went by while Robert and William toiled in the fields and respected the cycles of nature. When they ploughed William noticed that for some of the fields the work seemed easier than a year or two earlier. He asked his father why.

Robert took in a deep breath before replying 'Well William I think that is because of your work. You have removed many of the stones that my plough brought up. This is why the work is easier. When it comes to your turn to be the ploughman, it should be easier still.'

Together they ploughed on and found that they could work more than the single acre that, since time immemorial, had been the area a man and his horse was expected to achieve in each day's work.

There was another surprise during that spring ploughing season. One day the men woke to find a great herd of cows in the lane outside their little home. The cows were moving slowly from the position of sunrise in the east to the position of sunset in the west. There were men too leading them in that direction. They had long sticks in their hands and pushed the cows this way and that and sometimes gave them a healthy slap on their rumps to keep them moving. What was happening? These men and their animals had never been here before.

The story soon emerged. The men were cattle drovers who had, for years, driven their prize black beasts along a well-worn road from the Pentland Hills near Edinburgh to Carlisle. The reason was simple. Economics. The English paid more for them than the Scottish. The drovers were paid well too, although theirs was a hard life, living outdoors in all weathers. Traditions, however, were to change in that very year.

The drove road further east belonged to a wealthy Duke who farmed many thousands of acres in the Borders. During the last autumn drive, there had been problems. The cows had strayed far and wide, destroying crops. The Duke had banned them from crossing his land and deployed an army of gamekeepers, ploughmen, and other agricultural workers to ensure they kept off. The drovers had got the message. They were up against the most powerful man in the area and, as usual, no one was prepared to stand up to him.

The drovers had needed a new way and had asked the Earl of Brackenholm if they could cross his land. After some thought, the Earl had agreed. His land extended mainly in a north – south direction and was only five or six miles wide in an east – west direction, the way the drovers would go, and there were tracks they could use for the most part. At the usual droving speed of 10 to 12 miles per day, they should need not more than one day to cross his estate. He had thought of another advantage. He could send some of his cattle to the lucrative English market by tagging them onto the drovers herd. Both he and the drovers would benefit from this new arrangement.

William walked with the drovers across the Earl's land and heard the stories about where they were going and what they did. He would remember it well, and looked forward to seeing them again in the autumn. There would be a cattle drive twice a year, in autumn and in spring, to help break the monotony of working in the fields.

* * *

As autumn came there was another change. Robert Neal the ploughman started to feel somewhat tired at the end of his day's work. He put it down to increasing age and allowed his son William to handle the plough when no one else was looking. He was pleased with the result. William had a fine eye for a straight furrow and was strong. The horses responded to his touch, but he was still slower than his father had been in his prime in reaching each end of the field. Speed would come with experience and it was better to plough properly than to rush. The result was that the fine acreage that they had ploughed in the past gradually became slightly less and on some days was far less than they both wanted. Robert started to develop a dry cough but hid it from his son.

William had noticed, and asked his father what the matter was.

The reply 'Oh it's nothing really' was less than reassuring, particularly when William noticed that the rope around his father's waist was tied in a tighter knot than before. He thought his father might be losing weight, but their food was poor and neither could be called excellent cooks. Once again, this was their lot in life, and they had to deal with it.

Robert made every effort to ensure that his son did not find out about the blood he sometimes coughed up. There was no point in worrying William when he knew that he would be much better come the spring.

8

Christmas 1805 and Hogmanay came and went, and as winter started to turn into spring of 1806, the hunting season was in full swing for the local gentry. Naturally, the Earl was Master of his own pack of foxhounds, and the Master always prided himself on being in the forefront behind the hounds and being able to jump any of the obstacles that might be met during the chase. That was until the fateful day in February. Good living had taken its toll, and the Earl could easily be described as portly, although he would never allow that word to cross his ears.

It should have been an easy jump over the stone wall. For some reason that was never explained, his horse was spooked, jumped it badly, and reared up on its landing, throwing the Earl off his mount. The beast fell down on top of his master. As the horse struggled to its feet, the Earl lay still underneath, his neck broken.

The chase stopped as riders dismounted to see what had happened. There was no doubt the Earl was dead. His head was at an abnormal angle and no doctor on earth could bring him back to life.

The Earl's son John, who was a much less enthusiastic huntsman than his father, reached the wall, pushed through the crowd of dismounted riders, and saw that his father was dead. He was the Earl now, and there was to be changes on the estate.

With great gentleness, the late Earl's body was slung over a horse which was led slowly back to the big house. The hunt was abandoned. Someone would have to tell the Countess the news, and that sad duty fell to her son and the new Earl.

* * *

The Countess, who unknown to her, had become the Dowager Countess, was sitting with her embroidery in her day room. She thought she heard the sound of horses returning earlier than expected, but decided she must have been mistaken and went back to the task in hand, stitch after stitch.

John rushed into the house and called for the butler who came out of his pantry to meet him.

'Yes sir.'

'Where is my mother, the Countess?'

'I think she is in her day room sir, but she may be in her dressing room.'

'Where is her maid?'

'In the servant's quarters sir.'

'Then get her now and tell her to wait outside my mother's rooms until I call her in.'

As the butler turned to carry out his orders, John ran upstairs to the area of the house reserved for his mother. He knocked on the door of her bedroom. No reply. He repeated the task on the dressing room door, the withdrawing room door, and then the day room door.

'Enter' came the imperious command, and so he went in to find his mother alone sitting with needle and thread in her hand.

'John my dear, you are back earlier than I expected. Were there no foxes today'?

'Not really' came back a hesitant and mumbled reply 'but I have some very important news for you.'

'Well tell me then' demanded the Countess sitting up and looking forward to hearing the latest gossip.

There was no easy way to give her the news that she was now a widow so he just said 'there's been an accident and father is dead.'

'What happened'?

John did not know all the details as he had been at the back of the field of riders, so he just repeated his words 'there's been an accident and father is dead' adding 'I'm the Earl now.'

With those last four words, the reality of the situation hit the Countess like a thunderbolt. She began to wail and weep in a demented way, which John found very disturbing. He had not cried even one tear when he saw his father lying back there hardly an hour ago.

He turned and walked out of his mother's room to find her maid outside the door. Had she been listening to the conversation? He neither knew nor cared. He had a funeral to arrange and an estate to run, so all he said was 'go to your Mistress now, she needs you.'

With that instruction he walked down the corridor to the grand staircase deep in thought, his mind already made up about what he was going to do. For that, he quietly thanked his education at George Heriot's Hospital. The teachers had instilled in their pupils to be decisive. Decisiveness and then adhering to these decisions was the mark of a gentleman. And, of course, he was a gentleman.

As he reached the bottom stair and stepped into the hallway the butler was waiting for him.

'I thought you might want me Your Lordship.'

So he did know what had happened, but then one of the hallmarks of a good butler was that he knew all that happened in such houses. He must remember that for the future. His words were carefully chosen.

'You may have heard that there has been an accident during today's hunt. My father, the Earl, has been thrown from his horse and has been killed. There is much to do. You will tell the household staff what has happened. They are to go about their work in silence.'

'I want you to send for the steward of my lands, the estate carpenter, my coachman and have the head stableman immediately available. I want to see the housekeeper too and Mr Robertson the Minister and the head huntsman.'

'Yes my Lord.'

Good. The man knew his place, and with that John, the 3rd Earl Brackenholm walked out of his house and round to the stables. As instructed the head stableman was already waiting for him. He must have known he would be needed. As the Earl approached he knuckled his forehead as a sign of respect and said 'I was sorry to hear about this accident my Lord. It is a great tragedy for us all.'

'Yes. Where have you put my father's body?'

'Over there on clean straw. We have covered him with a blanket.'

John walked over to find his father's body. They had treated him with the reverence due to his station in life. John turned back the blanket then searched through his father's pockets. There were a few coins ready to tip the hunt's whippers-in at the end of the day. Well, they would not be having them as John put them into his own pocket. He removed the late Earl's watch and chain and attached them to his own waistcoat. When people saw that, they would know that he was in charge. Finally, he removed the signet ring from the little finger of his father's left hand and placed it on his own. The face of the ring was inscribed with the family crest, and he would need that to seal the many letters and documents he would be sending in his new role.

He replaced the blanket over the late Earl's face. He has already decided that his father would be buried in his hunting clothes. There were two more orders to give.

'Look after his body for me and post a guard overnight.'

'Yes my Lord.'

'Then take out the horse my father was riding today and shoot it.'

'But she's a fine mare, just 7 years old, and fully broken in. I would prefer not to have to shoot her. Please spare her my Lord.'

John would have none of this. 'I have given you your orders. That horse killed my father. I want her shot now. Then, give the flesh to the hounds and burn the rest. Get rid of the remains off my land by tomorrow. That horse killed my father and I want rid of it.'

'But, but…' the stableman wanted to continue objecting but knew it was no good, 'yes my Lord. I will arrange that but I will need to borrow a pistol.'

'You have your orders. Just do it.'

And with that the Earl left the stables and returned to his house. Where were the other people he had sent for?

* * *

He did not have to wait long. His butler entered and announced 'I have the steward and carpenter waiting for you my Lord. Where would you like to see them and which one first?'

His steward had seniority in the hierarchy of the estates staff so he would have to take precedence over the carpenter.

'My steward in here'. Now that was a surprise, and so the man was showed in. He had removed his hat and bowed his head to the new Earl. He too expressed his condolences.

'I was so sorry to hear this sad news your Lordship.'

To his surprise the word 'thank you' flew out of his mouth. 'We have much to do. I want you to tell all the estates workers what has happened and that they have a new Lord and master.'

'Yes my Lord.'

'Then on the day of my father's funeral they are to line up on each side of the lane to the Kirk and they shall bow their heads when the hearse passes. They will not be allowed into the Kirk during the funeral service.'

Now that was another surprise. 'As your Lordship pleases, but what if it is snowing on the day of the funeral?'

'That will be for them to manage. You have my orders, now see to it that they are obeyed to the letter.'

The steward did not think this was a very good start to the regime, but orders were orders so he muttered, 'yes, my Lord.'With that he begged leave of his master and went to carry out his instructions. His workers had respected the old Earl and would want to show their respects but not like this.

* * *

The next person on the list was the carpenter. He would not be seen in the Earl's rooms and so he walked to the servant's rear door.

'I was so sorry to hear this sad news your Lordship' said the carpenter as he also knuckled his forehead in respect to the new Earl.

This time a 'thank you' did not pass John's lips. His instructions were simple 'I want you to make a fine oak coffin for my father and make sure it is lined with lead. How long will you need to do this?'

The carpenter scratched his head to give him time to think. That was an unusual request. Coffins he had made before, but lined with lead! 'About a week, my Lord.'

'You will make my father's coffin in two days. Take what extra men you need from other work. I will not have my father's body lying on straw in the stables for longer than that. Have you the lead for the lining?'

'Yes my Lord. We always have some to repair the roof of your house when that is required. I will ask the plumber to make the lining, although I do not think that has ever been done before.'

'You have your orders. See that they are carried out to the letter.'

So the carpenter bowed his head in acknowledgement and set off to carry out his orders. They were tall orders and he would have to work through the night to complete his work for the new Earl's deadline. Why he wanted a lead lining was a complete mystery.

* * *

The next man on his list was his coachman.

'I was so sorry to hear this sad news your Lordship' said the coachman as he also knuckled his forehead in respect to the new Earl. Another man with the same words. Then he knew. That is what the butler had told them to say. Yes, he really did need to watch that man.

'I shall want the family coach to take my mother and I to the Kirk for my father's funeral. Make sure it is ready and we have a matched pair of horses to pull it.'

The coachman knew that this would be another tall order. The family coach with its crest painted onto the doors had lain idle in a barn for the past several years. The late Earl preferred to ride his horse, even to the Kirk on the Sabbath and he was used to driving the Countess in a small carriage. He knew why. The late Earl preferred, unlike so many of his fellow landed gentry, not to show off his great wealth in front of the estate workers, on whose labour he depended for all his money.

'My Lord, that coach has not been used in years. You may recall that your late father preferred to ride everywhere.'

'So you had better get it ready then. And, by the way, I will be using it every Sabbath in future and I shall expect it to shine.'

'Yes my Lord'. What a great deal of work that order would mean.

The Earl's next question was more surprising. 'Do we have a hearse to carry my father's coffin to the Kirk?'

'No my Lord.'

'Why not?'

'There has never been a need for one before.'

'Why is that?'

'Well, it's before my time, but I thought your grandfather, the first Earl, had died and was buried in London. There is a stone in the Kirk for that.'

John remembered now. 'And for my grandmother?'

'Her family took her away to their own graveyard for burial my Lord. There is another stone in the Kirk for her.'

Yes there was. What an interesting conversation. The man could read. Where has he learned that?

The new Earl gave his next order. 'I will not have my father 's coffin carried to the Kirk on a farm cart. Do you hear me? I require you to make something better than that. I shall want to see your plan tomorrow. You may use as much help from my workers as you need.' And with that he turned his back on his coachman and went to find his next appointment with the head huntsman.

* * *

'I was so sorry to hear this sad news your Lordship' said the Huntsman. Here was another man trying to curry favour.

'Tell me, now that my father has passed away, who will be the Master of the Hunt?' asked the Earl.

'Well my Lord, it is your pack of hounds so rightfully you are the Master.'

'In that case, as a mark of respect for my father there will be no more hunting until I say so.' He failed to add that he would much prefer to stay in the warmth of his house rather than out in the cold fields. It was a good excuse for him. He also decided that he would be looking very closely at the costs of keeping this pack of hounds as soon as it would be decent to do so. Perhaps it was a luxury he did not want to afford.

* * *

'I was so sorry to hear this sad news your Lordship' said the housekeeper. She has also been told by the butler what she ought to say.

'I shall need a black coat for my father's funeral service but I do not possess one. Does my late father have one?'

'No, I don't think so my Lord. His favourite colour was always blue. He said that was the colour of our flag, and I know he has a brown one and of course his red hunting coats.'

'But no black?'

'No my Lord. I think it would have been difficult to modify a coat of your father's. He was several inches shorter than you, and if you beg my pardon, a little stout.'

'Well then, you had better send for some black cloth and a tailor to come here and make me one as soon as possible.'

'Unfortunately that may be a little difficult. The nearest tailor is in Selkirk and he may not have any black cloth. We would then have to send to Edinburgh and that would take nearly a week there and back even on a fast horse. Then there would be the time needed to make your coat.'

She did not add that the tailor in Selkirk was her brother-in-law and he would refuse to travel to Brackenholm. She knew he had not been paid for more than three months since he made the late Earl's last hunting jacket, the one he was wearing when he was killed. She also knew that, unlike some aristocrats who never paid their bills, that the late Earl always did pay, although sometimes it was more slowly than his suppliers might like.

'I fear my Lord that it will not be possible to make your coat in time. I do have a suggestion.'

'Well.'

'There is a new fashion that allows gentlemen who do not have their own black coats to wear their darkest coat with a black armband on the left sleeve. I could make an armband for you for tomorrow my Lord.'

Now that was a good idea. It would save him both time and money. He ended the interview with a word he did not use often 'thank you.'

* * *

39

He saw his next visitor in a small sitting room off the hallway of the main house. It would not have been seemly to make a Minister of the Kirk enter through the tradesmen's entrance.

Mr Robertson greeted him 'I was so sorry to hear this sad news your Lordship, a bad business. I shall pray for the repose of your father's soul.

That was a little better. Perhaps it was what Ministers were taught to say during their training. The man was here to discuss the funeral arrangements not sink to his knees in supplication.

They discussed the words and the readings, then moved on to other arrangements.

The Earl announced 'I have decided that my workers will not be in your Kirk for the funeral service. That will be reserved for ladies and gentlemen only. I have ordered my workers to line the route to the Kirk instead. That is how they will show their respects to my late father.'

'But what if it snows or rains?'

'They will still have to attend, and that is that.'

Mr Robertson affected a little cough. 'May I raise another matter with your Lordship?'

'Go on.'

'Where in the Kirk's burial plot would you like your father's last resting place to be?'

'He will not be there.'

Now that was a shock. 'But, my Lord, that is the only consecrated ground for burials in our village,' came the surprised and technically correct reply.

'I've just told you he will not be there.'

'Then where pray my Lord?'

'I shall have his coffin brought back to this house. I have ordered it to be made lined with lead to help with the preservation of my father's earthly remains. I intend to build a mausoleum overlooking our estate where he, and when the time comes, my mother, I and any other family members can lie forever.'

'When I took my grand tour, this was a common practice in Italy for all the noble families. The Romans did this too. I already have a design in mind. You can find a way to consecrate it if that is what we must do. Now good day to you sir, we have much to do.'

And with that, a very perplexed Mr Robertson left the Earl's house. It was not a good start to the new Earl's rule. Just what would he tell his wife? There was something wrong with this man and he could not quite put his finger on it.

As soon as the Minister had left the Earl found paper, quill and ink and made a surprisingly good drawing of the mausoleum he had planned for his family's repose.

It was quite simple but of classical design with a rectangular room. At the front there would be a large oak door, four Grecian columns supporting a pediment and a simple slated roof. He would have the family crest carved into the stone with the family motto '*Semper audax*'. Always brave.

He thought he had been very brave with the decisions he had already made on this momentous day, and smiled with his own pleasure at the shock he had delivered to his servants.

* * *

On the next day his housekeeper asked to see him. She brought with her a wide black band and asked to place it around the Earl's left upper arm. The Earl nodded his head in consent.

Once the band was in place the Earl looked at it and said 'I like that. I want you to make some more, enough for all the servants in my house to wear them until my father's funeral. Off you go.'

And with that the housekeeper made a little bob in acknowledgement of her orders and went to carry them out.

* * *

Two days later came the time for the inspection of the lead lined coffin. The carpenter was instructed to take it to the stable where the 2nd Earl lay. His son inspected the work. Not too bad, a bit rough in places but then there had been so little time. His comment hardly gave credit to his carpenter for all the sleepless hours he had spent to complete his task on time. 'I think it will do. Now I want my father lain to rest in your coffin. I intend to bury him wearing the clothes he has on now. He was a great huntsman, and I think it is most fitting don't you?'

The carpenter could only nod his head in agreement.

So other grooms from the stable were called to help and with a degree of gentleness that belied their muscular bodies, they laid the late Earl in his coffin.

'Now close the lid and screw it up tight' was the next order.

The carpenter did as he was told although with the hardness of the oak he had chosen it did take quite some time.

41

The Earl watched over him until the task was completed.

'Now get some more men. I want this coffin taken to the main hall of my house. My father can lie there, where all can come and pay their respects, until we take him to the Kirk for his funeral service.'

* * *

He then called over the head stableman. 'Have you got rid of that horse that killed my father yet' the Earl demanded.

'Yes my Lord.'

'Completely.'

'Yes my Lord.'

'What did you do with the bones?'

'We threw them in the deepest part of the river my Lord.'

'Which river?'

'The river Bracken at the western edge of your land my Lord, where it's at its deepest. They say it is three or four fathoms where we put them.'

'That will do', and with that the Earl walked away.

If only he had known the truth. The head stableman and the head huntsman had connived together. They could not bear to see such a fine mare put down on the whim of their new lord and master who was showing all the characteristics of being a petty tyrant. They had hidden her away and intended to ask the cattle drovers to take her to England and sell her there. It was theft and a hanging offence if they were caught, but the lure of money at the Earls' expense had proved to be too great a temptation. After all, the drovers would be due in a few weeks time. Meanwhile they were the only two people who knew where the mare was, and it would be an easy matter to provide hay and fodder for her from the stores they controlled.

* * *

The Earl's next visitor was a stonemason, Mr Dunbar, called to the estate from their nearest town, Selkirk.

'They tell me that you are the best stonemason for miles around'.' Is that true' was his Lordship's opening gambit.

'They do say that I am the best man my Lord.'

'Then I shall expect your very best work won't I?'

'Yes my Lord.'

'This is what I want.'

42

With those words the new Earl pulled out the drawings he had made on that fateful day when his father had been killed. 'These are my plans. I want to build a mausoleum for my father's remains, and for others of my family later.'

Mr Dunbar was quite surprised. He had been shown very good drawings indeed, and although a scale had not been given, it was quite clear what was wanted. He had been given worse plans from men who called themselves architects.

'I understand my Lord, and where would you like this to be built?'

'Come with me.'

The two men walked together up a slight rise in the ground until they reached a small copse overlooking the great house on its north side with some open land at the front.

'Here. There is a fine view of our house, and the door will face south, getting the sun's warming rays onto the front.'

'Yes my Lord, this would indeed be a fine place for your mausoleum. There would be little wood to fell and I think the ground would easily take the foundations that must be dug.'

'When can you start?'

'Not yet my Lord. We have to finalise the size and agree the materials for the walls.'

'I want the very best stone.'

'Then do you have a quarry for this stone on your land?'

'No.'

'Then we would have to bring in all the stone we need from elsewhere by cart and that will be quite an expense.'

'I'm not made of money you know.'

'Then my Lord may I suggest another way of building which will look just as good.'

'Tell me.'

'Your plan shows a building a thousand feet square. That is too large and expensive. A building of about 250 feet square would be one quarter of the cost, and if it were 20 feet long and 15 feet wide that would suffice. There is no quarry here. I would use ashlar.'

'What is ashlar?'

It was then that Dunbar understood that the man he was dealing with was a fool. Every builder in Scotland and every pupil who had been to George Heriot's Hospital in Edinburgh knew that its façade that faced the Grassmarket entrance was fronted in ashlar stone. Dunbar decided to appeal to the snobbery of the Earl.

'It's the latest fashion much used in London to save costs. We build the walls in brick and then render the outside with plaster, then draw lines into the plaster to make it look like stone. Afterwards we paint the walls white to make them stand out more. It would look good here'. He failed to tell the Earl that the white walls would require a further coat of limewash at regular intervals to keep them looking good. That would be future work for him.

'When can you start?'

'Not yet my Lord. I have a further suggestion that will save on costs and improve the look. If you have just two columns at the front, one on each side, then your fine oak door will stand out more. It will also save too as they can be made of ashlar also.'

'The Earl was warming to this man. He was deferential, as he expected, but also looking to be economical. He liked that and said 'when can you start?'

Mr Dunbar knew well the ways of the gentry who would agree to one thing then during the course of the building work would demand changes at no further cost to themselves. He would not be caught by those tricks from this man.

'Well my Lord, if we have agreed to the size and method of construction I have suggested, the next stage is for the very fine drawings you have made to be redrawn to show this.'

'I want you to get on with my work.'

'No Sir. I do not work like that. Good day to you'. And with that the mason started to turn and leave his Lordship standing open mouthed. The man had insulted him. Sir. Not your Lordship, a man who was now in quite an quandary. He wanted the building, this was a man who could build it at reasonable cost so his words came out of his mouth almost without his thinking 'Please wait.'

Please, now that was a word he did not use very often. He was used to issuing orders and being instantly obeyed. Here was another man whom he would have to watch.

Mr Dunbar stopped and turned back to face his Lordship and said 'Yes my Lord.'

'I think it would be best if you told me how you like to work.'

'Good', thought the mason. That was better. His Lordship did have some manners after all. He had been warned about the man who had made such a bad impression on his workers in the first few days after his elevation to the peerage. The new Earl had not realised that servants gossip, servants know what is really happening in a house, and servants who may have to suffer the whims of despotic masters will tell others to stay away. The mason had had experience of the gentry before. He had been taught his trade by his father, who desperate for work, had agreed to work for one of these people. His father had never been paid because it was claimed he had not followed a verbal plan. It was his father's word against the gentry and it was all too certain who would lose. His dying advice had been 'make sure you agree in writing'. This was quite possible as the son, this mason was literate, whereas his father was not.

'Let me explain. I wish to see a final plan of the building you propose for me to build. We will both sign that to confirm we agree the design. After that there will be no changes, and I will build exactly to plan. We also have to agree the costs. I cannot give you the cost today until I have examined your final plan before we both sign and determined what materials might be needed, how much, and where they might be obtained. We will then have to arrange for cartage and that will add to the cost which you must pay directly and immediately. If you do not pay, I shall stop working for you.'

'Next, I need to see if there are materials on your estate that could be used. I am told you have a good carpenter working for you and he has oak in place. He can make the doors to your plan. Next there may be materials lying around your estate we may be able to use. There may be stone I can use for foundations and in other places. I shall need to be shown your land so I can see if there are materials here that will save your purse.'

'Next, it will take several months to build, even at the smaller size we have agreed. There may be labour from your workers to dig the foundations to my satisfaction, but I need to bring my journeyman masons and bricklayers here. There will need somewhere to stay and will need to be fed at your Lordship's expense. They do get a might hungry with all their efforts. They will need to be paid weekly too.'

'Then we will need quicklime and sand. I will need to make a lime burner for that and need much firewood. From where will it come?'

'Next your plan shows best slate for the roof. The best grey slate comes from Wales and is much in demand. There will be the costs of shipping to consider. However, there is an alternative source from Westmoreland, just over the border in England. It is somewhat cheaper but of a greeny grey rather than dark grey colour. Which would you prefer?'

'There is the fee for my own services too. Lastly, I do not start work ever until we have a written agreement drawn up by my lawyer to sign to confirm our arrangements.'

45

At first the Earl stood in silence dumbfounded by the sheer cheek of the man telling him how matters would be. Then he thought again. This man, Dunbar, knew his business, and it would be hard to find another mason from the area. Perhaps they could all read his mind as he was planning to default on paying at the end of the work on the grounds that his plan had not been followed to the letter. He knew he had been beaten. How could this workman have known? But then he did not understand the nature of backstairs gossip and family connections that had issued quiet warnings about him.

Eventually the Earl smiled at the mason and said 'yes indeed you have given me much to ponder upon. I appreciate your candour and desire to keep down costs while providing me with my mausoleum for my family's future. I think we should meet again in about ten days' time, after my father's funeral to discuss this further.'

'I agree my Lord' was the reply and Mr Dunbar nodded his head in respect and turned and left a dumbstruck Earl. Who had done this to him? He knew when he had been beaten and he hated that thought.

9

The day of the funeral arrived. It was bitterly cold, a sleet driven by a northerly wind beating down. The coachman had excelled himself. The family coach gleaned as the snowy droplets melted on its surfaces. The man had made a hearse from a small cart. It was drawn by two dark horses who had black plumes of feathers fixed to the headpiece of their bridles. The cart had a wooden cover over the coffin and it looked like the top had been painted black. Where had they found the paint?

The estate workers waited in line before the Kirk. They shivered in the cold. Robert Neal's cough had not improved. In fact, it was worse and he was spitting out small droplets of blood. He felt very tired but did not understand why. His son William stood by his side.

'Father, you are not well today, let me walk you home. It is madness to be here in this weather.'

'William, we must stay, it's our duty and God's Will.'

There was no reply that William could give.

The cortege arrived. The mourners were already in the Kirk, keen to be out of the bitter, biting wind. Several beefy men manoeuvred the handcart with its coffin into place and the Earl and his mother, the Dowager Countess, led in the procession. Mr Robertson brought up the rear as planned.

As he reached the door, Mr Robertson turned to the waiting estate workers and raised his right hand to give a blessing. His words were quiet but clear 'In the Name of the Father, the Son and the Holy Ghost, depart in peace.' He then turned, entered the Kirk, closing the door behind him then said the time-honoured words of requiem: 'I am the resurrection and the life sayeth the Lord, he that believeth in me, though he were dead, yet shall he live' as he followed the coffin and commenced the service.

What had the Minister said? 'Depart in peace', the message was clear. The estate workers had been given permission from Above to leave their imposed vigil, and so silently they returned to their homes to seek shelter from the dreadful weather this day had brought.

William helped his father home. It was indeed a blessing for them both.

It was also a quiet victory for Mr Robertson. That had been his plan, his divine guidance, when he suggested the funeral arrangements with his Lordship. It was unchristian to leave lowly workers who had little say in their day-to-day destiny out in the cold indefinitely.

The funeral service lasted, as the Earl had wanted for nearly 2 hours. When he and his fellow mourners left the Kirk his workers were nowhere to be found. They should have still been in line. Where were they and why weren't they where he had ordered them to be? John, 3rd Earl Brackenholm, was raging and was determined to find out who had flouted his orders.

He never did. The only explanation he received was that there had been a misunderstanding.

Later he sensed that the Minister, Mr Robertson, seemed more popular with his flock, but perhaps his work and the Sunday School his wife organised had made them more godly.

The Earl had been humiliated by his own workers. They would pay for that.

* * *

The next day the Earl required the presence of his Head Huntsman. The man arrived and acknowledged the presence of one of his betters by knuckling his forehead.

'You sent for me my Lord.'

'Yes. A few days ago, I told you that there would be no hunting for the time being as a mark of respect for my father.'

'Yes my Lord.'

'Well, I have decided that the Brackenholm Hunt is no more. It is closed. Finished. Done with.'

'But my Lord, your father would never have done that.'

'I have and I will.'

'But what about the hounds, and my men and their families?'

'Get rid of the dogs any way you want. You and your men are dismissed from my service.'

'But where will we go?'

'Anywhere, someone will have you. I want this done within the week. You are to report to me in seven days' times that my instructions have been carried out to the letter. If you do not, then not only will you all be dismissed, you will be dismissed without references. I want you off my land.'

The Huntsman was stunned. Why? What had they done to deserve this punishment? Where would they all go? There were families to consider. All he could mumble in a shocked voice was 'yes my Lord.' He turned and left the presence, and then a wry smile came to the corner of his mouth. He had a share in a hidden mare.

John the 3rd Earl smiled too. That would show his workers who was in charge now, and would save him several hundred pounds a year. He already knew where he was going to spend that money. He turned to his plans of his mausoleum. At least during his time on his Grand Tour, he had seen how Italian masters had made their drawings for their builders. He had learned well and would put that to good use. Then he could demand the presence of the mason again and get on with his project.

* * *

February turned into March, and the air became tinged with warmth. Robert Neal had expected his cough to improve as winter moved into spring, but it had not. If anything, it had got worse. He was still spitting droplets of blood and he was so very tired. He must get well soon, the ploughing season was fast approaching.

* * *

On the seventh day the huntsman found the Earl's Steward and told him 'I am required to report to his Lordship today. I have done his bidding.'

'What do you mean his bidding. He has said nothing to me.'

'His Lordship has ordered me to dispose of my hounds. He has closed the hunt - more's the pity.'

'He has done what?'

'He has closed the hunt and dismissed my men and I from his service.'

'The fool. His father would be turning in his grave if he had one.'

'Aye, but we have to obey him.'

'And the dogs?'

'I have kept the best bitch in whelp for myself. I have given some to the Duke's hunt and the rest have been shot.'

'No. His father spent years improving the breed.'

'Yes, but I have one, so at least the breed can continue wherever I go.'

'Where will you going?'

'We are dismissed from his service and his land by today. We will have to walk.'

'No you will not. I will find a cart so you and your family and belongings and those of your men can be taken where you will. If it requires two carts I will find two carts for you. I will not stand by and see faithful servants treated like this by that man.'

49

'And if he dismisses you too for your generosity?'

'He will not find out, and even if he does I might decide that I do not want to work for him. I know my trade well, and this estate even better, and if he wants to improve the yields his father had started he will need me. He never learned from his father. He needs me more than I need him.'

'Will you tell him we have gone. I cannot face the man. He may be one of my betters, but I shall never forgive him for what he has done.'

The Steward nodded his head in agreement. 'Let us find those carts. I will not have you walking in this weather. The tracks are icy and no place for wives and children.'

They left together and the Steward was as good as his word. He later returned to the grand house and asked to see his Master. When he was shown into the presence he said 'Your Lordship, I have to report that the hunt is closed and the men have left your land. I saw them go.'

'Very well' was the terse reply.

The Steward bowed and left, the Earl returned to his drawings. He would send for the mason the very next day.

* * *

When the Earl sent for his mason, he expected him to return with his messenger. He was outraged to hear that the mason had other work to finish and would not be able to attend until the next week. He was an Earl, and when he sent for a workman he expected him to be available immediately. That was the order of affairs in the year of our Lord 1806. His mood blackened. Had he made a mistake in his choice of builder?

That evening, he and his mother sat alone for supper served by their butler. There was an absence of small talk as they ate, not least because the Earl was still brooding about his builder. His father's coffin remained in a locked barn, and he had promised his mother that he would build a proper resting place for them all.

Eventually his mother pushed aside her plate and asked him 'when do you think your mausoleum will be finished my dear? I am anxious to see your father laid to rest.'

'The plans are drawn up, I have found a builder and he has promised me that he will commence the work very soon'. It was a lie. He had still to agree the details and the man had insisted on a written contract. It could be weeks and likely months before the work was complete. Thank goodness that he had specified a lead lined coffin to slow the rate of decomposition of his father's body.

His mother's next question disturbed him even more. 'Do you think, my dear, that you will take a wife soon?'

No he did not. That was not part of his plan, so again his reply was designed to give him room for manoeuvre while keeping the old lady happy, and more importantly supervising the running of his household. 'Well mother, this is something I must think seriously about. I have only recently returned from my Grand Tour and have yet to meet all the young ladies in our area. I am sure you would want that I should meet as many as possible before I make my choice. It is very important that I find the right one, don't you agree?'

The Dowager Countess did not agree. She was born in an age when young women were married off to whoever their father and mother thought the most suitable match. This was how important families increased their wealth and influence, and the size of their estates. Wives obeyed their husbands even if their husbands had mistresses. She had been fortunate. The late Earl had never taken a mistress although she suspected that her son may follow that practice. She was totally unaware that he liked male company. She also gave a guarded reply 'I will think about who the most suitable young ladies might be. We can discuss them over supper on another evening.'

With that, she left the dining room for her withdrawing room, sat down at a small writing desk, found paper and a quill, and started writing a list of names. As she worked, an occasional name was scratched out – not her. Who else? Gradually her list grew longer and her thoughts deeper.

Meanwhile the Earl sat at table and pushed his glass forward as a sign to his butler that he wanted it filled again. Once this was done he took a sip and thought about some of the young ladies to whom he had already been introduced since his return home. There were few, and all had ridden to hounds. He would have none of them whatever his mother might think. He intended to have a good time, marriage to produce an heir could come a little later.

* * *

In early March, he received a message that his builder was ready to see him so a time was fixed for two days hence. John would be ready for him.

As his butler showed the builder into his study he noticed that the man had a sheaf of papers in his hand. The builder was the first to speak 'good day my Lord.'

The Earl's reply was a less than friendly 'Hmm. I have the new plans here.'

'Then may I inspect them.' So the builder walked across to his Lordship's desk and looked through the plans. They had been well drawn as he expected. This man could be a draughtsman or even an architect if he tried. He decided to flatter the Earl.

'These are excellent plans my Lord. You have the gift of draughtsmanship. I am pleased to agree them. Shall we sign them together as I proposed last time we met?'

The Earl nodded his head and picked up his quill pen and, with a considerable flourish, wrote his signature. The builder added his in a neat fine copperplate hand.

'Now that is completed when can you start on the building?'

'Not yet my Lord, we still have to agree on the terms of our contract if you recall.'

The Earl did, and wondered how long that would take for a lawyer to draw up and how long it would be before work could start. His response was short 'the contract.'

'Yes my Lord, the contract. You may recall the terms I stated when we last met. I understand that you wish the building to be completed in the shortest possible time. I anticipate it will take about 4 months to complete providing the weather is favourable, so I have taken the liberty of having a contract drawn up for you to save time.'

'A contract. Do we really need that?'

'Yes my Lord. You will remember that it is an essential condition without which I will work for no man, however great that man may be.'

The cheek of it. He would work for no man. Then the Earl noted the last few words, however great, so the builder was saying he was a great man. And so he was. He was Earl of Brackenholm. He softened his approach. 'Then I must read this contract.'

'Here you are my Lord.'

Then the Earl started to read. His worst fears were realised. There was no way that he could build his mausoleum, on which he had placed great store, and had announced for all the local gentry to hear at his father's funeral without this man. He had been outwitted by a common labourer and that was not how the world should be. He was a Lord, and Lords ran the affairs of the country.

He read on:

The builder to set out the size.

His own men to dig the foundations to the builder's satisfaction.

He was to buy all the materials from suppliers designated by the builder.

Ten builders to be housed and fed, and what was this, to be provided with a gallon of beer each per day. That was new.

The builders to be paid each week, to be paid if materials were not to hand and if the weather prevented any work, and even worse, if they were not paid on time and in full, the contract would immediately become null and void. They would not work on the Sabbath.

And so the conditions went on until he came to the last clause. The builder to be housed in his servants' quarters, fed and looked after, and what was this, his fee, sixty guineas. That was outrageous. He read on. Twenty guineas to be paid immediately, a further twenty when the walls were built and a last twenty guineas when the work was done. Even worse, the builder was to stay in his house until the final part of his fee had been settled. He had been well and truly caught and there was no way back. What could he challenge?

The Earl put down this contract and said. 'These are very severe terms. I see that your men will not work on the Sabbath day. On my estate, my workers are required to attend my Kirk. I expect your men to do the same.'

'No my Lord, they will not. They are free men and can choose for themselves whether to attend your Kirk or not.'

'And you, will you attend my Kirk?'

'No my Lord, I will not. I do not share your belief in your God.'

Even more outrageous behaviour from this man. Who did he think he was? But the Earl needed this building. His next question caused the builder to give an inward sigh of relief. 'If I agree to this contract when could you start the work?'

'Today is Thursday. I can begin on Monday next if you can provide me with men on that day to dig the foundations. That should take about one week. Then when the materials in the quantities I have specified in my list are here, my men and I will build you the finest mausoleum in Scotland.'

'Where is the list?'

'It is on the last page of our contract.'

The Earl looked again at this sheaf of papers. Yes there it was. Tons of this and that. The man had done his homework , but it would cost a fortune. 'And what will you do between the making of the foundations and the arrival of all these materials?'

'I shall supervise the carpenter to make the doors, seek materials on your estate if there are any to be had, and build the lime kiln my Lord.'

The Earl picked up his quill again and signed the contract. He handed this instrument of torture to his pocket to the builder who also signed. There was a copy for each of them.

'Good day to you then. Until Monday next' spoke the Earl.

'Not yet my Lord, our contract says you will pay me the first twenty guineas today if you please.'

Had he heard correctly, or had he missed something in all those flowery legal words. With great reluctance, he opened a drawer in his desk and drew out a leather bag from which he counted out twenty golden guineas, not one more or one less, and handed them to the builder.

'Thank you my Lord.'

'Until Monday next then.'

The builder bowed his head, gathered up his papers and turned to leave. He had done well. Very well. This popinjay, this fop of a Lord would pay. He had arranged to snip his master's bill with the suppliers of materials for this building and would indeed fill his coffers. His suppliers knew what to do. As he left the grand house, he began to whistle a merry tune.

* * *

The Earl rang for his butler who entered immediately. He had been waiting for this master's call having heard his conversation with the builder through the secret hole he had made from his pantry to the Earl's study. It was a common practice. How else would a butler know what his master wanted and what was happening in the household?

'You rang my Lord?'

'Yes, fetch my Steward from wherever he is and whatever he is doing. Now!'

'Yes my Lord.'

The butler bowed his head and left. Clearly his conversation with the builder had left him in a foul mood. He would have to warn the household staff to tread carefully today. But then, he saw himself as the real master of the household. He ran things, although his Lordship thought he did so himself. Clearly that man had much to learn about his place too.

* * *

When the Steward eventually arrived over an hour later, the Earl got down to business straight away.

'As you know, I intend to build a mausoleum for the remains of my father and for the rest of my family. I have agreed with a builder who will do the work.' He made no mention about some of the onerous terms of the contract, that was none of the Steward's business. 'The builder will commence digging the foundations on Monday next. You are to provide him with any help that he needs, and have available, let us say six strong men for this task.'

'Yes my Lord, let me think who they might be. It will be done as you order.'

With that, he too bowed his head and left. He would have to move men from other duties in the fields for this. It would slow the preparations for sowing crops later in the season, and no doubt, his Lordship would complain about that. He knew who he would send for this work. It was his job to know.

* * *

A cold, wet Monday arrived. As William and his father arrived at their place of work for the day they were intercepted by the Steward who ordered 'come with me', so they followed him. On the way they were joined by four more workers, one a fellow ploughman. The Steward led them up a rough path to a partial clearing in the wood his lordship had agreed with his builder would be the site for his mausoleum. The builder was already there waiting for them. He had left his home on the previous day, the Sabbath, but then he did not recognise the importance of that day to so many others, and rode from his home to Brackenholm. He had brought with him the tools of his trade which were lying in front of him.

'Here are your men' said the Steward, then, turning to his own workers ordered them to follow the instructions of the builder to the letter. 'Do as he says.'

Through years of practice the builder knew how to motivate a workforce and it was not by giving such harsh orders with their underlying threats. He began 'I need your help for the next few days. The Earl has decided to put a small building here overlooking his land'. He did not say a mausoleum, they would probably not know what that was and the details of what was to be built were his to share with his employer. 'We will clear the land, then, I will place pegs to show where the building will be. After that the foundations need to be dug. Once that is completed you will be able to return to your normal tasks.'

Digging foundations would be even harder work than ploughing a field. At least there were horses to help with that work. William gulped, his father coughed and spat out another blood-tinged gobbet of phlegm. The other four men looked at each other and shook their heads in disbelief. Why had they been chosen? Fortunately, the builder had persuaded his lordship to reduce the size of his new edifice, otherwise the task of digging foundations would have been massive. The five men and William men did not know this but the builder did, and was much relieved he had done so.

The work began. As luck would have it there were no large trees to cut down, only a few saplings at what would become the rear of the building. To his son's surprise Robert Neal kept coughing and stopping in his allotted tasks to take a deep breath. He did not look well and this hard, physical labour in cold, wet weather appeared to be making him worse. William whispered in his father's ear, 'father, take a rest when you need to. I will work twice as hard for us both so no one will know.'

The work continued. It was back breaking, as they dug deeper along the lines laid down by the builder. In places, the ground was down to solid rock after hardly a yard's depth, but in one place, at a rear corner the ground was soft and the men dug deeper and deeper and deeper over an ever wider area and still they did not reach bedrock. The first week came and went but the foundations were not complete in the one place. By the second day of the second week, despite their efforts there was no sign of bedrock and they were over eight feet down from the level of the land. The builder stopped the work and walked into the wood with his axe. He found a nice straight tree and cut it down, removed any side branches and sharpened one end to a point. This would be his testing rod.

He carried it back to the foundations and told his workforce 'I do not know how much more land we will have to dig to reach the underlying stone. I have made this rod. What we will do is to place it in the bottom of the trench you have dug and hammer it into place. Then we can see how much further we must dig. The rod was held and William given the honour of hitting the free end with a large hammer. Down and down the rod went into the earth until the builder called 'Stop.'

It was now quite clear to the builder that there had to be a fault in the rock at just this point. They could dig forever and the land would become more unstable. His men were tired out. It was unfair to ask more of them, but he had a plan borne of years of experience in his trade.

'I think we have dug far enough now, but the rock we want to find is deeper yet. I have a plan. We will fill this hole with stones up to the level of the bedrock, and that will be enough to give us what we call a stable foundation. Now where can I find enough stone?'

'Excuse me sir' came a voice from amongst his workers. It was William. 'I know where we can find the stone you need. I have been clearing the fields my father has ploughed of stones and there are several big piles now. There may be enough.'

What a good lad he was. He might just save them all, for what the Earl did not know would not harm him. The instruction was the simplest one he had given for weeks 'show me'. With these words ringing in his ears, William led the builder from the place where he and his father had sweated so much. He would take a circuitous route to those fields. It would give his father and the other men more time to rest.

After half an hour of walking the builder had come to recognise the ploy of this young man. He smiled. His smile grew wider when they eventually reached the first field. There, neatly piled by the edge were hundreds of stones, tons of it. This was what was required to fill the void they had unexpectedly found when digging the foundations. What was needed now were horses and carts to transport the stone from here to there. They walked back in silence to the building site to find five men resting and talking together. One man had a cough and was spitting onto the ground. He noticed the spittle was blood-stained. That was not good and he knew what the problem was, but dare not say. He also noticed the likeness between that man and the youngster who had taken him to the fields and so proudly shown him the results of his labours in gathering stones lifted by the plough. Father and son.

The builder's next task was to find the Steward and ask for horses and carts to carry the stone from the fields to the foundations. There were but two available only so he commandeered them and their drivers, explained what he wanted them to do and that they should be ready first thing tomorrow to move the stone. He then walked to the foundations where his workers were still resting. He knew what he would do. 'I want you to drive that wooden measuring rod into the ground until it is level with the rock we have found.' This was to prove to be a major error of judgment. 'Tomorrow we will be bringing stones from the fields to fill this hole. I want three of you here to unload the carts and three of you there to load the carts.' With that he pointed to Robert Neal and two other men to stay and William and the other two were detailed for cart filling. He was pleased with his choices. It was easier to unload, carts could be tipped up and their contents deposited for the most part into the hole, and there would be periods of rest between deliveries. Robert Neal needed to have a lighter workload.

Although it was only mid-afternoon, to their great surprise, he dismissed the men to their homes. His Lordship had never done that, but they knew that for the next few days they would have to work like the devil to complete the foundations.

* * *

The very next day, the work to load the carts with stone and unload them into the foundations began. Each cart could only carry about one ton of stone. It would be a slow process to fill the massive hole, but, at least there was time to rest between loading the cart.

All in all, twenty cart loads were required, and there were still heaps of stones left at the side of the fields that Robert and William had ploughed.

* * *

The Earl heard the noise of the loaded carts passing along the tracks and called his Steward and asked 'what is that noise I hear?'

'It is carts delivering stones from your fields to your building site my Lord.'

'Why?'

'It is on the orders of your builder my Lord. He has told me this will not only save you money but will clear stones from your fields. Do you wish me to send him to you?'

'No. You deal with it.'

'Yes my Lord', and with that the Steward bowed and left. He did not fully understand why the builder required this stone, but the man knew his trade, and he had the instructions of giving this man any assistance he needed. That is what he would do, no questions asked.

* * *

The filling of the hole took the rest of that week and was completed early on the Saturday morning. It had taken a week longer than expected to complete the foundations but the builder was not concerned. He was living in the Earl's servant's quarters with all his food found. He could live like that for weeks until the supplies of brick and sand arrived. Then he remembered, he had a lime kiln to make.

When the last stone was in place, he thanked his workers and dismissed them for the day.

'Sir, we will have to report for other work on the estate now.' That was Robert Neal speaking.

'No you will not. Your time has been given to me for as long as I want it. I shall want your work until sunset today. Your work here is done. The work I now require from you is to go home and rest. Next week you will have to return to your usual duties.'

The men nodded their heads in acknowledgement and left the building site. Just who was this man who gave them this gift which made their lives easier? The Earl and his Steward never did. They worked them to the bone.

10

On the following Monday Robert and William returned to their fields and their plough. Robert's cough was worse and he was so tired. At times, he no longer had the strength to hold the plough, and passed that task to William. He had taught him well. The furrows were just as straight as he had made for over twenty years. Nobody would be able to detect the difference.

William's concern for his father grew, but as always Robert made light of his fatigue 'I will be much better when we have summer here and the weather is warmer' came the stoical reply. William wanted to believe his father's words, but somehow he could not.

* * *

On the second Sabbath in April there was a buzz of excitement amongst the Earl's estate workers. The cattle drovers were at the edge of his land and would pass through on the next day, the Monday. Meanwhile they had to attend the service at the Kirk.

As was the new pattern, the 3rd Earl arrived by coach with his mother, no horseback for him like his father. His father had always attended the Kirk in a plain wool coat. He did not want to show off his great wealth when compared with his lowly workers. Not so his son. Not only did he arrive in state but his usual dress was an embroidered silk coat the must have cost more than the yearly pitiful wage he gave to his men. Not only that, he had several of these coats and seemed to enjoy flaunting them in front of all.

The Minister, Mr Robertson, did not like this display, but could say nothing. His own position depended on the man. He knew ill would become of the man at some time and some place hence. He did not know where or when. He should have prayed for the Earl to change his ways. He could not, and that troubled his conscience from time to time, less frequently as the weeks passed.

* * *

The cattle drove passed through the Earl's estate as planned on the Monday. For some reason, it seemed slower than usual, but then an interesting meeting had taken place in secret between the head drover and the Earl's head stableman and former head huntsman who had re-entered the estate despite instructions that had forced him to leave some weeks earlier. The meeting concerned a certain horse. Eventually a deal had been struck. There would be a three-way split between them of the monies raised by the horse's sale. They knew the risks when the mare was handed over at the western side of the estate at the end of that day.

Meanwhile, unaware of what was happening in the drove, Robert and William were ploughing a field together. Robert kept coughing and spitting, until he had to hand over to William to complete their day's work. They had not met their target of ploughing an acre a day by the time both returned exhausted to their humble home.

The same happened on the Tuesday when William took on even more of the work. No stones were removed from the field on that day.

* * *

Wednesday came when William wanted his father to rest at home. 'I can plough the field for us today father, while you stay here. You are not well.'

That was quite the wrong words to say. Robert, who had never missed a day's work in his life stood and said what he always said on these occasions 'it's my duty.'

They both went off to plough that field, but Robert could not work the plough. He was too tired but for why? He sat in the shade and watched his son with pride. He had taught him well and he would be as good a ploughman as himself, in the long tradition of their family calling. He continued to cough and spit, but his spittle contained more blood stains than before. Perhaps William was right after all and he was unwell. He coughed again and cried out in pain. This time was different. There was a trickle of dark red blood at the corner of his mouth. He coughed again, and another trickle of blood came. He yelled for his son, as an even larger trickle of blood oozed from the corner of his mouth.

William heard his father's cry. He had never cried out like that before. He stopped ploughing and ran over to his father and saw the blood at his mouth dripping down onto his chin. Something was very wrong. He helped his father lie down in as comfortable a position as he could find then instinct kicked in. He knew what to do. He ran to find help.

There was nobody in the next field or the next, but in the third field he found another ploughing team. He ran across the rough furrows calling out 'help, help'. They stopped. 'Help my father is ill, come and help me.'

William was near to tears as he repeated his demand. The men left their work and ran back with William over the two fields to find his father.

Robert was lying where William had left him. There was a large pool of blood by his mouth. He was dead. He had died of consumption which had eaten away his lungs and blood vessels until his pulmonary artery had given way under the strain.

William had seen death before with his mother, sisters, and brother. He could not believe his father was dead. He was such a big, strong man and now he was gone. Now he was all alone in the world. For the first, and last time in his life, the tears came and flooded down his cheeks uncontrollably.

The other ploughmen knew what to do. They unhitched the horses from the plough, then lifted Robert's lifeless body from the ground and gently lay him over the horses which they led back over the fields to what was now William's humble abode. They placed the corpse on his bed.

There were other tasks to complete. After a brief discussion between themselves, one of the ploughmen left. He had to report to the Steward what had happened. The other took William's arm and guided him out of the bothy, onto the lane and walked with him into the village. Their first stop was at old Mrs McPherson's house. She would know what to do with Robert's body, then on to see the Minister.

As was the custom, the ploughman and ploughboy went to the servant's entrance of the minister's house and knocked on the door. It was opened by a maid. 'We wish to see the Minister' came the urgent demand from the ploughman while the ploughboy could only nod his head in agreement through his tear clouded eyes.

The maid went to find Mr Robertson who was in his study thinking about his next sermon. He answered her call and followed her to the back door where he found man and boy.

'You had better come in and tell me how I can help you.'

They followed the Minister into his house where he led them to a small room with a table and chairs. It was the room where his own small household staff ate their meals. They all sat down.

Through his tears, William explained that his father had not been very well for some months but had expected to get better. They were ploughing together when his father took a rest only to cough up blood. He had run for help, but when he came back his father was lying in a pool of blood and was dead. They had taken his body back to his own little home and that is where he now lay.

'Let us pray for him' and so all three bowed their heads for a few minutes until Mr Robertson said 'may he rest in peace.'

He then turned to more practical matters and discussed the arrangements for Robert's funeral and burial. It was agreed that would take place on the following Saturday afternoon. They were just about to leave when Elizabeth Robertson, warned by the maid that something was afoot, entered the room. She saw William's tear stained face and went and put a motherly arm around him. 'What has happened?'

William repeated the story he had just told her husband as best as he could through sobs and more tears. He had loved his father dearly and would miss his strength and support. What was he to do now?

Finally William said 'I must go back to my father now.'

'No' came an emphatic reply from Elizabeth. 'You must stay here until after the funeral, then, go back. We will look after your father until then'. Her husband was taken by surprise by her offer, but he knew better than to argue with his wife when she had made such important decisions. He merely nodded his head in agreement. Food was prepared and a room found for him, and he stayed where he had been told. William also knew that arguing with the Minister's wife would get him nowhere.

* * *

On the Thursday the field where William and Robert had worked the previous day remained unploughed.

* * *

Late on the Friday morning there was another visitor to Mr Robertson's house. This time he knocked on the front door and was admitted by the same maid who had answered William's knock just two days before. He was bidden to enter. It was the Steward of his Lordship's lands and he was looking for William. He had been told where to find him.

'I wish to see William Neal. Fetch him for me,' came the curt instruction.

The maid did a little bob of acknowledgement and went to find William, who followed her to the front of the house. He had not set foot there before. It was so different to the servant's quarters. He had never seen such luxury.

The Stewards next words were 'come with me William Neal', and so the pair left through the front door, walked through the village and headed towards the great house and its complex of buildings, eventually reaching a building containing the room the Steward called his office. William went in with him and stood in silence. What did this man want at this time?

His answer came a short while later when a man dressed in a fine silk coat entered the room. It was the 3rd Earl. William knuckled his forehead in acknowledgement of his Lord and Master.

The Earl wasted no time and got down to business 'they tell me your father is dead.

'Yes my Lord.'

'Then who will plough my field?'

'I can your Lordship, my father taught me well.'

'How old are you?'

'Sixteen my Lord.' It was a little lie. He would be sixteen soon, but he thought that it was better to say he was older.

'Well if you are only sixteen, then you cannot be a ploughman, you can only be an apprentice. You will be indentured to me.'

Yes my Lord.'

'And as an apprentice you can only earn half the wages of a proper ploughman until you are twenty-one. I shall also charge you rent for your house.'

William gasped and said 'why?'

'It's that damned man Pitt taking two pence in every pound tax so you can help to pay it.'

William had never heard of Pitt, whoever he was, and tax he had read about. He did the sums in his head. Thank goodness Mrs Robertson had taught him to count as well as read and write. He would hardly have a quarter of the pittance his father had earned. That could not be right, but he could not argue. He remained silent.

The Earl's next words shocked him even more' when will you bury your father?'

'Tomorrow afternoon my Lord.'

'Then I want you to bury him in the morning and be in my fields catching up with the time you have lost to the plough in the afternoon.' With that he left the room. That would teach him, he thought.

The Earl was wrong. It would not teach him. William decided there and then that he would not work for the man. He would be little more than a slave, and his education, albeit in secret, had taught him that slavery was wrong. He must think what to do as he walked back to the minister's house deep in thought.

He knocked on the back door of the house and after a few minutes the door opened and he was bidden to enter by Mrs Robertson herself.

'Where have you been William?'

Containing his tears William told he the story of his confrontation with the Earl and what he had been told to do.

Elizabeth had other ideas. She too had heard what her husband had said about the new Earl, and she seen him in the Kirk as well. She knew he was a bad lot and his treatment of William, who had become to her like the son she would never have, was beyond words. The Earl must be stopped.

She sent William to his room and sought out her husband.

They whispered together, lest anyone hear what they were plotting, after which Mr Robertson walked into the grounds around his Kirk.

* * *

Saturday came and the burial service was conducted with great reverence by Mr Robertson, after which Robert Neal's body was laid to rest in a freshly dug pauper's grave.

William thanked him and then asked to be excused attendance at worship in the Kirk on the next day, the Sabbath. He explained 'Sir, I need to be alone with my thoughts and my bible tomorrow.'

Bible, where had he found that, and then Mr Robertson realised and stayed silent for a moment then said 'William, you are a brave lad, I will pray for you whatever you do.'

With those words in his ears, William returned to the bothy. His plan was working.

* * *

On the next day, the Sabbath, the Earl and his mother arrived at the Kirk in their coach and their finery as if nothing had happened. The service followed its usual course, although Mr Robertson did mention Robert Neal by name and asked for their prayers for his immortal soul. Most of his congregation would pray as he asked. He knew of at least two who would not.

As he left the Kirk, the Earl called Mr Robertson over to him.

'Yes my Lord.'

'I see that my new apprentice ploughman William Neal did not go to worship. Where is he?'

'Yes my Lord. He wanted to be alone today and asked my permission to be absent. Given the circumstances, I gave this to him.'

'Hmm. And why was he not in my field yesterday afternoon ploughing? I ordered his father's funeral to take place yesterday morning.'

'Yes my Lord. We tried but alas his father's grave had not been dug in time and we had to delay.'

'Very well' and with that the Earl turned away and walked back to his coach.

Mr Robertson smiled. He knew why the funeral had not been held until the afternoon as originally planned. His walk in the grounds on Friday had had a purpose. He had instructed the gravediggers to work slowly and not finish their task until the Saturday morning late. That was the outcome of his whispers with his wife. What a clever lady she really was.

11

After his father's funeral, William walked back to what was now his modest home, although with the Earl's announcements about what he would pay, that turned his father's pittance wage into his own slavery. He would never work for such a man. The first stage of his plan had been to get Mr Robertson, the Minister, to agree that he could be absent from the Kirk service tomorrow.

He had some basic cooking skills and with some of the food that had been left he made some oatcakes. The remainder he ate, then collected the few meagre possessions he had into a small bundle with his most precious possession, his bible, hidden in the middle. He was ready.

As dawn broke on the Sabbath, William was already awake. He ate the one oatcake he had left unpacked, collected his bundle, then left the bothy for the last time. He ran westwards following the trail of the drovers. He would join them and follow them to England.

As he ran he remembered a passage from his bible, Deuteronomy, Chapter 32, verse 35, '*To me belongeth vengeance and recompence; their feet shall slide in due time: for the day of their calamity is at hand, and the things that shall come upon them make haste.*' God may have promised that, but he had revenge in his own heart for the treatment that the Lord had given his father. He did not know where or when that might happen, but one day he would exact the most terrible revenge he could on that man. An eye for an eye.

He let the thought pass as he ran. At least the cow pats left behind by the drovers herd showed the way he was to follow.

* * *

As Monday dawned, William was not at the plough. The Steward was informed and decided he would find that lazy, good-for-nothing apprentice ploughman and give him a good whipping to liven him up. He would never be late again.

He started his search at William's bothy but he was not there, neither was he at the Robertson's house, nor in any of the other places on the estate he expected to find an errant lad. Where was he?

* * *

Tuesday came and William was still absent from his duties. The Steward came to the only conclusion that he could, and perhaps should have reached on the previous day, that William had run away. He would have to tell his Lordship.

The interview with his Lord and Master did not go well. 'I have to report my Lord that William Neal is not at his plough and cannot be found. I think he might have run away.'

'What?'

'Yes my Lord, I think he might have run away.'

'Then find him and bring him back here. He is my indentured ploughman and I need my fields prepared for sowing my crops.'

'How my Lord?'

'Set the hounds after his scent. They will find him.'

'I cannot my Lord. You may recall that the hunt and the dogs have been closed.' He made no mention that most of the dogs had been shot dead on his Master's orders.

'Then send out some men to find him. He cannot have gone far.'

'In which direction shall we search first my Lord?'

'In which direction would you go if you wanted to run away?'

'To Edinburgh my Lord, our capital city where there are so many interesting things to see, the castle, Arthur's seat, The High Kirk - St Giles cathedral, the shops, and that is where he could find paid work easily.'

'Then look there', and with a wave of his hand he dismissed the man. Whatever next.

The Steward was a worried man. He collected two of his underlings who could ride and they saddled up 2 more horses, then, started to ride towards Edinburgh. As they rode they asked anyone they met if they had seen a lad of William's description. They had not. After three days, the Steward decided that they must return to Brackenholm. There was no sign of William. Perhaps he had run in another direction, but which one? They gave up the chase.

William had run in another direction, the opposite direction to his pursuers. He was over the hills and far away, and had been gone for three days before the hunt for him had begun. His plan had worked. He had told not a soul of his intentions, not even Mrs Robertson.

* * *

William had run on the Sunday until he was bursting for breath. He could not stop. He knew he had to get away as far as possible that day when he was sure no one would be looking for him. The Earl would want him back. He had indentured him as an apprentice ploughman, and although no document had been signed or he had been asked to make his mark (the Earl did not know he could read and write) he was sure some charge would be made against him. The gentry ruled the Courts, and who would believe his word against that of an Earl?

Eventually William slowed down, stopping to walk in between bursts of running. He had found a new way of rapid travel on foot. As night came he found shelter in a wood and made a makeshift bed by collecting together fallen leaves to form a softer place to lie than the hard ground. He ate one oat cake. He did not know how many days it would be before he met up with the drovers. Finding water was easier. There were many streams running down the hills at which he could take his fill.

On the Monday, William followed the same pattern of running and walking that he had found so effective in putting as many miles between him and Brackenholm that he could. He needed to find the drovers soon. They would protect him from the Earl's men, who he expected would come in hot pursuit of their fugitive. He would not go back whatever he had to do.

Tuesday arrived and William came across an unexpected problem. The cattle tracks and their droppings had divided to both the right and the left. Which way should he go? He had no coin the throw in the air and land as either a head or a tail to let fate decide for him. He chose the track to the right and ran on for several more miles. Then the track stopped and there was a large area where cattle had been. The ground was trampled down, there were hoof marks everywhere and dung aplenty. He had chosen the wrong way. He knew what had happened. The herd had been driven to this place and had been stopped. They had been forced to go back the way they had come. He should have taken the track to his left. He retraced his steps wearily. Where were the drovers and their beasts?

The drovers had had a very hard time this year. They had not been able to follow the traditional route that for years had been their path to the rich markets of England. On two occasions, armed men had blocked their path. Their Masters had given orders that no cattle were to cross their land and they would follow those instructions to the letter. Their positions depended on it, and like so many who had orders to follow, they had families to be fed. There was no choice in the matter. The herd had to be stopped in its tracks, and that was that.

These delays had slowed down the progress of the herd and its controlling drovers considerably. They were not where they should be, getting close to their destination in Carlisle. Several days had been lost, and the beasts were beginning to lose both weight and condition. They were becoming less valuable by the minute. Why were there so many difficulties this year? Then they knew. It was because of the Duke's actions they had encountered further east in the early part of the drive. He has told others other members of the so-called gentry what his intentions were, and they had followed his lead.

* * *

William retraced his steps to the divide in the drover's tracks that he had found earlier in the day. He took the left-hand path, combining running and walking once again to ensure he covered the necessary miles to escape the Earl.

By late afternoon on that Tuesday, he saw the herd ahead in the distance. He had found his objective, but his instincts told him not to join them and ask for their help on that day. It would be better if he caught up with them during the following morning. They would be closer to England.

He found what shelter he could and lay down before eating his last oatcake. He would have to find other food soon or continue feeling very hungry.

* * *

Midway through the following morning, he caught up with the slowly moving herd and sought out the head herdsman.

'Sir, can I come with you to England?'

'No, we are too busy and do not need help from a mere lad.'

William repeated his request 'sir, can I come with you to England?'

'No', then the herdsman looked again at William. He thought he recognised the lad from the time they had passed through Brackenholm. What had happened? He was running away was the only conclusion he could reach was that someone from that estate would chase them and take him back. He could not help the lad.

'Sir, I can work for you if you take me to England.'

Then the herdsman had an idea and asked 'can you lead horses?'

'Yes sir, I have led my father's plough horses while he was still alive.'

So, that was the reason. His father had died and that was the cause of his running away. He could not have known of William's meeting with the Earl and its outcome. That was the reason William was fleeing.

'Perhaps I can find work for you. We have a horse that we are taking to market with our cattle. If you lead that mare with us you can follow. There will be no pay for you, but we will share food with you. What do you say?'

'Yes sir.'

That was better. If anyone found that he had a stolen horse then he could blame William. The lad had followed them with the animal. He must be a thief, but we did not know that. He reckoned that nobody would believe William's story. He had his alibi.

* * *

With that agreement, William was introduced to the horse and instructed to follow at the back of the herd. He complied. He knew about horses. He had followed the plough and led the plough horses for his father. He stroked the mare's muzzle as a way of getting to know her. She was quite frisky, but with his gentle words and handling, she calmed down and allowed herself to be led along the trail.

During the day, William had more time to look at the horse. She was a powerful animal that had been loved by someone, not a herdsman. As he looked again at the horse he thought he recognised her. Was she the horse the late Earl used to ride? Yes, he thought she was. If he was found with her he would be called a horse thief, and he would hang for this crime.

He had to make another plan.

* * *

After a long day's drive William was sitting with the drovers eating his modest evening meal, when one of the men told him they were in England and Carlisle was only two miles away. They would be there on the next day and take some of the cattle, and the horse that William had been leading into market. No, I will not lead her into Carlisle to market. They hang horse thieves in England too he expected. It was time to put his plan into action.

As the camp slept, in the dead of the night William walked silently to the mare where she was hobbled to prevent her running away. He stroked her nose and patted her down for the last time, then picking up his few belongings he ran away for a second time. He would not go to Carlisle market. Nobody would brand him as a thief. He knew right from wrong. Despite his poor start in life he was honest.

He walked then ran in silence with the pole star at his back. That was one thing he had learned from the drovers. That star pointed north, and north was back into Scotland, the land of his birth, and to which he could never return.

William knew his destination. He would go to London. He remembered Mrs Robertson telling him it was the largest and wealthiest city on earth. It was the place where his bible had been printed by Mr Thomas Guy. That was the place for him.

Fortunately there was a clear sky and full moon to light his way over fields, tracks and streams until he reached a wood. He decided to hide there and rest. The drovers would be too busy with their herds to come looking for him and he doubted that the head drover would say he had found a runaway horse. That animal would be sold, probably several times over, and no one would ever find out from whence she came.

William trudged south. In his hurry to flee from Brackenholm he had made a mistake. He should have brought the flint and his father's knife with him. He would have been able to light a fire to keep himself warm, although that could have brought his presence to the notice of villagers or farmers who lived in the area. Perhaps it was for the best that he shivered in the cold night air despite finding shelter from the wind in a convenient area of woodland. He had to keep walking towards London.

* * *

On the next day, he was able to leave the hills and walk towards a river valley. Alongside the river was a well-marked track where carts had been driven many times. There were ruts in the road where the passage of vehicles over time had worn into the earth. This was easier, and so he was able to travel far on that day until he came to a place where another river, rushing off the hills came in on his left-hand side. Which way should he go? Last time the right-hand path had been the wrong one to take. This time the decision was easy. The deeper ruts lay on the right-hand path. That would be the way to take, although he could see in the distance the loom of high hills. He hoped the track found its way between them and he would not have to climb again into wild moors above the sheep pastures. Only time would tell.

Time did tell. The road started to climb and its ruts showed that any passing traffic had had difficulty here. Why did nobody use this track? Where were the farmers or perhaps a coach travelling north? He speculated on the answer to pass the time. In reality this was sheep country with just a few ploughed fields deep in the valley close to dwellings. The coaches were absent too. That winter had been harsh preventing journeys along an already difficult terrain. The company had fallen into debt. Its coaches and horses had been put up for sale. Its owner was afraid he could not pay his creditors and would be thrown into a debtor's prison.

As William walked and ran south beyond the high hills, he came across the occasional village or small township. His instinct was to detour around them, sometimes adding many miles to his journey. Then he had yet another thought to ease his journey to faraway London. He would hide at night to the north of the settlement. Then, be awake as the sun rose, and walk through the houses at the crack of dawn before anyone was astir. It would shorten his journey. He was rationing the food he had taken on that night he left the drover's camp, but was always hungry. He needed to find more food soon, but where? It was still spring. There was little food to be had in the hedgerows except for some dandelion leaves which left him hungrier. Any fruit trees had long since been harvested and the corn had yet to grow. Fortunately, the days were getting longer and had been mercifully dry. He could find water easily from the many streams and rivers from which to quench his thirst. He had found that by soaking the stale bread in some water held in the palm of his hand, it would soften and be easier to eat. He could even lick the palm of his hand so that none went to waste.

After five days, lady luck smiled on him. About a mile ahead, the road was being crossed by a hunt in full cry. William waited until it had long gone then continued his walk south. As he walked over the area where the hunt had been he saw something shining on the ground. He stopped and bent down to investigate and to his surprise found a penny coin that must have fallen from one of the huntsmen's pockets. It was his now. He would be able to buy bread later, but not in the next town.

He was down to his last piece of beef and reckoned he had but two days food left. He needed to speed up the rate of travel. After all his efforts to leave servitude under the Earl of Brackenholm, he did not want to fail now, or be found dead from hunger on the road to London.

PART 2 – THE TRAVELLER

12

Two days later William reached a major obstacle in his journey. There was a very wide river to cross. This river was different to any others he had had ever seen. It ran in a straight line as far as he could see to both the right and the left, but the water did not move like any normal river. It was still, and yet there was a well-worn path on the far side, and a narrow what looked to be slippery and winding path on his side. He had reached the Bridgewater Canal. This time he turned left and walked on. After a few miles, and about an hour later, there was a narrow, arched bridge over the canal. To the left there was a well-worn track to a village at the top of the hill. He would not go there. He crossed over the canal on the bridge to the wide track. It had to be used regularly, there were many horses hoof marks in the ground, and more than one horse too, and fresh horse droppings. He had found some kind of civilisation at last. He followed this track to his left. The walking was easy and the path level, after all those times when he had had to climb up and down those hills. By now it was quite late in the day and dusk was falling. As was his habit, he found shelter and ate the last of his food. Perhaps the good Lord had spared him after all. That night it rained heavily. He shivered again as his tattered clothes soaked up the water.

By the next morning, the rain had ceased but the track was heavy with mud from the overnight rain, making the walking more difficult than some of the wilder parts he had just left. As he walked he saw something he had never seen before again. There was a horse coming towards him along the track but what was it doing. There seemed to be something floating in the water next to the horse. As he got closer he could see that the horse was pulling the boat through the water. What was this and where was he?

Then his keen eye spotted a man standing at the back of the boat. He had something in his hand. As the horse, which was leading the boat on a rope came level with William he stopped and patted the animal, who stood still too. The boat did not stop on its path through the water and as it came closer the towing rope dropped into the water. The man at the back of the boat reacted and moved the rod he held, the boat's tiller, to stop his barge dead in the water. Before he could shout out at this interfering lad to leave his horse alone the lad spoke out 'Excuse me sir, where am I?'

'Sir', he did not get called that in his work as a bargee.

'Excuse me sir, where am I?'

The lad's words were not spoken in the local dialect, or any dialect he had heard before.

'Excuse me sir, where am I.'

'This is the Bridgewater Canal.'

'Excuse me sir, what is a canal?'

Now that was an interesting question. The answer would require some thought and he did not have time to waste. 'It's like a level river that barges, my boat can move on pulled by my horse.'

'And where does the canal go. I want to go to London.'

'That is a long walk from here.'

'Yes sir. I'll walk there.'

So, this was a determined lad. Where had he come from and why did he want to get to London were questions the bargee would have liked to ask but he had a cargo to carry and would only be paid when it reached its destination. William's next question surprised him even more.

'Where can I buy bread?'

So the lad had some money. He had asked politely, and that deserved a proper answer.

'If you continue to walk down the towpath you will reach Worsley. There is a baker in the village who will sell you bread'. And very good bread it was too. The bargee had bought some just yesterday and the remains were in his cabin.

'Thank you sir', and with that the lad ran off. He had learned something new, what a canal was for and that he was walking on a towpath, an easier way to travel than over the hills. He was now far away from Brackenholm. He could not be caught now, or could he. William resolved to continue to be very careful.

William stopped running then walked towards Worsley. As he did so he came across two other barges travelling towards him. This time he did not stop to stroke the horses but gave a wave to the bargees. They waved back. He next came across another barge, this time going in the same direction as he, but William was faster and again waved to the bargee. He noticed a name on the side of the barge, *Bridgewater No 13*. Thirteen, now that was an unlucky number for some people.

As he came towards a group of houses he saw a number of barges tied up in a line in front of what looked to be a wooden barrier over the canal. He had found a lock. As he looked he saw another barrier a little further down with two open gates. But where was the water? It was at a lower level than where the barges were waiting. Fascinated, William watched what was going to

77

happen. A man came out of a little building and walked to the open gate which he pushed closed using a long piece if wood attached to the gate. Then one of the bargees walked across the planks to the other side of the canal, then down to the other gate which he also moved until both gates closed in a 'V' pattern. Then the man from the building turned another handle which produced a sound of rushing water, then to William's surprise again the space between the two pairs of gates filled with water until it reached the level of water where the barges were moored. The two men then opened the gates nearest the barges two of which then moved side by side into the water. The open gates were closed, then there was another rush of water but this time the level between the two sets of gates fell until it reached that of the next section of the canal. Then the other gates were pushed on by the men and two barges moved forward and set off on their way. There was something else. On some of the barges there were women and children, sometimes lots of children from mere babies to young men nearly as old as he helping to work the boats.

William had just witnessed for the first time in his life how a canal lock worked and the way of life on the water for so many families. It was commonplace on the canals of England. He could have stayed and watched the operation repeated, but as this was early afternoon he wanted to find the baker's shop he had been told about earlier in the day. He saw how he could cross the canal to the other side and copied what the bargee had done. He walked across the top of the gates. It was a good job he had good balance. He did not want to fall into the water and get wet again.

When he reached the other side, he walked to the little building and saw that the door was open. He rapped his knuckles on the open door, as he had been taught to do before entering a building, and walked in. The man was writing something in a large book.

'Excuse me sir, I have been told that there is a baker's shop here in Worsley. How may I find it?'

The man, who was the lock keeper, looked up and nodded then said 'what do you want there?'

'I want to buy some bread sir.'

'Do you have any money?'

'A little' came back the cautious reply.

Satisfied, the lock keeper gave him directions to follow the track up the hill where he would find Worsley. The baker's shop was next to the local inn. It was easy to find.

William walked up the hill. It was not too far before he found the little cottages that made up the township of Worsley. At least he was in the correct place. As he reached the inn, there were loud noises coming from it. He peeped in through the open door where he saw several men, who looked as if they had come from the barges still moored in line waiting for their turn to pass through the lock, were drinking mugs of ale. That was not for him. The baker's shop was indeed next door. William saw in the window several large loaves of bread. A smell, which made him want to eat came out of the open door. Should he go in? William decided to see what would happen. A woman of the town came in with a basket on her arm, then one of the loaves in the window was taken out. A few minutes later the woman came out of the shop with a loaf in her basket. The same thing happened again until there were just three loaves left in the window. It was now late afternoon.

William walked into the baker's shop and asked 'excuse me sir, please can I buy one of those loaves of bread in your window.'

'That will be tuppence.'

'But sir, I only have a penny. Will you sell me half of a loaf then?'

What cheek! 'No I will not.'

'But what happens if the loaves remain unsold at the end of the day.'

That was a good question. 'They feed my family. Now go.'

William left the shop but continued to stay outside and look in the window. He thought what would happen if those three loaves remained unsold when the baker closed up for the day. Surely there would be enough bread to feed his family with just one or perhaps two loaves. So he waited until the time came for the baker to close his door. As he was doing so William walked in and repeated his first question 'excuse me sir, please can I buy one of those loaves of bread in your window?'

'They're tuppence, have you any more money?'

'No sir I have a penny so can I buy half a loaf now?

'They're tuppence.'

'But sir, do your family need all three of the loaves you have left?'

They did not. The reply was a hesitant 'maybe.'

'Sir I have not eaten in three days (a slight exaggeration) please sell me half of a loaf.'

The lad did look gaunt and tired and did look like he had not eaten for three days as he said. The baker relaxed a little. He did not need three loaves for his family. Two would suffice, and he could not sell today's bread tomorrow. He would need to bake afresh as always. One loaf would go to waste or to his hens. He could afford to be generous, after all a sale was a sale and he would have another penny in his pocket.

'Very well, I will let you have a loaf for your penny, but you will have to promise to return on another day and pay me the penny you owe me.'

William nodded his head in agreement. The deal had been struck. William handed over his penny, the baker gave William his loaf. William had learned another valuable lesson, be prepared to haggle over the first price he had been given. He left the shop happy. The baker wondered if he would ever be paid that extra penny as he closed the door for the day.

* * *

William walked down the hill back to the canal with his prize under his arm. He would walk on further then find a sheltered spot and eat something. He would have to make this last several days. He slept well that night. He was free.

13

When he awoke the next morning he was surprised to find a horse eating grass next to where he lay. It looked like one of the horses used to pull the barges along the canal. The horse had a halter around its head attached to which was just a short length of rope. The rope had a frayed end. William now knew what had happened. The horse must have broken free sometime during the night. There was no barge moored near where he had hidden for the night. Then he remembered where he had seen the horse before. It was the one he had seen towing Bridgewater No 13. That barge was nowhere in sight. It must lay moored back the way he had just come. He rose quietly so as not to frighten the horse, then caught hold of the halter rope. The horse, well trained that it was, let him. William now had control and retraced his steps. He hoped to find the barge soon and return the horse to its rightful owner.

* * *

As darkness fell on the previous day four barges were the last vessels to be let through the lock to the lower water level. They had moored up for the night in line ahead a short distance downstream with barge number 13 nearest to the lock.

There were four men, the bargees from these boats talking together. Three were facing in the direction they would travel later in the day, the other was facing towards the lock. The man facing the lock was waving his arms in the air and shouting 'where's my horse... thief... stolen...ruination...can't deliver my load...dismissal...debt...woe is me...ruination.' The other men listened but had no answers for their fellow bargee.

Then around a slight bend in the line of the canal they saw someone leading a horse towards them. As the horse and man came closer the three of them recognised the horse. It was number 13's. They began to smile. This annoyed the other man. He shouted and raged even more and demanded to know what was so funny about his stolen horse. The reply was laughter. Eventually he demanded to know what was so funny and was told 'look behind you.' As he did so he did not know whether to give thanks for his horse's return or to send for any officer of the law he might find to arrest what was undoubtedly the thief. He did neither and stayed rooted to the spot as William drew level with the group.

'Excuse me sir, but I found this horse wandering further down the canal. I recognised him from one of the barges I saw earlier yesterday near the lock, and have brought him back to you.'

'No you haven't, you stole him and became afraid you will be hung as a thief, so you have brought him back.'

'No sir, I am not a thief. I have brought him back. Look at this rope.' And with that he held up the short length of rope he had used to lead this horse back to its rightful owner. The rope was frayed.

It had clearly failed allowing the horse to run away to where William had found him.

The bargees looked at the rope and muttered amongst themselves for a few minutes while William waited. He could have run away, but that would have let the men believe he was a thief. He waited in silence.

Eventually the owner, bargee number 13, was convinced by his fellows that his horse had strayed and he was lucky that an honest lad had brought him back. What could he say? He mumbled a brief 'thank you and sorry I called you a thief.'

At that William merely nodded his head and turned away to retrace his steps along the miles he had lost through his honesty. 'Wait', came a shout. William turned to face the man who had branded him a thief without waiting for all the facts to become known. 'Where are you going?'

'To London'.

'I am going that way. If you come aboard my barge I can at least repay you for the wrong I did by taking you with me.'

'To London.'

'Towards London', and with that William stepped aboard the barge.

'I cannot pay you' said William.

'I cannot pay you either or give you a reward for the return of my horse. If you help me with the lock gates I can share my food with you.'

William just nodded his head. The deal had been struck. The bargee held out his hand to seal the deal. William held out his hand and the two met in a firm grasp. William looked him straight in the eye. He had learned another lesson. That was how bargains were sealed.

The bargee's final question was simple 'what is your name?'

'William Neal.'

'Well Willy, my name is Jeremiah Barnes. I was named after a prophet in the bible'.

'Yes Sir.'

So the two, man and lad, set to work together to harness the horse ready to pull the barge further down the canal. They were the last of the four to leave their overnight mooring. As they passed the place where William had found the horse, he pointed out the spot to Jeremiah. The response was just a wry smile.

* * *

The other three bargees were far ahead. What a story they would have to tell in the inns and byways as they traversed the canal. It had to be true, number thirteen was an unlucky number.

* * *

That evening, as it grew dark, Jeremiah and Willy as he was now called, moored the barge against the canal bank. They made sure that their horse was well and truly tied with a new piece of rope and that he had an area of grass to graze. They went into the little cabin where Jeremiah produced some bread and cheese, and bottles of ale. They sat at a little table lit by a flickering glim. There were no wax candles for them. The beer was a new experience for Willy so he drank just a little until it was explained to him by his newly found companion that the bargees never drank the water in the canal. They drank ale. It eased their tired limbs after a day's work and helped them sleep so they claimed.

After their simple meal, Willy found his bible, removed it from his pocket and started to read only to find Jeremiah questioned what he was doing. Willy explained that he was reading his bible and then had a thought. Would his companion like him to read about his namesake.

The reply was a rather rough 'maybe' so Willy found the book of Jeremiah in the Old Testament and started to read '...*I ordained thee a prophet unto the nations. Then said I, Ah Lord God behold, I cannot speak: for I am a child.*'

They decided that these words were hard to understand and that in future, if Willy was to read stories from the bible it was much better if they were parables from the New Testament. They could understand that message, especially following the school classes of Mrs Robertson, already so many weeks behind William.

The next day followed the same pattern. The barge headed slowly southwards as their horse plodded down the canal towpath. For William, each day was a benefit; he was further away from Brackenholm and unlikely to be captured and returned there.

At the end of the third day Jeremiah moored his barge by a group of others. He and Willy could see a house with lights in the window a short distance ahead. He ordered Willy 'follow me.'

So follow him Willy did until they came to the front door of the building they had seen. Above the door there was a swinging sign proclaiming for all the world to see 'NEW INN'. As Jeremiah entered, there was a lull in the noise and a shout of 'has he brought his horse?' followed by peals of laughter. Clearly the story of his missing horse had already preceded him along the canal and was now common knowledge amongst bargees and other canal users. He found a table close to the door and beckoned his new found friend Willy to join him. They sat in silence. After some time one of the inn's serving wenches came across to their table and asked what they would like to eat and drink.

'Two of your meat pies and two jugs of ale' came back Jeremiah's reply.

It seemed like an age to the two watermen from barge number 13 before the wench returned with their order and placed it down on their table to even more laughter and nudges of elbows into the ribs of their companions from the other patrons of that tavern.

'Eat and drink up lad,' were the next words from Jeremiah. So Willy, his boat lad, tucked into the best food he had ever eaten. He found great chunks of meat in a thick gravy topped with a crust. He had never seen the like before and soon his dish was empty. He was hungry, and thirsty too, as his jug of ale soon followed the pie into his belly. Jeremiah also ate in silence. When he had finished eating and drinking he said to Willy 'come on lad', then put a few copper coins onto the table to pay for the meal, such as it was. They left the New Inn in silence and walked back to their barge as more peals of laughter came from the place of their humiliation.

William could not understand why. He had done nothing wrong in returning a stray horse to its rightful owner, yet he was being made fun of by the other users of the canal. Life did not seem fair. That night he was too upset by the turn of events in that hostelry to read from his bible. He hardly slept. Where was his life leading him?

* * *

The next morning Jeremiah walked back to the New Inn and purchased bread, cheese and beer, their staple diet. He did not intend to stop at any other hostelry for the time being, until the story about his horse had become too old.

He returned to the barge and together he and Willy, as he called William, harnessed up their horse and set off to travel as far as they could down the canal that day.

That night they moored by the side of the canal and for the next two nights.

On the third night, after the humiliating incident at the New Inn, Jeremiah moored the barge for the night in a small town. There was a much wider canal here and barges moored up on both sides. A bridge linked the two banks. By looking under the bridge William could see that the canal started to make a long slow turn towards the right, rather than following the near straight line that had been its previous course. That night it rained very heavily. The noise of the rain drumming on the cabin roof woke William several times. At least for this night he was not sleeping rough in a wood or a corner of some field. His clothes were dry.

The next morning the rain continued to fall and gradually lessened in intensity. Jeremiah seemed in no hurry to set off further down the canal. Perhaps it was the rain that kept him together with William in the little shelter on their barge. He was strangely silent and seemed deep in thought and so to pass the time William read his bible to himself. Eventually Jeremiah gave a deep cough to clear his throat and said 'Willy I need to talk to you'.

'Yes sir.'

'You might have seen that the cut (that was his word for the canal) has started to head in a different direction towards the setting sun.'

'Yes sir.'

'Well it is now heading towards the sea and away from where you need to go.'

'Yes sir.'

'If you stay with me we will reach the sea where you may be able to get a boat going to London but you would have to pay and you have no money do you?'

'No sir.'

'There may be a boat that would take you if you worked, but you have never been on a ship like that have you.'

'No sir.'

'There is another danger.'

'And what is that sir?'

'The press.'

'The press, what is that sir?'

'It's called the press gang. These men are sailors from the King's Navy. They have the right to force you to join their ship. You could be away from

85

home for years. They can take men from boats carrying cargo too. They caught me many years ago, but I earned the right to be discharged. If you try to get away and they catch you, they hang you. So never get drunk with ale, and stay well away from London's river when you get there.'

'Yes sir'. That was another very important lesson that William had learned. He would not head towards the sea. He wanted to ask how his present mentor had gained his freedom, but decided that was one question to many.

'Now Willy if you head in that direction' at which Jeremiah pointed to the south east, 'you will come to an important town called Birmingham. From there a new cut goes all the way to London. I know about it because some men tried to get me to move there, but I said no.'

'Why sir?'

'They did say that there were many more locks to go through than on this cut. That would be hard work for a man of my age and they have tunnels.'

'What's a tunnel?'

'Well it's like a long hole made through a hill. It's dark and scary and they do say they are inhabited by ghosts. That's not for me.'

'But what should I do?'

'We are staying here today and will go into the town and find a friendly inn and have a hot meal, perhaps a good meat pie again. I think I know where to go this time. Then we will rest and perhaps you could read me more of your best bible stories. Tomorrow I will have to move down to the sea and you will have to leave and walk to Birmingham. You have been a good friend to me these last days and you brought back my horse. I cannot pay you for that, but I will buy you bread and cheese to see you on your journey. They have a local cheese here called Cheshire and I think you will like it. Come on Willy, let's go and find that inn.'

With that, they left the horse securely tied up and walked into the town, down narrow streets, and turned this way and that until at the end of a narrow lane they reached their destination. There were no noisy shouts and laughter as they went in to find a few men drinking their ale and talking quietly to themselves. Jeremiah was welcomed by two men with a nod of the head and a lift of their mug. They were amongst friends this time, and were able to eat and drink their fill in peace.

The next morning Jeremiah went into the town and returned with a well-filled sack that he gave to Willy. 'Here you are lad, to help you on your way. Now when you reach the cut from Birmingham to London you will find it is easy walking down the towpath, but it is a long way. You may be able to find a barge to take you there. Try this. Find a lock and sit and wait for a barge to come along, then help with moving the lock gates as you have done for me. The older the bargee the better, as he will be more likely to want your help.' In silence they harnessed the horse to the barge and got ready to travel down the cut. William stepped ashore with his sack of food and other meagre belongings, not forgetting his faithful bible. He and Jeremiah looked at each other for a few seconds and smiled, then Jeremiah said 'bye Willy lad, God bless you.'

'Bye Jeremiah, God bless you too.'

With that William turned and started to walk in the direction of Birmingham. Jeremiah geed up his horse and his barge started to move downstream. He had a tear in his rheumy old eye. He wished he had fathered a son like that. He dared not to look back; neither dared William.

14

This time William felt much bolder and walked down muddy tracks and lanes. He had food so he could never be charged with theft in any of the towns or settlements he passed through. He was still careful to seek shelter at night in a wood or under a hedge. After two days he came across the tell-tale signs that a herd of cattle had passed, and were going in the general direction he hoped was still the way to Birmingham. There seemed to be fewer animals in this herd than the one he had followed to escape from Brackenholm to England. Maybe this was another sign from God to show him the way. He decided to follow the herd and trust to providence, and the Almighty. Perhaps his late father was correct after all 'this was God's Will'.

Eventually he came across a herd of about 100 animals. They too were black, like the herd he had followed in the Scottish borders, but were a little smaller, as were the drovers who were fewer in number than before. As he came nearer he heard their voices. They were speaking in a foreign language. It had to be because William did not understand a single word they said; there was nothing he recognised from the English language.

He greeted the first man he met at the rear of the herd with a friendly 'good day sir' but there was no reply. William walked on past the cattle until he found the man at their head, leading the way. He repeated his greeting 'good day sir' but found the reply hard to understand. He slowed his pace to that of the herd and started to ask questions.

'Where are you from; where are you going; are you going to Birmingham; can I walk with you?'

The answers came from this man in singing, halting English. They were Welsh from Ynys Mon. Yes, they were going to Birmingham. They had previously driven they cattle all the way to London, but that was too far now. There was a new place, yes it was Birmingham, and they were going there because its population was growing fast. They made many things there, and there was a good market for their animals. It was nearer than London so they could make three journeys per year rather than two and earn more money with less effort. Yes William could walk with them but he would have to find his own food and even if he helped keep the cattle on track he would not be paid for his efforts. Fortunately, Jeremiah had been very generous with his food parcel. He could eat sparingly and make it last. He had done so before and it would not be the last time, he supposed, that he would have to be careful again.

The drovers and William walked the miles towards Birmingham together in silence. They had some difficulty understanding each other's language so silence was the best option. One day when William's food was nearly exhausted the leading drover pointed ahead to what looked like a haze in the sky. It was not haze but the smoke from all the coal fired manufactories in Birmingham that hung low over its dwellings. They were nearly there. There were more buildings than William had ever seen in his life before, and they seemed to stretch as far as the eye could see.

William did not know what he might find amongst all those buildings and their narrow streets. Would he be safe there? He decided that he would adopt the strategy that had served him so well earlier in his journey. He would walk to the south and avoid the town. After all, Jeremiah had promised him that he would reach this new canal that would lead him to his goal of London, the richest and largest city on earth according to Mrs Robertson. He believed both her and Jeremiah.

He was surprised to find that there were well worn tracks leading in the direction he wanted to go. His sack of food was nearly bare, he needed to find more soon, so he ran then walked and ran then walked for that day then found the best shelter he could for the night. Although summer was already here, that night it rained heavily. He was cold and wet and hungry the next morning. He had to reach that canal soon, so he ran and walked until gradually the warmth returned to his tired body. He just had to find the canal.

In the early afternoon, he reached his goal or he thought he had. Was this the canal to London? It was much narrower than Jeremiah's Bridgewater canal and there were no barges in sight. He turned south and walked slowly along the towpath. Where would it lead him to?

About an hour or so later he found why there were no barges where he had just walked. He had found them at not one lock but three, one after the other to take the canal to a higher level. There were barges queued up at both lower and higher levels and another stuck in the first lock. Men everywhere were shouting to each other all making claims about who should be first to go up or down the flight of locks. When William reached the scene of the confusion he could see why. There was only space for one barge at a time in the lock, and these boats were much narrower than those of Jeremiah and his fellow bargees.

There were two men, who William presumed were bargees standing with their fists raised and looking to want to indulge in fisticuffs to decide who was first. There shouts continued 'I'm first,' 'no you're not I am.' A crowd of other boatmen was beginning to gather with each side cheering on their

89

respective champion. Just before the first blow was landed, there was a stentorian shout from the back of the crowd 'stop that' and into view marched the tallest and strongest looking man William had ever seen. 'What's going on?' he shouted to make himself heard above the general noise. The hubbub quietened for a second or two, then began again with opposing claims to who was first. The big newcomer shouted again 'be quiet, now.' It was the voice of command so silence fell. It was a practiced voice of command from a man who had been a sergeant in the British Army and used to giving orders. Silence fell on the gathering.

The former sergeant turned to one of the antagonists and asked 'What is your problem?' The answer came fast and furiously 'I'm first because...' 'No he wasn't came' an interruption from the other would be prizefighter. The response from the sergeant was immediate and dreadful 'I told you to be quiet; you will have your turn for your say so in a minute. Be quiet or else.' The threat was real. A little peace descended on the gathering while the sergeant thought for a minute. He would have to decide who should be first between these two angry men. In reality, the sergeant was the keeper of the three locks. He should have been at his post just to prevent such an altercation but had left for purposes he was not prepared to reveal to anyone. He would have been dismissed his post if anyone had found his little secret. His years of army training and experience kicked in. 'You men', he pointed to the braying mob of bargees who had been urging their respective champions into a fight just moments before, 'go back to your boats now.' Slowly, sulkily, and with shuffling of feet, that order was slowly obeyed. The arena cleared.

'Right you two, if you give me any more trouble your barges will never pass through my locks. I will send you back from whence you came, do you understand me.'

Both bargees did. If they were sent back it would be they who would be dismissed and without work, however poorly paid as it was, their families would starve. Silence reigned.

The lock keeper stood up to attention, as he remembered from those many parades, to demonstrate his importance to these undisciplined men. He wished they had been privates in his old regiment, they would have fought his way, the King's enemies and not each other. It was decision time.' As I see it we can sort this out in one of three ways. You can fight each other until one of you drops, but that will take time and your fellow travellers will not like that. I can decide who goes first, or if I choose, who waits until everyone else has cleared my locks, or we can have a wager. Which will it be?'

Somewhat reluctantly both agreed on the wager.

Good. That was common sense returning to this little fracas. The lock keeper put his hand in his pocket and brought out a shiny silver coin and showed the head of King George III on one side and the tail on the other to prove to both that there was no fake or trickery. 'This is my King's shilling. It was given to me when I first joined the army so be careful with it. You,' he turned to the bargee from the lower level 'will toss this coin in the air, and you, he turned to the bargee from the upper level will call out heads or tails. Whoever wins will go first, the loser will go second. Is that agreed?'

Both men nodded their heads in agreement so the wager took place. As luck would have it the bargee from the upper level won. That would speed the process of clearing the backlog of boats.

The sergeant made sure the King's shilling was handed back to him.

'Right you, get your boat out of my lock, moor up and then come back here' was the order to the loser.

'Right you, get your boat moving into the locks now' was the order to the winner 'then when you have cleared the lock you will moor up and come back here, and if you think you can keep going you will have to reckon with me.' He had judged his man well, that was what he would have done, but his work required him to travel up and down this cut and he now knew that he had been issued with no idle threats.

The lock keeper then marched down to the lower level and ordered the bargees to come with him, then repeated the exercise at the upper level. He now had a squad of men and he would put them to work like soldiers. His plan was simple. In order to speed the process, he put a man at each gate, one on each side, and another man to control the paddles that opened and closed the water channels to fill and drain each lock. They would work to his command, open this, close that, water here, and that would speed the work. He smiled, it was just like the old days having men to obey his every order.

William had observed these goings on from the opposite bank of the canal. He had never heard the like before and was fascinated by the way that a little authority and a clear plan had turned a frightening scene into a hive of purposeful activity. He had learned another lesson. He then noticed that no one was moving one of the lock gates. They were one man short, and as the gate was on his side he walked forward, put down his now empty sack and prepared to follow orders. By now the days were longer and well before sunset all the barges had cleared and been sent on their way. The locks were empty.

The towpath had changed sides to the opposite bank. William crossed over by walking along the top of the lock gate and had started to turn towards what he hoped would be London when that voice called 'you there'. He stopped in his tracks.

'You there, which boat are you from?'

'None sir.'

'Then what are you doing? I saw you working the gates on my orders.'

'Walking to London sir. I happened to be passing and saw you were a man short.'

'All the way to London.'

'Yes sir.'

'No you're not.'

'Then sir, please tell me how I can get to London?'

'Well now, you have helped me so I will help you. This is the canal to London, down there', and he pointed in the direction William had started to walk, 'but you're not walking.'

'But sir, if I do not walk how will I get there?'

'Leave that to me.'

'How sir?'

'I said leave that to me. I can find a boat to take you there, if there is where you must go.'

'Thank you, sir.'

'Now where will you sleep tonight?'

'I will find shelter in a wood and curl up there.'

'And if it rains?'

'Then I will get wet sir. It has happened before.'

'And what will you eat?'

William knew his sack was all but empty, but did not want to admit his hunger. 'I have a little bread sir.'

He was not believed. The lock keeper knew when a man was not telling the truth, his army experience had taught him that skill. 'If we walk a short way towards London, I have a cottage. You can sleep there for the night under my roof, and we will eat together.' He had a rabbit collected from a local poacher and some of the early vegetables that grew in the little garden he dug and planted, and there would be a rich stew tonight.

William joined him for another hearty meal. He wondered if everyone in England ate as well as this, meat pies, stew. How different from his oatmeal diet from what was now distant Brackenholm.

15

For the next three days he worked the locks with the sergeant, as he liked to be called. When the locks were free of barges looking to pass through, the sergeant left William in charge and disappeared. William dare not ask where he went, but each evening they ate well. The sergeant started to tell William about all his adventures while he had served in the army, of the wars he had fought, the wounds he had received and the comradeship of standing shoulder to shoulder next to a friend in a line of battle. William listened and learned. He liked the idea of comradeship, but thought he could never be that brave. No, the army was not for him if that was what the life was like.

On the next day a heavily laden barge moored up ready to pass through the flight of locks. On this occasion the sergeant and the bargee had friendly smiles, and from the snatches of conversation that William heard, a friendly banter. William also noticed that on one occasion the bargee gave the sergeant what looked like a mock salute. After this barge had reached the upper level, its horse plodded on for only a short distance and stopped opposite the sergeant's cottage when the bargee jumped ashore and tied up his boat. William wondered if this was to give his horse a rest as he walked back. When he reached there the sergeant was all smiles. 'William my lad, I want you to meet with Joseph. He was a corporal in my regiment, and is a good man. I have arranged for him to take you to London, but you must promise to help him work all the locks on the way. You won't get paid, but you will get your food. Do you agree?'

William did agree. His immediate response was 'thank you sirs'. He held out his hand to shake that of the other men. The deal had been struck. But there was no movement in the direction of London that day. The sergeant and his corporal sat down with a large jug of ale which there proceeded to share while telling each other stories from their army days. 'Do you remember when?'

'And what about?'

Fortunately only one barge wanted to pass through the locks while the pair of old soldiers were reliving their glory days. It was William who saw it safely through.

* * *

The next day corporal Joseph and William set off for London. If William had hoped to be transported on the barge and to save his legs he was going to be disappointed. For most of the day his duty was to lead the barge horse down the towpath. They made slow progress. Joseph did not seem to be in any great hurry to get his cargo to its destination, but each day they were miles nearer to William's goal, London.

On one day, they had to moor up behind a line of other barges. Joseph explained that they had reached Braunston tunnel and it would take nearly a day to pass through its two miles or so length. There was no room for their horse. William would take the gelding over the hill on the path to reach the other end of the tunnel and wait there while Joseph steered the boat through.

'How do you get through if the horse can't pull us?' asked William.

'Well' said Joseph, 'we have to employ men called leggers and what they do is walk the boat through by pushing against the tunnel walls. It's very hard work. At least here two boats can pass side by side, so there will not be the delays that we found at Sergeant's Lock.' That was a good name for it, William would remember that for all his days.

'I was told that ghosts live in the tunnel' explained William.

'No, that's just a story we tell to keep people away.'

* * *

Joseph and the barge entered the tunnel propelled by the leggers. William walked their horse up the hill and down the other side to wait. At least on this day he had not had to walk too far.

The two met up later that day on the London side of the tunnel. While they were eating their evening meal and drinking their ale, William asked Joseph if he had seen any ghosts.

'No, I told you it was just a story.'

They travelled on towards London until they had to moor up again in front of another tunnel mouth. Joseph explained that this was Blisworth Tunnel, the longest in the world. It was nearly 3 miles long and taken years longer to build than expected. Joseph told William that at first the barges could reach the London side of the tunnel, then had to be unloaded and pack horses used to carry their cargo to the other side where another barge could be loaded up for the ongoing journey to Birmingham. At least that was in the past now.

The next day, when Joseph's turn came he and the leggers set off down the tunnel while William walked their horse over the hill. That took him an hour, and so again he had to wait for his barge and Joseph to arrive. Again, during their evening meal William asked Joseph 'are there ghosts in this tunnel?'

This time Joseph took some time before answering 'Maybe. They do say it is haunted by some of the men who were killed while the tunnel was being dug, but I have not seen the ghosts.'

William then knew that Jeremiah Barnes claim that tunnels were haunted by ghosts was probably true. He resolved to keep out of tunnels. That was another lesson learned.

* * *

They continued their journey towards London. As they got nearer to the capital Joseph warned William that they would be coming to several flights of locks and he would need his help again to navigate through them. He explained again, as if teaching a raw recruit in the army his drill, what William had to do. 'These are much quicker because boats can pass side by side, like we saw in the tunnels and there is less room to make a mistake.'

'Then why was Sergeant's Lock not built like these then?'

'That William is a very good question, but they do say that the canal owners ran out of money to build a double lock. They will live to regret it, because, as the cut gets busier, they will have to build another set alongside the old ones. Serves them right if it costs them more.'

That was another lesson for William. Make sure you have enough money to build for future expansion when the time comes.

* * *

They travelled on through the locks until they came to what William thought was a big lake with lots of barges moored alongside its banks. Here the canal cut divided, one arm to the right and the other to the left. Here there were two inns, one on either side of the canal. Joseph pointed them out to William. 'That one over there is called 'The Barge' and this one is 'The Bull's Head'. We are at an important place called Bull's Bridge. We'll stay here for the night but we are going to eat there' and he pointed towards 'The Bull's Head'. 'We are going to eat our fill of hot pies and drink our fill of ale.'

They walked over to their chosen hostelry and entered through a battered wooden door. There were immediate shouts of recognition and welcome for Joseph from the customers who were enjoying the inn's delights. It was clear to William that Joseph was a well-known and well liked member of the bargee's fraternity. How different from that first inn he had entered with the unfortunate Jeremiah Barnes. They ate and drank well are returned to their barge for a well-earned good night's sleep.

The next morning, Joseph explained again what was happening to the course of the cut. 'That way', and he pointed to the right, 'takes you to Brentford and the river Thames. That's the river that goes right through the middle of London and down to the sea. It's very busy, there are ships bringing goods in and taking them out to the rest of the world. I went from there after I joined the army.'

With that comment William was quite certain that he did not want to go that way. He remembered Jeremiah's story about 'the press' and being forced to serve for years on a Royal Navy ship. He intended to stay as far away from the river and being caught as he could. But where did the other way go? Joseph explained that too.

If we go the other way that takes us to what is called Paddington. That's a little village a few miles from the centre of London and that's where we are going. When we get there, we will unload all those crates and parcels, then, they will be taken all over London to where they need to be.'

William was greatly relieved by this turn of events. He tried not to show his relief, but perhaps Joseph had noticed. It did not matter. They set off for the two or three days it would take to reach this place called Paddington from where William would find the city of his dreams that his mentor Mrs Robertson had described so long ago, and the place where his trusty bible had been printed. It was the greatest city on earth he had been told. William intended to find out for himself.

16

While William was making his slow way to London there were changes taking place back at Brackenholm.

As they dined each evening, the dowager Countess and her son John discussed their future. It would have been truer to say that the Countess talked and John listened. The conversation rarely varied. Which of the ladies on my list do you think would be the most suitable wife for you. The reply was always the same. 'I am still thinking about them. You have made me spoiled for choice Mama.'

The truth was somewhat different. Each time he had been presented with a list John, the 3rd Earl, had thrown it into the fire and watched as the piece of paper burned and was lost to sight. He was much more interested in his mausoleum project which was nearing completion. Mr Dunbar and his men had worked hard but then they had been blessed with exceptionally fine weather for that time of year in the borders. The walls were up and plastered, the roof trusses fixed and soon the slates for the roof would be fixed in place. Just another few days to wait.

At last the mausoleum was complete, and all it needed now was a blessing from Mr Robertson, the Minister, and his father laid to his final resting place. Then John could put into place the next part of his plan.

On the evening his father had been placed in the mausoleum it was John this time who spoke first at supper with his mother. Now that was unusual. His mother listened intently. 'Mama, now that father has been lain to rest in what I want to be the final resting place of all our family members, I think the time has come for me to take my seat, as of right, in the House of Lords in London. I know our dear father never did, but I think it will be important for the future of our estate if I find out so much more about how our country is run and make as many important friends as I can there.'

'That is not what I expected to hear John. I have spent a great deal of time trying to find a suitable wife for you here for our estate.'

'Yes Mama, and I am so grateful for all the trouble you have taken. I do think that in London there may be there possibility of meeting a rich heiress, I am told there are plenty looking to make as fine a match as I would be, and I would like to explore that if I may first. If I am unsuccessful, then of course I will return here and we can discuss who might be best for me to marry from your lists.'

As there was no other reply the dowager Countess could make, she merely replied 'hmm, let's see then.'

In truth John had no intention of looking for a wife in London, well not at first. What had the great Dr Johnson said *'he who is tired of London is tired of life'* John's plan was quite simple. He intended to spend money from the estate on a house suitable for a man of his station in life, to enjoy all the pleasures of London, and then when he was older, say forty or even fifty years old, he would take a much younger wealthy wife who would give him the heirs he knew he would need. She could look after and pleasure him in his old age. It had been done before by other aristocrats and would no doubt be done again. It was his turn now.

He discussed how he would reach London with his steward. The final plan was that they would have to ride to Scotland's capital, Edinburgh, and they would travel together until they reached a coaching inn at the Old Town. The roads, such as they were, were poor and there was no certainty that his carriage would get through. That was not the Earl's first choice of travel, but it would have to suffice. Once they had reached Edinburgh the Earl could pay to be taken by stagecoach to London. Earl John knew the city well from his schooldays. He had no desire to stay there longer than he had to. It would only take 4 days with overnight stops at coaching inns along the way where he could eat, drink, and make merry. Perhaps there would be a serving wench or even an ostler to share his bed. It was cheaper than the mail coach which could reach London in 2 days, an unheard of speed. When John had to return to his estate that would be a quicker way to travel if need be.

There were tearful farewells at Brackenholm. The Countess still had her doubts about the wisdom of her son's plan, but she was powerless to stop him. The estate had been transferred to John on her husband's death, and although there was provision for her to be housed and fed for the rest of her days on God's earth, she hoped she would not be sent to some dower house. She liked the great house, so perhaps, for the next few months while John was taking his seat and making new contacts she would be able to enjoy all the trappings of luxury her status gave her. She sent John on his way, with an instruction to write to her often, but if she had known how long it would be before her son returned she might have had more concerns.

John was quite clear in his own mind. He intended to stay in London and enjoy the city's life for as long as he could before he had to return to the wild border lands that were his. His education at George Heriot's Hospital and his Grand Tour had opened his eyes to other things in life than working the land, although he had never worked the land in his life nor ever would he. There were others to do that and make money for him to spend.

As expected the journey to London took just over a week in all. Although he did not know it, John, the 3rd Earl of Brackenholm had arrived in London on the same day as William. It was perhaps fortunate that their paths did not meet then. The Earl had arrived at Smithfield in the city. William was several miles west at Paddington Basin. John had also somewhere to stay with a friend from his Grand Tour days. They had been writing to each other in secret for some months. It was a miracle that he had been able to keep this from his mother. His next task was to find a way of taking all his baggage and himself to that address in the new smart part of London, what people were calling the west end, where the people of quality shopped and lived. It was nearer to Parliament too, but his plan was to spend as little time as possible there, just enough to be able to write an occasional letter to his mother about that place. After all, he would have to pay for the mail coach to Edinburgh, and then by horse for his letters to reach Brackenholm. He had other things he wanted to spend his fortune on.

17

While the Earl had arrived in London in the relative comfort of a stagecoach, William had walked the towpath leading the barge's faithful horse to its destination, Paddington Basin. The basin was alive with the activity of other barges loading and unloading under the direction of men with papers in their hands controlling the hustle and bustle around them. 'See those men' pointed out Joseph to William, 'they are tally clerks, they check everything in and out, or are supposed to, but you have to watch what they do. They can cheat you, and some are not as honest as they claim to be. You can help me because you can read and write.'

William helped Joseph and other men to unload the barge. It was heavy work lifting out the crates and making sure they were placed in one pile ready for collection later. As William watched what was going on he saw how a fiddle was worked. A parcel or box was taken from one pile and placed on another smaller, but growing pile elsewhere. So that was how the system worked. He was there to make sure nothing was taken from what he now regarded as his delivery, and nothing was.

When this store, the warehouse had been closed for the night and padlocked tight, William returned to the moored up barge to find Joseph. He told him what had been happening, although Joseph clearly already knew all the tricks of the trade that might happen to his delivery. All he received for his labours was a 'well done' from Joseph. He was so tired he fell into a deep sleep without eating. He dreamed about a life in London, but would his dreams ever come true?

The next morning, after a meagre breakfast on the remains of their bread, Joseph put his hand in his pocket.

'You are a good and honest lad, William, and have been a great help to me these days past. Here is something for you.' With that he withdrew his hand from his pocket and held out a shilling coin.

'Is that for me?'

'Yes, you have earned it.'

'But I agreed with you and the Sergeant that I would not be paid.'

'Yes, but I think you deserve this. You will need money to buy food and London is a very expensive place to be.'

'Thank you', and with that William took the offered coin and put it into his own pocket.

'Now William, would you like to earn another shilling?'

'How?'

'Go and join the army. They will give you another shilling, the King's shilling. They feed you, give you uniform clothes, and a good life.'

William had remembered the stories of battles, death and foreign places that Joseph and the Sergeant had reminisced about those few days ago. That was not the life he wanted for himself. He had fought for too long to escape a life of servitude to an uncaring employer to give that up now only to be told what he had to do. He merely nodded his head, as if in agreement with Joseph. It would soon be time for them to part company.

* * *

Joseph walked with William from their barge towards the massive wooden gates that marked the entrance to the basin and its warehouses. As they did so they came across a line of empty horses and carts with their drivers waiting to collect whatever needed to be delivered to customers in that growing metropolis they called London.

'Joseph, which way do I go to get to London?'

'Well, it's a big place, where do you want to go to?'

'I don't know. What do you think?'

Joseph had known since the time they had first met that William was a runaway from somewhere. He did not know where, and this was a question that was never asked. Men did what they could to survive, and for the men of their class life was hard. They had to stick together. Comradeship was everything. The army had taught him that. He did know what to do. Move William on so he could return to his barge, load up with his next cargo, and make the return journey to Birmingham. That was his life now. At least he had his friend the Sergeant to meet. He would have more stories to share now.

Joseph looked along the line of carters for a friendly face. Who did he know? As he surveyed the ranks there came through the gates an old horse and tired looking man who he knew. Here was another old soldier. Joseph approached this man and began a conversation. On two or three occasions, he turned and pointed towards William. Another deal was being made. Once this had been completed Joseph beckoned the waiting William to come forward. William advanced to the horse and cart, Joseph and another unknown man and was concerned about what he would find there. He need not have worried. Old soldiers have a way of looking after each other, and this is what would happen again. William's luck was holding.

The deal was quite simple. William would help load when it reached its turn in the queue, and unload the cart when it reached its destination in London. The carter, who would not give his name, would take William back to his lodging where he could stay for a few days until he found out where he would go in London. The place he would end this day was called St Giles. What William did not know then, but soon found out, that this was a notorious rookery, a haunt of thieves, drunks, prostitutes, and the poorest of the poor. There was one advantage, the authorities were too scared to enter St Giles. He would be safe from both press gangs and army recruiters. As before the deal was sealed by a shake of the hands between William and the carter.

It was a pity thought Joseph that William wanted to make his way in life in London. He was a good helping hand on the barge and could have made a life there. They had been a good team together.

As they faced each other for the final time Joseph drew himself up into that position of attention he had learned in the army and threw William a salute. William, who had had no army training followed suit and returned the salute as best he could. They shook hands. 'Goodbye William, good luck' were Joseph's final words, 'thank you sir and I wish you the same.' They turned and went their separate ways. William climbed onto the cart, Joseph walked towards the warehouse to find his next load. Neither man looked back. The future for both of them lay in different directions.

* * *

The cart, with William aboard moved off and passed through the warehouse gates onto a well-worn and rutted track through fields towards a collection of buildings in the not too far distance. That was London, spreading towards the west, away from the original development called the city. They reached a cross roads. The carter pointed ahead and said, 'that's Tyburn Way, they used to bring prisoners along there for hanging over there' as he swung his arm to the right towards a large open space. He turned the cart to the right down a well-developed road with a wall on the left until he reached a gated opening into which he turned. William was amazed at what he saw. There were large houses on either side of the road, then, as the cart moved on its way they came to a large grassy square with grand houses all around. William had never seen the like before and asked 'Is this London?'

'This is where the nobs live and where we will be delivering or boxes', at which he pulled up outside what seemed like the largest house of all. It had a large front door with windows on either side and reached upwards with four layers of windows that got smaller as the building rose up to its roof.

'Right lad, off you get, and help me with these boxes. They got down and found a box about ten feet long and two feet square. It was not as heavy as he expected, so he asked 'what's in here?'

The carter looked at the label stuck to the front before replying 'a clock.'

William was not surprised when, instead of taking the clock to the front door, they carried it down a narrow path and into a small courtyard to the rear door where a servant in a smart uniform was waiting. He opened the door and instructed them to bring their delivery into the servant's quarters. This was no surprise to William. After all, he had had the same experience those months ago in Brackenholm before he set out on his adventure. As they turned to leave William saw, on the opposite side to the servant's door, a stables, coaches and a rear entrance. So this was how the wealthy lived in London.

The pair completed their deliveries to similar properties in the area that William learned was called 'Mayfair'. Some houses were larger than others, some taller, but all exuded wealth beyond anything William had previously experienced.

At the end of the day, with all their deliveries completed the carter turned his horse and wagon away from the setting sun across another wide road and into another area of London. This was very different to Mayfair. The lanes were narrow, there was the stench of animals and the people wore rags and were barefoot for the most part. The houses were broken down. The place was ugly and depressing. After a few twists and turns down the lanes the carter turned into a cobbled yard. There were other carts there and a stables for the work horses. A fat man who was wearing brown woollen clothes of good quality and leather boots was standing at the entrance and marked down their return. The man had a misshapen nose and one ear larger than the other. He was the owner of the carting enterprise, a hard man, who had made his money as a prizefighter before setting up in his present business. When he saw William he shouted out 'who's this?'

'A lad from the barge at Paddington Basin. He's been helping me today.'

'I'm not paying him you know.'

'He does not expect to get paid, but he could be a good worker for you.'

'Maybe, but I don't need another hand yet.'

The carter showed William where to put their cart after they had unhitched their horse. They removed the harnesses from the horse then rubbed down and fed another gelding. To his surprise the carter found that William did not need to be told what to do. Where had he learned to look after horses? That was a question William would never answer however many times he would be asked.

Their work done and the horse fed, the two left the stable yard and walked out into the lane and turned towards the maze of buildings.

'Stay with me, and welcome to St Giles.'

They walked through filthy foul lanes and past slums where ragged, barefooted children sat on doorsteps. There were women inviting them to come and join them. Most were unkempt, some ugly, and some pock-marked. William had not seen the like before on any of his travels. St Giles was squalid and depressing. Why had William come here? His answer would be to escape poverty and servitude, but what he saw here was much worse poverty than he had experienced back in Brackenholm, while the people he saw seemed to accept the conditions they lived in. He thought he should never have left, but he was here now, and could not go back. How different was this area to that just a short distance away where he and the carter had made their deliveries. The difference was that of chalk and cheese.

Eventually there reached a building that was perhaps more broken down than any of the others in that lane.

'In here' said the carter, and pulled William's arm to make sure he came along through a battered door that was nearly hanging off its hinges. The smell was foul as the two climbed stairs to the top floor and found one small room. There, William found a woman with lank greasy hair and a care-worn face nursing an infant on her breast. There was a pile of dirty straw in one corner and a scurrying sound – a rat. This place was far worse than the bothy home he had lived in just a few short months ago. His parent's house had always been as clean as their meagre resources could make it. This room had never been cleaned in months, if ever.

The carter spoke first again 'this is my wife and baby son, meet Wilson.' He had forgotten William's name.

William thought for a moment, to say William seemed far too grand a name for these surrounding. He reverted to his name given by Jeremiah Barnes 'I'm Willy.' It was simpler that way.

'Yes, Willy, he's going to help me with the cart and can stay here.' At that a corner was pointed out 'you can sleep there.' There was no straw just a hard wooden floor. Willy would have to curl up there as best he could. Worse was to follow.

'You help me with the cart and you can stay here rent free. I'll not pay you a penny piece though and there may be some bread to eat if you're lucky.' It was clear to Willy, as he now was called, where any money went, the carter drank his fill in a local alehouse while his wife and child and food would always be the last consideration. When the carter threw him a corner of a stale loaf of bread he knew that he had made a terrible mistake. He would have to escape again.

The carter knew what he would do with Willie. He could work with him during the day and when he could he would turn him into a prize-fighter. He was a big strong lad, and fit. The carter dreamed of managing his protégé and of the money he would make. He would have to start the process carefully. Thus, when they were waiting for loads the carter told Willy that he would have to look after himself and this was the way to do it. Stand like this, hold your fists like this, punch like this and that, defend yourself like this. It was basic training and another lesson for him he would have preferred not to have. Was London, his dream, really like this nightmare?

18

His chance to escape came at the end of the first week in St Giles. It was a Sabbath as Willy would have called it, although the locals here called it Sunday, that was something of a day of rest, although as far as he could tell, none attended the Kirk, or as he had now learned, the church or chapel. It was a new language. The carter had gone out leaving Willy with his wife and child. Where had he gone and when would he return? Willy got up and walked to the stairs, then, as there was no one in sight, he walked down them as quietly as possible to the battered front door and looked outside. There was no one there. What luck that was, so he slipped out of that dreadful place and walked a short distance to the corner of the lane, a crossroads. Which way should he go? He decided to take the middle path, straight on this time. He remembered when he had turned right into a dead end on his journey from Carlisle, and he had turned left at other times. Forward march, as the Sergeant would have said, was his choice this time.

The lane took him deeper into the rabbit warren of narrow lanes and dead ends that was the place called St Giles. There were women standing about inviting him to join them, but he ignored them as he did for children playing in the mud and detritus that was their natural environment. Willy walked on until he saw a wider road ahead. He knew where that was. It was the boundary road across which he could not be sure he would be safe. As he pondered what to do next, he heard shouts coming from the next corner. He increased his walking speed from the gentle amble it had been once he had passed the first crossroads after his second escape. As he got nearer the shouts became loader. He could hear what was being said.

'No, leave me alone' said one voice.

'We want your magic cards' said another, while a third said 'if you don't give us them I'll kill you.'

'They won't work for you, leave me alone.'

'They will, and I want them. I want them now.'

'No, leave me alone, help.' That was the first voice again.

Willy reached the scene of the activity in a few seconds more. He found a smaller lad of about his own age, or maybe a little older, held against a wall by two bigger young men. One of them called out 'for the last time, give us your magic cards.'

'They're not magic,' came a mournful cry.

Willy did not like what he saw. Two men bent on hurting or killing a lad of about his own age. Without thinking he acted. He ran up to the nearest man put his left hand on his shoulder to turn him round. As the man was turned to face him, Willy punched him hard on the nose using his right hand and the new found skills that the carter had taught him just a few days ago. When the man put his hands to his face to stem the bleeding from what was a broken nose, Willy hit him again with a left into his belly. As the man doubled up, Willy hit him again with a right to the jaw. The man crumpled and fell to the ground, knocked out. It had taken but a few seconds to reduce the odds.

The second man, having overcome the shock of seeing his fellow thief knocked to the ground yelled out 'you' then pulled out a knife and started to wave it in front of Willy's eyes. 'I'll get you for that.' He lunged forward, but Willy was quicker and stuck out a leg. His assailant tripped and fell to the ground. As he stuck out an arm to save himself from the fall, the knife left his hand and clattered to the ground. Quick as a flash Willy ran and put his foot on the knife. That would even things up a bit. The man stood up and realised he had lost his weapon and his advantage. He made to fight Willy then thought better of it. He has seen what had happened to his mate who was now getting up from the floor, dazed and confused from Willy's knockout blow.

With a parting 'we'll get you for this' the knifeman picked up his mate and the two staggered off leaving a frightened third person who shrank back against the wall who cried out 'please don't hit me.'

Willy had no intention of hitting him. He bent down to pick up the knife. It was his now, so he stuck it in his belt. It was quite sharp, and he would have been badly injured if the man had hit him with it. He walked over to the cowering figure. He remembered what friends did to seal a bargain and held out his right hand with the words 'I'm Willy.'

The would-be victim held out his hand in return, 'I'm Billy.' The two hands met, the pact had been sealed. They could both relax now the danger had passed.

Willy was the first to speak 'what did they want and what's magic?'

Billy said nothing for a while. He needed to recover from his ordeal at the hands of those two would be assailants, and all for a pack of cards. He put his hand in his pocket and pulled out the cards and showed them to his new-found friend Willy.

'What are those?'

'Playing cards.'

'I have never seen anything like them before.'

'Let me show you.' Billy opened out the cards to show their patterns of red and black and different numbers of shaped spots. He explained about the four suits, hearts, clubs, diamonds and spades, about the numbers one to ten and that number one was called an ace, and the cards that had pictures of a king, a queen and a knave. Then with a quick flick of his hands he mixed the cards up and held them out in a fan shape to the surprised Willy. 'Choose a card but don't let me see what it is' came the instruction.

Willy chose a card.

'Now look at the card and remember which one it is.'

Willy did as he was told. He had chosen a seven of clubs.

'Now put the card back anywhere you like.'

Willy followed the instruction and saw that Billy then mixed the cards up as he had done before, he called it shuffling. Billy then held the pack out towards Willy and told him to take the top card and look at it.

Again Willy did as he had been instructed, took the top card and looked at it. To his amazement it was the seven of clubs, the card he had picked at random from amongst the fifty-two others.

'Was that the card you chose?'

'Yes, but how did you do that?'

'It's magic.'

Willy now understood what he had heard. The two assailants had wanted the cards because they thought that it was the cards themselves that were magic. They were not and never could be. The magic was in Billy's hands.

They repeated the trick several times. On each occasion the top card was always the one Willy had chosen. The next time was different. On this occasion when Willy was asked to look at the top card and if it was his, the answer was a resounding 'no'. What had gone wrong with the trick this time?

A smiling Billy put his hand behind his head and pulled out a card asking 'was this your card?'

It was.

'How did you do that?'

'It's magic.'

Willy had to laugh with his newly found companion and wondered how he performed such tricks. He knew that would always be Billy's secret, and try as he might he just could not work out how it had been done.

They chatted together for a while. With his lowland Scots accent Willy was clearly a runaway from somewhere, but where. They exchanged names, ''I'm William Neal, but they call me Willy.' 'I'm Billy Bow.'

'That's an unusual second name, how did you get that?'

'It's part of London, over there, and where I was born so they say, so that is what I am called' answered Billy as he pointed to the eastwards.

'Where do you live Billy?'

'I have my own secret place where no one will find me. Where do you live Willy?'

'Nowhere.'

'Do you want to stay where I do then?'

'Yes please, but only for a few days until I can find somewhere else.'

Billy Bow knew that would be difficult to do. Most of the rooms and houses in St Giles were broken down and rat infested. It was the place for criminals and the poorest of the poor to live, those who had nowhere else to go. He had another idea. Perhaps he could persuade his saviour to go into business with him. Willy could protect him, he had shown himself to be very good at that, and now he had a knife he doubted if he would be attacked again. The two would be thieves would not try again he hoped and word would spread that Willy should be left alone.

'How do you get food Billy?'

Now that was another interesting question. Billy had served his apprenticeship as a street urchin and knew how to survive in the streets of London. He could pick a pocket for a coin or two if times were hard, he knew how to steal food from stall-holders in the various markets. He also had his business. He was an entertainer, but not in the sense of the actors and actresses who played on the stages of the increasing number of theatres that were springing up in the west end of London. He performed his card tricks to the wealthy patrons of these places in the hope that some kind soul would reward him for his skill with a farthing, or if he was lucky even a penny. The real trick was to appeal to the ladies who would then tell their husbands to give a copper to him. Most of the husbands were mean, and fortunately for him they did like to pander to their wives. He got by. Now if his new friend Willy collected the money while he performed his tricks, they might make more together, and more importantly, Willy would make sure that no one tried to rob them. Willy would be his protector.

He explained his plan to Willy. Would Willy like to join him? As Billy mentioned each of the survival tactics he had learned, Willy merely nodded his head. So that was how you had to live in London. It was not the story he had been told by Mrs Robertson in faraway Brackenholm, but he had little choice. Here was a young man, older than himself, offering to share his, at times, nefarious skills.

His adventures during his flight from the Borders had taught him to never look a gift horse in the mouth. Here was his gift, the second since arriving in London, that is if you considered the basic course in pugilism he had received from the carter.

It was an easy choice. He put out his hand to Billy who took it for the second time that day. The bargain was sealed. Willy then put his hand into a pocket in his threadbare clothes. 'I've got this' as he pulled out the shilling given to him by the Corporal, Joseph the bargee.

Billy's eyes opened wide when he saw the silver coin. 'Where did you get that? Have you run away from the army?'

'No, it was given to me by another friend.' He then mentioned the barge trip down the cut and what he had done to help. He had earned his shilling honestly.

Billy knew then that they would eat well on the next day, the Monday. He knew which sellers were honest and those who tried to sell inferior food at inflated prices. He understood his city with all its quirks and foibles, both the good and the bad. 'Come on Willy, let's go to my place.'

Now where was that? The two set off across the road to what Willy knew was the place where the quality lived, so near to St Giles, but so far away in privilege and wealth. They went down a back lane to a row of fine houses. Billy stopped at one and pointed to a small door about six feet above the ground. 'That's where I live. It's over a stables. They use that door to take in straw and hay for the horses, but never lock it. I climb up and make my bed under the straw. Come on, I'll show you.'

With that Billy climbed like a monkey up to the door and opened it and beckoned Willy to follow him. After one or two false starts Willy found the foot and hand holds between the brickwork and climbed in too. Billy closed the door. They had arrived.

PART 3 – AN HONEST YOUNG MAN

19

For the next three years the two men, as they had now become, worked together. Billy showed Willy all he knew about staying alive in London. He taught Willy how to pick a pocket if he had to, how to steal food and how to hide in the hay loft they still called their home. They were lucky. If any of the stable hands had found them they would have been thrown out in an instant, but none did. Perhaps someone knew they were there and turned a blind eye. It did not matter which was the case. They were safe and warm and dry. Billy also showed his friend how he obtained his supply of playing cards. That was in a different part of London called Belgravia. Here there were houses where the rich could come and play cards, and it was rumoured, play cards for money. The cards were only used a few times for some reason and were then thrown out. Billy could climb the wall into the yard where the rubbish was put and steal what cards he wanted. It was as easy as that.

Their main business was entertaining theatre patrons each evening. As arranged, Billy played his tricks to his audience while Willy collected their meagre offerings and made sure no one tried to rob them. Willy was Billy's protector and partner, sometimes in crime. They had found a way to survive, and could buy some of their needs from time to time.

In return for being taught to be streetwise by Billy, Willy returned the favour. He taught Billy to read and write. The one thing Willy steadfastly refused to do was to join one of the street ladies for their form of entertainment.

The days passed. Autumn turned to winter when the pickings were poor and then to spring in the year of our Lord 1810. It was a time for change. This came when the newspapers announced that there was to be the public hanging of the notorious highwayman Jack Jackson at Newgate Prison. The date and time was set and it was anticipated that there would be a huge crowd to watch the spectacle. The gentry could pay, and pay well for any room overlooking the site of the gallows, while the citizens of London could watch in a great crowd. The newspapers even claimed that there would be ten thousand spectators for the event. Such a large crowd gave the possibility of rich pickings. They would want to be entertained while they waited for the main event, seeing Jackson swing on the end of the hangman's noose, and who better to entertain them than Billy with his magic card tricks. It was an easy decision to make for Billy and Willy. There was money to be made there and so they set off early and walked the two or three miles from their lodgings over the stable, along Newgate Street to the prison walls. A vast crowd was gathering, pushing and shoving each other to obtain what each spectator deemed to be the best vantage point. Vendors were selling their wares, piemen their pies, bakers their bread, charlatans their patent cure-all medicines. It was a seething mass of humanity. Sadly for Billy and Willy none were interested in their card tricks, all eyes were towards the gallows themselves and conversations about how well Jackson would die and how long it would take. It had been a mistake to come here, and it proved to be an even bigger mistake when Billy was surrounded by a large crowd of latecomers and pushed into their midst. For the first time in over three years Willy and Billy had become separated and there was no way that Willy would be able to fight his way through this mob to join his friend. They would have to meet again after the hanging, but where?

Willy was now at the back of the crowd as the unfortunate Jackson was escorted up the gallows steps with a prison warder on each side. It looked as if his arms were tied to his side. There was a tradition that the condemned would address the crowd before being despatched to meet their Maker. What would Jackson say? The mob, for that is what the braying crowd of London's citizens had become waited. Silence. They waited again. Silence, then a hood was placed over Jackson's head then the noose. That was part of the entertainment lost. Then the trapdoor opened, Jackson gave one kick and then was still.

At the moment Jackson fell Willy turned his eyes away. He was disgusted with himself for having been persuaded by the thought of rich picking to come to Newgate. As he averted his gaze, he saw, for the first time, a well-dressed gentleman turn his eyes away too. Perhaps this man had been as disgusted by the spectacle as had Willy. Then he saw something else. A grubby hand moved out and removed a watch from the gentleman's pocket. He had, in the parlance of St Giles, been dipped.

Willy would never be able to explain what he did next. Perhaps it was some primeval instinct or the training he had received from Mrs Robertson and Billy Bow, he stepped forward and bumped into the pickpocket to distract him, then picked his pocket and retrieved that watch.

By now the gentleman was walking away purposely from the crowd. He had his head down and was clearly unaware of his loss. Willy ran after him calling out 'Sir, sir' but the man walked on oblivious to the shouts behind him. Willy ran on still calling out until he reached his target when he called out again 'Sir, Sir, stop.'

113

The gentleman turned and lifted his walking stick. He would defend himself, if necessary, from this assault on his person by a ruffian. He increased the speed of his walk.

Willy increased his walking speed until he was ahead of the man. He turned and yelled out at the top of his voice 'Sir, sir, stop, please, please.'

The gentleman halted. He had been surprised to have the word please used by this ragamuffin standing in front of him. He raised his stick for protection.

'Thank you sir, you have lost this.' With that, Willy held out his hand to show the watch that he had dipped the dip for.

'Well, bless my soul, it is my watch, thank you for returning it.' The gentleman knew he had been lucky. It was a fine gold watch, valuable, and a present from his wife. He would have been in trouble if he had returned home without it. He did not know how he had lost his watch, but could guess. He took his valuable back from Willy's hand and placed it in a pocket of his woollen coat. 'You could have kept it.'

'No sir, they would have hung me for a thief.'

Now that was an interesting comment from his rescuer. It was also true. 'You must have a reward for our honesty'. He then put his hand in another pocket and drew out a golden guinea. 'Here you are.'

'No sir, I cannot take that. Nobody would believe how I had that much money. They'd hang me for a thief.'

Now that was a surprise to the gentleman. Here was an honest man facing him who did deserve a reward, but what? 'What's your name?'

'Willy', but with his accent it sounded like woolly.

'Woolly, that's an unusual name.'

'No sir, Willy, William.'

'William, and do you have another name'?

'Yes sir, William Neal.'

'Well bless my soul, that is my name too.'

'Yes sir.'

'Well William Neal, I want to give you a reward for bringing back my watch. What is it to be?'

'Sir, I want proper work.'

Now that was an interesting reply too. His namesake wanted proper work and perhaps he could provide it. He had a large household and would find something for this other William to do. 'Very well, come with me'. At that he turned and started walking down one of the lanes. Willy, as he still was, followed making sure that he walked a pace our two behind. The gentleman turned from time to time to make sure William was following him. He was,

114

but always a step or two behind. Somewhere in his life the other William had been taught to respect his betters. That was a good sign.

After a few twists and turns along the narrow streets they arrived at a green painted carriage, similar to the one the new Earl, as William remembered him, used to attend the Kirk. There was a coachman sitting on its box waiting for his master. As they arrived the gentleman called out to his coachman 'Brampton, this is William, he's coming home with us.' William understood what to do. He climbed up to join Brampton while his newly found mentor climbed inside the coach, then rapped on the roof with his stick. With a shake of the reins, Brampton's horses bent to their task and the coach moved off. Where were they going? They turned and headed westwards.

In his excitement about his reward, William, as he had now become, had forgotten about Billy. He would find him later. It was nearly two weeks later, on a Sunday, that William was able to escape the Neal household and go looking for his friend Billy. He searched high and low, in all their usual haunts, but Billy was nowhere to be found.

20

Although William and John, the 3rd Earl Brackenholm has reached London on the same day by very different routes, their paths had never crossed. At first the Earl had stayed with friends from his Grand Tour at their splendid home in Chelsea. This had proved satisfactory for the first week or two while John found his bearings, but he soon decided that it was too far away from either Mayfair or Belgravia, the two areas where the real action was for him to stay in Chelsea. In any event, he did not wish to presume on friendship for overlong and looked for alternative accommodation. He could afford to buy one of the more modest terrace houses in either Mayfair or Belgravia, but decided, for the time being, until he was sure where he wanted to live, to look for rooms to rent. As usual he was in luck. The elderly widow of a knight of the realm could find rooms for him. In truth, she needed the rental income, and John knew that, and, as always with members of the ruling classes, this aspect of the arrangement was played down. However, there would be strict rules of etiquette that John would be required to follow. There was to be no alcohol drunk in the house, he was forbidden to bring lady companions there unless they were potential marriage partners and chaperoned. The front door would be locked at precisely 11pm timed from the striking of the clock on Westminster Abbey. There would be no gaming or playing of cards, and so the rules went on.

The deal was agreed with the proviso that should John wish to leave he would give one month's notice. In contrast, if he fell foul of any of the house rules, he would be required to leave immediately and there would be no refund of his rent. For proprieties sake it was not called rent, but his contribution towards the household, and that would be in advance each month. Where had he heard formidable negotiations before? He remembered Mr Dunbar, the builder of his family mausoleum. Perhaps this lady had been taking lessons from him, or he from her?

John moved in and made sure he complied with the rules of his accommodation. If he wanted female company, there were plenty of places where he could join a courtesan, a lady of the night, for their mutual pleasure. He might even find a favourite in the fullness of time. If he wanted male company they would have to be far more discreet, but it could be done as he had found before. There were gaming houses where he could play cards, theatres for concerts and plays if he so chose, and gentlemen's clubs a short walk away. He mused that Dr Johnson had been correct after all when he said *'he who is tired of London is tired of life'.* There was so much to do to fill his leisured days. He had also to consider the House of Lords, the excuse he had given his mother for his escape from the Borders, but that would come later.

Now that he had found a settled address, at least for the time being, he decided that he had better write to his mother. What would he say? After some thought John decided that he would not dwell on the many pleasures of London that were ready and waiting for those with money to spend, but say more about the efforts he had made to find lodgings of which his mother would approve. He wrote about Sir John's widow who had taken him in, all the rules of the house that he was obliged to follow, how near he was to the Houses of Parliament and how he intended to take his seat in the House of Lords.

Many years later, when the records of Brackenholm came under other scrutiny, it was the only letter from son to mother ever found.

John sealed his letter using wax and the signet ring he had taken from his father's body, then, arranged for a servant to take it for delivery by mail coach to wherever in London the collection point was. That was none of his business; a job for lesser mortals.

He was tired after all that mental effort and needed relaxation, a game of cards possibly. No, that also required mental effort, bodily relaxation was called for. He left his lodgings and made his way to a house of so called ill repute. Which of the ladies would take his fancy today?

* * *

A few days later John decided that the time had come for him to take his seat in the House of Lords. As was his usual practice, he had not determined what he had to do beforehand. He wandered casually to the entrance he had been advised was for peers of the realm and knocked on another oak door. It opened and John was faced by a flunkey in a black coat, white knee breeches and brass buckled shoes. 'You called sir?'

He had seen and heard too many rude servants before so he announced himself in the most determined voice he could muster 'I am John, 3rd Earl Brackenholm and I am here to claim my birth right and take my seat in the House of Lords.'

'No my Lord, they are not sitting today.'

What did the man mean not sitting, and then he understood, this was the term they used when peers met for debates.

'I do not recognise you, have you taken the oath yet?'

117

'What oath?'

The flunkey decided that this man, calling himself an Earl was an imposter. However, his speech was that of Scotland, he was young, and maybe he was an Earl. Discretion and training came to the fore.

'I see my Lord. Your Lordship's House has its rules. Would you follow me please.'

John followed the man through what seemed like a maze of narrow corridors until they came to another imposing oak door where they stopped. The flunkey knocked on the door and waited to be called to enter an oak panelled room lined with shelf upon shelf of books. 'Excuse me sir, I have with me the Earl of' he paused until John supplied the answer 'Brackenholm', 'who says he wants to take his seat.'

The man behind a desk piled with papers looked up. He was also dressed in a black coat, but at his neck he wore an extravagant, and clearly expensive, lace cravat and a wig. He exuded an air of authority that John had not seen very often. The last man to confront him like this was his old headmaster at George Heriot's Hospital, his alma mater. This was the Clerk to the House of Lords who was perhaps the most important man for that august body. He knew everybody and everything and controlled all their Lordship's affairs. He might not be a Lord himself, but his influence stretched beyond that of the man who sat on the Woolsack, the Lord Chancellor. The Clerk was a busy man who did not suffer fools.

'Well?'

John decided that he would restate his case 'I am John, 3rd Earl Brackenholm and I am here to claim my birth right and take my seat in the House of Lords.'

'Are you? Do you have your Letters Patent?'

'My what?'

'Your Letters Patent that will have been issued to you by the Lord Lyon, King of Arms, as I detect that you are from Scotland. I shall have to read them.'

'That; I left it behind', along with a large quantity of other papers.

'Then my Lord, I am unable to assist you.'

'What else do I need to do?'

That was better. This puppy had lost some of his brashness. He intended to take him down a peg or two more.' This is what you need, your Letters to prove you are who you say you are. We have not met, and I do not recall your father ever sitting in our chamber.'

'No sir, I believe he never did. He loved his land too much.'

118

That was better still. He would teach his Lordship more about the ancient institution he expected to walk into.' Once I am satisfied with your Letters, the next stage is to find two of your fellow noble Lords, of similar rank to yourself, who will sponsor you. Can you do that?'

'I don't think so, and would appreciate your help.'

That would be given reluctantly, but as Clerk, he had no other course of action than to suggest sponsors, but he would make sure that there would be men to decline that post. 'As your father never sat here, I presume that you have no ceremonial robes.'

'No sir, what do I need?'

'I suggest you see Messrs Ede and Ravenscroft.'

Who are they?'

'They, my Lord, are the oldest tailors in London. They make all our ceremonial dress, and that is something you must wear when you are introduced by your sponsors who will be dressed alike.'

John had not thought about ceremonial dress, it sounded like a very expensive cut of cloth that may only need to be worn once. He would have to investigate the cost.

'Then, when you are introduced you will have to swear an oath of allegiance to His Majesty King George.' There is one other matter to consider and that will depend on how long your tailors will take to prepare your dress. We only introduce new peers at the beginning of each Session of Parliament, and did so just a few days ago. I fear my Lord that you will have to wait for some time before the next session begins.' That part was not true, but the Clerk wanted to put off having to introduce Brackenholm for as long as possible. He had taken a dislike to the man. There was something not quite correct about him, but like Mr Robertson, the Minister, before him, he could not put his finger on just what it was at the moment. When the time came he would find out.

'I think my Lord that I have given you much to prepare. When you are ready, please come and see me again.' With that he rang a bell on his desk. There was another knock on the door and the flunkey entered and motioned to John, 'if you will follow me your Lordship.' John followed. He was being escorted off the premises.

The Clerk to the House of Lords gave a little smile. The normal practice was that fathers handed down their ceremonial robes to their sons who wore them only when occasion demanded, leaving them for storage and any repairs with the Court Tailors. Messrs Ede and Ravenscroft would have to make for Brackenholm from new and that would take time. He would make sure it did.

He took paper and quill and wrote a short note, then sealed it. He rang his bell again and asked for a messenger. When the man arrived his instruction was simple 'make sure this reaches that address before my last visitor does.'

* * *

As John, the 3rd Earl, left that imposing building he thought he may have been treated harshly by the Clerk. When he thought more he realised that he had learned a great deal about what he had to do before he could take his seat in that House. The Clerk had been offhand and officious with him, not deferential to his rank as he had expected. Perhaps senior officials of Government had to be officious. He decided not to find the tailors he had been directed to. No, now was the time for pleasure. He made his way to a favoured establishment.

* * *

Several days later, once he had asked for and been given directions, he presented himself at the modest establishment with gold lettering on a black background over the window *Ede and Ravenscroft*, and a hanging sign 'T*ailors established 1689.*' He had found the place, 93 Chancery Lane. He walked in and was greeted by an elderly, grey haired, stooped man who asked 'can I help you sir'?

The reply was affirmative then John said 'I am Earl Brackenholm and I require the correct dress so I can be introduced into the House of Lords.'

'And when would you like this for my Lord.'

'As soon as possible, in the next few days will do.'

'With regret your Lordship that would not be possible for us.'

'Well if you cannot meet my requirements tell me who can?'

'There are no other tailors in London who are allowed to make your robes.'

He had been sent to the correct establishment after all. It was time to speak more quietly. 'Then, I am pleased to be here at your shop. Tell me how long it might take for my, what did you call them, robes?'

'My Lord, do you know what your robes will look like?'

'No.'

'They are made of red silk, and for an Earl have to be trimmed with three rows of ermine. That is the winter coat of stoats you know.'

John did.

'My Lord, we have no ermine left in our stores. We will have to wait until more arrives after next winter before we can commence your order.' That was also not quite true. The Earl could have been measured and the robe prepared leaving the ermine to be added later. If you would like to leave your address we will send for you when we can commence your robes.'

'And how much will this cost me'?

An astronomical sum was mentioned with the words 'and that will include your cocked hat.'

'Then my Lord, after you have worn your robes, we do take them for safe storage, repair, and delivery to the Lords when you next require them.' The tailor mentioned another large fee.

John gulped. He had not expected to pay so much just for sitting in that House. He decided to think again, but for the sake of propriety he did give his address. He made sure he did not mention it was only a lodging. He left the premises.

The tailor gave a knowing smile. He knew full well that address. It was that of another of his former customers who had passed away. He had also kept secret from John that he had a set of robes available for sale. They would need some adjustments, for a fee of course. They had belonged to another Earl who had died recently and who had had the misfortune to sire only girls. Thus, the law of the land meant that that title would be lost. What a shame, but he would find a buyer at some time. What was required was a successful war, when victorious generals and admirals would receive peerages as their reward for services rendered.

When the Clerk came to purchase his next set of clothes he would be able to mention what had taken place. Gentlemen's conversations with their tailor were as sacrosanct as confessions to priests, well almost.

* * *

It was eight months before John received a note from the tailors informing him that were now ready to make his robes and would he like to call on them for his measurements to be taken.

He ignored the note. In the intervening period he had made the new life he desired around the pleasures of London. He was too busy to take his seat in the House of Lords, and anyway, he had better things to spend his money on, personal pleasure rather than a set of robes he would only wear once.

What would he write to his mother now? He decided to fall back on something he remembered being taught at Heriot's, when you have nothing useful to say, say nothing. He remembered too the tawse that had been applied to his person for making inappropriate comments during lessons. He decided on masterly inactivity.

* * *

The autumn of 1810 arrived when the conversation between John and his gentlemen friends turned to the hanging of Jack Jackson, the highwayman, and what a great spectacle it would be. One of the group declared that he could find the best position to watch from a house overlooking the prison yard, but it would need payment to the householder. The question was how much?

'I think I can get places for us at five guineas a head.' John was surprised at that cost. He would have been more surprised if he had known that his so-called friend would be paying the householder just one guinea a head. John parted with his money. It would be something new to do.

* * *

One week before the hanging of Jackson a letter arrived at John's lodgings. It was unusual that the seals did not bear any imprint to show from whom it had been sent. It could not be important, so it was put aside for later. When John did open the letter it proved to be extremely important. It had been sent by his Steward from Brackenholm. It was brief and to the point.

'It is with great regret that it is my sad duty to inform your Lordship that the Dowager Countess has died peacefully in her sleep yesterday. I have instructed the carpenter to prepare a coffin like your father's for her.'

John sat down to let this news sink in. He had decisions to make. He needed to return to the Borders to arrange a funeral and his mother's internment with her husband in his fine mausoleum. The quickest, but most expensive way to return was by mail coach. It was reputed to take only two days. He needed to find a seat and would send one of the servants of the house to arrange that.

His second decision was to return his ticket for the hanging and ask for a refund. To his even greater surprise he was told that 'sorry, there are no refunds for this.' His friend would not change his mind, whatever John said, so he departed empty handed. His friend gave a wide grin once John was out of sight. Such was the demand to see this hanging, he could sell the ticket to another interested party for ten guineas, and so he did.

John also saw his landlady and explained the situation. He had to return home to bury his mother and deal with affairs at Brackenholm. He anticipated being away for three or four months and would she keep his room while he was away. The reply gave him another surprise.

'Yes but only if you pay me for this time in advance.'

'But I have to be away, that's not fair.'

Fair or not, an argument ensued. The outcome was not to John's advantage. He had been told to get out of the house and not return. He was not a gentleman. He would also lose the rent paid in advance for the remainder of the month. That was the agreement. Go.

John packed his belongings into the same trunks he had used when he first arrived in London. When he came to leave, the servants of the house refused to carry them downstairs for him or to arrange for their transport to the mail coach. It was an insult after all he had paid for his lodgings. He left in a raging temper.

* * *

The mail coach did reach Edinburgh in the two days advertised for the journey. It had been a rough ride in places, punctuated by a faster run when they travelled on turnpike roads. He was exhausted, but did stay at the coaching inn terminus of his country's capital city. He would arrange to travel to Brackenholm on the next day. His meal was poor when compared to the food he was used to in London and there were no serving maids willing to share his bed. His temper continued to rage.

In his hurry to leave London, John had not sent word when he would be arriving in Edinburgh. There was no one to meet him. In any event, he was probably there earlier than his letter would have reached his estate.

The next day John enquired about reaching Brackenholm. There was no easy way. The best that could be offered was a seat on the post chaise that would leave in another two days' time for Selkirk. No doubt he could hire a horse there and ride to his estate. Meanwhile he would be welcome to stay at the inn, for a price of course. John knew that his pockets were being picked by these people. Sadly, he had little choice but to accede to their demands. More money left his purse.

He finally arrived at his estate nine days after he had received that letter. He could not understand why, in these modern times it had taken so long. His final stage had been on a horse and cart making a delivery from Selkirk to his estate. He had been made to look a fool again. He found his mother's coffin lying in the hall, exactly as he had done for his father, the house in mourning and all the staff wearing black armbands again. That was pleasing and his spirits lifted somewhat as his butler said 'welcome back home my Lord on this desperately sad occasion.'

Yes it was. At least here he could give orders that would be instantly obeyed and he had a comfortable bed in which to rest and better food. He gave thanks in his mind for these blessings as he issued instructions for the Minister, Mr Robertson, to attend upon him the next day in order to finalise the funeral arrangements. He was also thankful that the design of coffin he had dictated for his father had been followed again. There was no smell of a decaying corpse to bother him.

* * *

The meeting with the Minister was short and to the point. The service would follow the form of his father's funeral attended by the gentry. John did relent slightly and agreed that his mother's maid, the butler and his steward should attend the Kirk too.

The discussion turned to the presence of the estate's workers as before. On this occasion, mindful of the embarrassment caused when they had left their stations at his father's funeral, and because he would also lose a day of their labour on his land, their presence would not be required. Mr Robertson breathed a sigh of relief. He would not have to practice another subterfuge.

The date was set, letters despatched to would be mourners, the coach and hearse ordered ready and the mausoleum door was unlocked. The occasion passed smoothly as planned.

* * *

Once his mother's body had been lain to rest John, Earl Brackenholm, turned his attention to the running of his estate. He needed it to provide the income for his life in London. He had no intention of remaining in this out of the way Borders village longer than he needed.

He had made his plans during that long journey north. He would reduce his expenditure by reducing the numbers of household staff to a skeleton. When he returned, as he knew he would have to in the future, it would be easy to recruit others. Meanwhile he could spend the savings.

He called for his butler and handed him the list of staff to be dismissed. It contained, among others, his late mother's ladies' maid, the coachman, footmen, and maids. He had retained the services of just two people, his housekeeper and her husband, one of the footmen. They could look after his property. His instructions to his butler were quite simple 'I wish you to dismiss these people from my service.'

When the butler looked at the numbers of his staff on the list he was so shocked he remained silent for a minute or so before he retained his composure. 'Are you sure you wish to dismiss so many of your loyal staff my Lord.'

'Yes, I will have no need of then, I am returning to my duties in London.' He had no intention of telling any servant what those duties were. Let them think he had an important post requiring his presence in the capital city.

'As you wish my Lord, but what about references?'

Now that was an important point. A servant leaving a household without references would be unemployable. He did not have the time or inclination to write about each one, the butler could do it. 'Write this then, whoever it is worked at Brackenholm for however many years they did. They gave satisfactory service. You can sign them yourself.' That would solve the problem.

'With respect my Lord, may I suggest that it would be inappropriate for me to sign the references. They should bear your signature and seal.'

'Very well then.'

The butler was dismissed from the Earl's presence to carry out his instructions. It would be very hard. These were men and women he had worked with for years. Some he had trained himself. He also knew that his dismissal would soon follow. So it proved.

John called his Steward into his presence and explained he had to return to his duties in London. He required his Steward to generate as much income as possible from the estate. He would be required also to provide a written summary of accounts on each quarter day. That would enable John to budget for his pleasures. All in all, a most satisfactory solution had been reached. He could return to London in the very near future with a secure income.

He decided to wait until those members of staff who he dismissed had really left his house, just to make sure his orders had been followed. Finally he signed the reference for his butler. All he could say was 'thank you for your service'. The man was in tears. He has spent most of his working life from junior footman, being promoted on merit, to be the family's butler. He had nowhere to go. The one saving grace was that he had never married. He would travel to Selkirk then Edinburgh. Surely, there, he could find a proper gentleman who would welcome his services and experience.

John's final interview was with the housekeeper and her husband, the former footman. 'I am entrusting my house to your care for the time being. I shall return when my duties in London allow. My Steward will pay you from now on.'

It was clear to both servants that would have to be on their toes and be expected to work even harder than before. Here was a man who would return without warning and expect to find his property in pristine condition. They would have to find ways to reduce their workload. At least they still had employment unlike so many of their friends and colleagues who had been so ruthlessly dismissed. It was a sad day.

The next day was much brighter for them. The Earl called for one of his stable hands, he had to keep some of them to look after the estate's working horses, to saddle horses and accompany him to Selkirk. Once there, he would retrace his steps to London, while his man rode back with his horse to Brackenholm. The tyrant had left, but for how long?

* * *

When he reached London, Earl John realised that he had been away for only six weeks. Perhaps he should have kept his lodgings after all, and perhaps it had been a mistake to argue with his landlady. That was water under the bridge and there was no going back. He had made many decisions for his future income. He had also received a legacy from his mother that was being held for him in an Edinburgh bank. He knew what he would spend that money on. He would purchase a small gentleman's residence in Mayfair or Belgravia, near to all life's pleasures, and have a small staff. He had sufficient money following the dismissal of what he thought of as the bloated numbers of servants at Brackenholm. He would employ a butler, a valet, a housekeeper, a cook and a maid. That should be sufficient. In his mind he calculated those costs and compared them with the costs his mother had incurred at Brackenholm with all her servants. There would be money left over to fund his lifestyle.

He was lucky again. One of the gentlemen card players and gamblers he knew had fallen on hard times. He called it bad luck, but the reality was he was a poor card player and a frequent loser. He was deeply in debt. John was able to purchase his house rather cheaply. The gambler was able to pay his debts and avoid the Marshalsea Prison, but what happened to the man afterwards did not cross John's mind. He had his London home and his bankers Overend Gurney had done all the work. He trusted them as they were

the banker's bank and the Gurney's were honest Quakers. Let his pleasures
begin.

21

The coach, carrying William aboard set off at a leisurely pace and travelled westwards through parts of London he did not know. It eventually arrived at an area William would later know was called Kensington, an area with new houses built around a large grass lawn, the Square, and turned into a 'u' shaped driveway in front of a very large white house with columns alongside the front door. The coachman, Brampton, gave William a nudge in the ribs and pointed downwards, the sign for him to alight. He then opened the coach door to allow his passenger to exit, and as the other William Neal stepped onto *terra firma* he said 'We're home sir.'

Mr Neal turned towards William. 'If you want to have work you can be an assistant to my coachman Brampton. What do you say?'

After a short pause there was a nod of the head. It had been agreed.

Mr Neal then turned to Brampton. 'Brampton, this is William. I want you to look after him and teach him how to be a coachman. He will be your assistant and follow your directions. I want you to take him to meet cook and get him a proper hot meal, then find somewhere for him to sleep. You will also need to get him his uniform. I'm sure there must be a spare coat or two somewhere below stairs.' With that he walked up to his front door, which was opened, as if by magic, by his butler. He was waiting for him. How did the butler know his master was at the door? That was one of his secrets. The front door closed behind Mr Neal, the banker.

Brampton was not sure whether to be pleased that he had an assistant upon whom he could load a lot of work or displeased because his own position might be threaten by this young upstart who had arrived from who knows where. He decided that, for the time being, he would follows his master's instructions and see where they led. He indicated to William to climb back onto the coach, then moved off. His matched pair of bays knew where they were going. They led out of the driveway, turned left, then left again and entered a stable yard behind Mr Neal's property. Their day's work was done. They would be unharnessed, led to their separate stalls, fed, watered and rubbed down.

William had seen a look of concern flicker across Brampton's face when he was introduced as the assistant coachman. He decided that it would be better never to tell that he had worked with horses from the age of eight years. That was his secret. He had to learn about coaches, that was new. He decided to follow the instructions of the coachman as best he could and learn another trade.

Brampton removed the cloak with its triple row of capes, the sign of a head coachman, revealing a smart coat made of dark green wool. William liked the colour and hoped he would be given a like garment. He was not disappointed. It was to become his favourite colour. He was then taken to meet the household's cook, a jolly, rotund, motherly woman who fed him stew and dumplings and asked if he wanted to try her plum pudding. He did, but it was very filling for someone who had been existing on or about the poverty line for so many years. William ate slowly and took in his new surroundings. He would like it here, that was until Brampton took him to the stables and up to the hay loft with the remark 'You can make your bed here for tonight.' It was hardly better than the secret stable he had shared with Billy Bow.

* * *

The next morning William woke at dawn, a practice he had followed for all of his life. He thought he was the first person in the household to awaken until he went down to the stable door and saw candlelight in one of the downstairs windows of the house; another servant with long working hours. He went back into the stables and started to make friends with the bays. He stroked their noses, gave them a wisp of hay each to eat and made sure they had fresh water. They responded to his gentle touch with wickers of pleasure.

Sometime later Brampton emerged from the servant's door ready to start his day's work. He was required to have Mr Neal's green coach ready and waiting at the front door at precisely 8 o'clock every morning except Sunday, ready to drive his master to his bank in the City of London, about 3 miles away. He would then return to Kensington, and if required take the ladies of the house, Mr Neal's wife and daughter, Charlotte, to whichever address they wished for their social engagements. Later, he would drive back to the City to collect Mr Neal at 6 o'clock in the evening for the journey home. This would make sure his master was home and able to change for supper at 8 o'clock. The house had well- regulated times. One matter Mr Neal prized above others was punctuality. William would have to learn that.

Brampton walked over to William. He was pleased to see him awake and nearly ready for work. He was not a lie-a-bed. He stopped, turned and pointed to the servant's door. 'Go and get something to eat. The housekeeper will see about your clothes later. You will not be required on the coach today I will be taking my master to work myself.' That was better. He had re-asserted his authority as Coachman to Mr Neal.

William walked over to the door that Brampton had indicated. It was the servant's entrance. He knocked on the door and waited. Nothing happened. He knocked on the door again with the same result. At his third knock the door opened. Standing inside the door was a young woman wearing an apron and with her sleeves rolled up to her elbows. 'Are you William?'

'Yes, how did you know?'

She did not answer the question. 'Come on in'. His arrival had been expected.

William entered the house and followed the woman, who he later found was one of the maids, down a corridor to a large room furnished with table and chairs.

'This is where we all eat'. William had found the servant's dining and meeting room. It was the place where all the gossip about Mr Neal's household and his guests began. It was empty. Where was everyone? As William was soon to discover they were going about their duties, having already breakfasted. Mr Brampton had failed to tell William that he should just walk in and join his fellow servants for their first meal of the day. 'Where have you been'?

'Waiting, nobody told me what to do'

Now that was an interesting piece of news to share. Brampton should have told William what to do and when to eat. The coachman was not the most popular servant amongst his fellows and this would do his reputation no good at all. The maid, whose name was Mary, motioned William to follow her and she led him into the kitchen to meet the family's cook for the second time. She was already busy with her preparations for her master's evening meal. There were fish and meats and vegetables already on a large table, and a roaring fire in an alcove. Here was the heart of the house.

'Hello again William, have you eaten?' asked the cook.

'No.'

The Cook turned to Mary the maid, who worked for her and who had been the early riser that William had noticed all those hours ago, and said 'get William some bread and cheese, and some milk to drink.'

Mary departed and soon returned with a large platter of bread and cheese as ordered in one hand, while in the other she carried a large jug. She handed William the platter and smiled at him. It was a come-on smile. William just nodded his head in thanks and tucked into his late breakfast. If this was how the family ate, he would never be hungry again. He said his own silent prayer of thanks to God for finding him such bounty. The truth was that his honesty, plus all the tricks he had learned from Billy Bow, had brought his reward. Mary's smile had worried him. He did not know what to do and there was no one to ask. His parents were long since dead and no one had ever told him how to respond to such a smile. He decided God would guide him in his own good time providing he read his bible regularly.

After William had eaten his fill, Mary showed him back to the servant's room, which she called 'our hall', sat him down and then left the room. William waited. What else was there to do? He continued to wait in silence until another older woman entered the room. She was tall and thin and had sharp facial features and was also wearing a long apron, this time over a dark green dress. Her sleeves were not rolled up, unlike Mary. She too was used to giving orders 'follow me William.'

William followed her to another part of the house when she led him into a room with a desk and chair behind it. She sat down on her chair in her office leaving William to stand before her, and then looked him up and down. He was nearly six feet tall she estimated and muscular, but with a flat stomach. He had been used to hard work and, she thought, a poor diet. That would change here. Mr William Neal was a very generous employer at a time when many of his colleagues were miserly and treated their servants like dogsbodies. Mr Neal expected a fair day's work for a fair day's pay, and with few exceptions that is what he and his family received in return. It was part of her job to see that happened, and if need be, she could be a harsh taskmistress. She had her standards to uphold.

'William, why do you have pieces of straw sticking out of your pocket?'

William brushed his hand down his clothes to remove the offending articles then replied 'it must be because I slept on straw in the stables last night.'

So that was where Brampton had put him, to make his own bed, and he had not told William about the servant's breakfast. That man would have to be watched and she would be the person to do it. She would have words with the butler, Reid, who, as head of the servants downstairs, could also be on the lookout for William's regards. It had been made very clear to them the previous evening by the Master that William had performed a very valuable service for him, but declined to say what, and he was to be properly looked after. She and Reid had failed last night. It would not happen again, but where could she put him? There were no spare rooms in the male servant's quarters.

That would be a decision for later in the day. Her first task was to find him clothes, both to wear while he was working around the house and for his public duties when out with the coach or a carriage. Mr Neal expected his employees to look smart in their uniforms made from his favourite dark green material. That was the household colour.

The housekeeper opened a draw in her desk, took out a book and consulted its contents in silence. What did she have? Those records would have made any army quartermaster proud. There were details of sizes and numbers of servant's uniforms that she had in stock. Although Mr Neal was a good employer, there was always a turnover of staff. Some left for other work, some, trained to the house's rigorous standards found ready promotion in other great houses, of which there were plenty in London, and a growing demand. Whenever anyone had left she had made sure that uniforms were returned and repaired ready to be used again when necessary. Now was one time when her system would come into its own.

She stood up and walked over to a cupboard and opened the door. Inside were hanging several green coats. She pulled out one and gave it to William 'Try this on.'

He did so, but the sleeves were a little short and there was more than enough room around the middle. William took it off and handed it back. He felt disappointed as he wanted to wear that dark green coat.

The housekeeper looked at her stock again and found another. 'Try this one.'

William did so again and this time the fit was much better. There was still some space around the middle, noticed by the sharp-eyed housekeeper, but that would not matter. It would hardly be seen, and with the hearty daily meals prepared by their Cook, William would soon put on some weight and fill out his coat. That was the coat, now for the rest. She found shirts and breeches and boots and a cloak, more clothes than William had ever seen or owned in his life. 'Here you are' came the pleased call as she handed them to William. She returned to her desk and took out a quill and ink and made some notes in her book, then went to a drawer and pulled out, what to William looked like a very large sack. It was so big that it would cover him from head to foot. 'Do you know what this is?'

William didn't, but thought he had better give a polite reply 'no Miss.'

That was precisely the response the housekeeper wanted. Had William been told what to say? She thought he had not, and that he was a very polite young man. Her given name was Guinevere, a name she did not like, and so she wanted to be called 'Miss G', as a mark of respect for her position as the senior female within the hierarchy of the household. She held up the sack to give William a better view. This is called a palliasse, and what you do is fill it with straw, tie the ends closed, and then you can lay on it. I promise you it will be more comfortable than lying on straw in the stable'

Her thoughts then turned to where William would sleep and keep his newly delivered clothes. William, I would have liked to offer you a room in the house but all the male rooms are already occupied. I have one room free in the female quarters, but you must not go there ever. If you are found there you will be dismissed immediately without a reference. Do you understand'?

He did, 'yes Miss G.'

'You will have to sleep in the stable for the time being, but I promise you something better as soon as I can find it for you.'

Yes Miss G.'

Now put down that pile of clothes and I will show you around the house.' She gave William the guided tour, both upstairs and downstairs, pointing out whose room was whose and Mistress Neal's quarters. Now that was a place to avoid.

The whole of the morning had been taken up by these arrangements. Miss G then took William back to the kitchen where Cook had a bowl of broth for them. William ate well, but why was he so hungry? Perhaps it was just Nature's way of making up for lost time in his previous life.

Afterwards William collected his clothes and returned to the stable, filled his palliasse with straw as instructed and lay back on it to rest. Miss G was right after all, it was more comfortable than lying on straw alone.

While he was waiting for his next orders William found his bible and began to read. He had not read for several days and hoped God would forgive him for his omission.

* * *

It was quite some time later when the coach driven by Brampton drew up into the yard. He called out for a stableman and for William. William hid his bible and walked down the stairs from the upper floor of the hayloft to meet the man whose instruction he had to follow. Brampton showed William how to unhitch the matched bays from the coach, then he handed the horses to the stablemen. He showed William where the coach had to be stored and pointed to the dirt that had been thrown up onto the vehicle from the streets of London. He found a wooden pail with a rope handle and gave it to William. 'Fill it with water from over there'.

Over there was a black metal pipe sticking out of the ground. On one side was a handle and at the front another pipe, a spout, from which drips of water fell to the ground. It was the house's water pump, but William had seen others during his apprenticeship with Billy Bow, and knew what to do. He raised and lowered the handle and water came out of the spout and filled the pail. He carried it back to Brampton and the coach.

'Your job, before you get to eat, is to wash all the dirt off my coach so that the paint shines like new.'

He gave William some rags and left him to the task. The water was cold, and William's fingers felt as if they were dropping off his hands, but work was work, so he put his back into the task.

An hour later Brampton returned to inspect progress. Where he had been for that time William did not know, but he did detect the smell of ale on the man's breath. William's work did not meet Brampton's standards and he was ordered to start all over again while his mentor disappeared through the servant's entrance no doubt to enjoy one of Cook's hot meals.

Eventually William finished and went in through the servant's door. His hands were blue with cold and he was shivering. He went to the servant's hall but no one was there, then he went into the kitchen.

'Where have you been William, you have missed supper again' asked Cook.

'Brampton made me wash down the coach twice with water from the pump. I'm cold.'

Cook knew he would be, so she sat him down in front of her fire and brought him some hot soup. 'I've saved this for you.'

'Thank you Cook.'

Cook had saved other hot food for William as well. The lad was exhausted and Brampton had no business making him wash the coach twice in cold water. She could argue with that man, but he was unlikely to listen. She had a better plan. She would make sure she had a cauldron or two of warm water for William, when he needed to wash down the coach. She also intended to have a word with the butler, Reid. His word below stairs was not to be trifled with. She would suggest that William must be called, whatever he was doing, to join the other servants for their evening meal together. That would sort Brampton out as he dare not upset the butler. Butlers had their master's ears and could drop subtle hints about the performance of their servants. There was the ultimate sanction for anyone who fell foul of the household, dismissal without a reference.

* * *

Cook's plan worked. William joined the others for mealtimes which were often substantial. There would be treats that he had never seen before. Cook explained that these were left-overs from the master's table, and particularly if he had guests, she would have to produce six, seven, or even eight courses. It all depended on the hostess, Mrs Neal's demands. They could be onerous and require Cook and Mary to work for twelve or more hours in the kitchen each day. Mrs Neal expected perfection with every dish and would readily criticise any that did not meet her expectations.

* * *

On the first Saturday evening after William's arrival, after supper in the servant's hall, each was called in turn to meet Reid the butler and Miss G. It was time for payment of their weekly wages.

William was called last and handed ten shillings. He tried to give the money back. It was more than he had ever seen in his life. He had only done the work he was asked. Miss G took him to one side and explained he had worked, he would be paid, and the money was his to do with what he liked. He could spend it on ale, or other pleasures, or he could save it. William chose to save his money; he now had eleven shillings, and would be able to add more each week.

He had already seen the outcome of so-called pleasures during his stay in the rookery. He intended to do better and would not waste so much as a penny.

* * *

Several weeks passed. One day when he had been away with Brampton all day with the coach he came back to hear hammering and sawing noises from the hay loft where he slept. What was happening? He found that a partition had been erected in one corner to create a room for him. At supper that night Miss G asked to see him. It's the best we can do for you for the time being, but there will be a door and shelves for your belongings.

If Brampton was displeased that William had his own room of sorts, albeit in the stables, he did not show it. William was cleaning the coach as instructed, and the time was now ripe to give him another task, the cleaning and polishing of the horses' harnesses. More instruction was given and received by William. He already knew what to do from his father's training.

He considered that he could do better than Brampton, but decided to work slowly, just as any beginner would.

He had also started to make friends with some of the other servants. He began to make friends with a man of about his own age who was being trained as a footman and valet. His name was Matthew Reid, so to distinguish him from the butler, he was universally known as young Reid.

* * *

More weeks passed. Then one Saturday night after William had eaten then returned, exhausted after his week's work to his little room, there was a great commotion from the house. Was it robbers? William ran down and through the rear door and into the servant's rooms. He was ready to fight for his master if need be, but that was not necessary. One of the footmen, George, was being restrained by Reid and young Reid. The story soon unfolded. He had gone out after being paid and got drunk, then on his return had tried to force his way into the female servant's bedrooms and been caught.

With some difficulty he was manhandled back to his room and the door locked behind him. He would be left to cool off until the next morning. Eventually the noise that George was making subsided as he must have fallen into a drunken stupor. He would be dealt with the next day.

Morning arrived and George was helped into breakfast by young Reid. His clothes were dishevelled and stained with vomit and he had a very bleary-eyed look. He did have a presence of mind to say 'sorry, it won't happen again', to the assembled company of household servants, but he knew what his fate would be. He was told by Reid the butler to collect his things, give back his uniform to Miss G and leave the house forthwith. There would be no reference.

As George was walking to the rear door to leave for ever, William managed to whisper to him 'what will you do now?'

'Join the army.'

What had that great soldier Sir Arthur Wellesley called his men 'the scum of the earth'. William did not intend to join them.

Thus, because of George's misfortune William found himself promoted from living over the stables to his own room in the house. He would not make the same mistake as George.

22

As the days passed William realised that he was learning his way around the gentrified parts of London. Brampton had shown him the route to and from the master's bank, which streets to avoid and where to go if there was trouble.

The pattern was always the same. Take Mr Neal to his bank each morning and return to the house. On some days they would be required to take Mrs Neal and her daughter Charlotte for visits to other fine houses. On other days they would take them to shops, and wait for them. If the sun shone they might ask to be driven around Hyde Park or Green Park or even down to Buckingham House, the residence of King George and Queen Charlotte. The usual vehicle for these trips was a light four-wheel chaise that was easier to drive than the coach. Brampton drove the ladies. William's duty was to open the carriage door and offer a hand of support when they alighted.

However, on every day it was necessary to return the ladies home in good time for them to set out to collect Mr Neal from his bank and return him home. The family also had a son, Jonathan, who was away at school. He would be returning home in the summer. The gossip was that he would join his father at the bank each day. Clearly, he was being groomed to succeed his father at that august institution.

* * *

The household gossip had predicted correctly that Jonathan Neal would join his father and travel in the coach to the bank from Monday to Saturday during his summer vacation from his school. Sunday was a more relaxed day in the Neal household. Unlike at Brackenholm, the servants were not required to attend the Kirk. Some were members of the Church of England, as were the Neal's, others followed Nonconformist worship, and some, like Brampton, professed no religion. William could not decide for or against the competing claims of the different church or chapel denominations. He decided he would read his bible until he would choose which branch of Christianity to follow.

On the Monday both William and Jonathan Neal boarded their coach at the prescribed hour. Brampton drove as usual. After alighting from the coach Mr Neal asked Brampton to alight from his box as he wanted a word with him. The word was an instruction wrapped up in a question 'When do you think it will be time for William to learn to drive my coach too?'

Brampton got the message. He hoped he was not going to be dismissed in favour of a younger coachman, but was re-assured that Mr Neal did not dismiss loyal staff without reason. He had better start to show William the ropes, or perhaps in this instance, it should be the reins. He would make sure that William had the reins in his hand when the time came to take the Neal's home. Perhaps he would choose a rough road to show who was in charge of the coach. Mr Neal would know what he had done. He would do that on another occasion pretending that there was an emergency and a need for a diversion.

He had not reckoned with William who had been working with horses since he was eight years old. William had watched how Brampton had handled the reins and decided that he was quite heavy handed, tugging unnecessarily hard on the bays mouths. The bays had been well schooled before Mr Neal bought them. William decided that they would respond just as well to a more gentle touch, and so it proved.

* * *

The summer months passed quickly, or so it seemed. The ladies wanted to be taken out on most days, particularly if the weather was fine and there was always the Neal gentlemen to deliver to and collect from the bank each day. The work was tiring. William was housed and fed well and Miss G was correct he had filled out around his middle to fit that dark green coat she had chosen for him.

In early September, on one memorable day Brampton told William he was not wanted. This was the day to return Jonathan to his School, and that was going to be the coachman's job.

Mr Neal stayed at home that day. William was delighted that he had been given the day off. It had rained heavily, and by the time Brampton had returned, he was cold, drenched and very late. The coach was more mud-spattered than William had ever seen it, but it was too late for cleaning that evening. William decided he would rise early, at the same time as Mary, the scullery maid, to ensure that his master's coach looked its best for the next day's travel to his bank.

* * *

For the next year William's life was that of routine. He learned to drive both the coach and the chaise and clean both together with the relevant harnesses for the horses. Brampton now left him alone to get on with the work and went out as often as he could. William thought that he spent his spare time in alehouses but never seemed to have a hangover when the next day's work was due.

William was given an increase in pay, to fifteen shillings each week. His food, clothing, and lodgings costs were met by his master, Mr Neal. He continued to save all his money.

23

The year changed to 1810. Although he did not know it yet, this would be the year that William's circumstances changed again. He was given another increase in pay, this time to 20 shillings per week, untold riches for that former ploughboy. If he had stayed at Brackenholm his wages would have been four shillings per week if he was lucky, and he would still have been called an apprentice.

Summer followed spring, and as September heralded the change towards autumn, Brampton again took Jonathan Neal back to his school for the year, again leaving William behind.

For some reason when he returned, Brampton made his way up the stairs to the hay loft. All he would say afterwards was that he needed to go there. As he descended the stairs he fell and landed in a heap at the bottom. He tried to stand but couldn't. His leg was bent under him at an odd angle and clearly broken. He called out for help but none came. His fellow servants were eating their supper and talking loudly to each other. His cries could not be heard.

It was some time later that William found him. He was drifting into and out of consciousness and in a bad way. William ran indoors for help and found both the Reids. Together the three men were able to lay Brampton down on a pile of straw in the stables and examine his wound. It did not look good. He had broken his shin bone and it was possible to see a piece of bone just protruding through the skin. That was really bad news. Men had had their legs amputated for less, and without a leg Brampton's working days as a coachman would be over.

Reid the butler found Mr Neal and explained what had happened, and that he had better call a doctor. He mentioned a name.

'No Reid, not him. He is a sawbones who only believes in bleeding his patients. I think that just weakens them more, but of course I am not a doctor and the medical profession swears by the practice.'

'I want you to send for Dr. Lind who lives in Harley Street. I have heard tell he will know what to do. He was a doctor in the Navy, and it was his work that has led to the use of fresh citrus fruit to prevent scurvy. He will have the experience and know what to do. Send young Reid and tell Dr. Lind I will pay his bill.'

Young Reid was despatched and told to make all speed to the address he had been given for Dr. Lind. He ran as fast as he could and found the good doctor's house. He banged on the door as loudly as he could and waited for a reply. He banged again, this time with a rapid tattoo of his fists. The matter was urgent. Eventually the door was opened by an elderly manservant.

'I need to see Dr. Lind now on a matter of great importance for my master Mr Neal.'

Fortunately, on this evening Dr. Lind was at home. He rose out of his chair in his study and walked to the front door of his house to determine what the commotion was all about. Matthew was lucky to find the doctor at home. It was his normal practice, although he had retired from the Royal Navy, to keep abreast of all the new developments in his profession. He had been out on the previous evening, and would be out on the next evening attending scientific meetings. Sometimes he just listened; on other occasions he was asked to speak about his experiences and research.

Young Reid explained what had happened, and that Mr Neal, the distinguished banker, had asked him to obtain the services of the famous Dr. James Lind.

'But I have retired from my profession.'

'Mr Neal is insistent that you attend his house sir, he will pay you well for your services.'

Money was not uppermost in James Lind's mind at the time. He had spent his adult lifetime caring for his fellow man after taking the Hippocratic Oath those many years ago. He could not say no.

He gave two instructions 'get my carriage now' and to Matthew 'wait here while I get my things.'

The manservant knew the doctor's coachman would not be pleased to be roused at this time of night, but duty was duty. Both men had served with James Lind in the Royal Navy and understood only too well the requirements of both duty and service.

It seemed like a very short time before the carriage was at the front door and Dr. Lind was telling young Reid to join him and give his coachman directions where to find the Neal house in Kensington.

The coach set off at a goodly clip, and soon arrived at the front door of the Neal's house. Reid opened the door and ushered both the doctor and young Reid into the hallway. I'll get the Master. Mr Neal had also seen the arrivals and joined the group.

'Where is my patient'? The doctor had taken charge with those time-honoured words. He was shown to the stable where he found Brampton moaning and groaning in pain, that had been dulled in part by the administration of frequent sips of rum.

141

Dr. Lind took scissors from his bag, slit open Brampton's breeches and examined the wound. There was one end of a broken tibia just penetrating through the skin, a compound fracture, that could easily lead to gangrene and the need for an amputation. The skin around the wound was covered in a matted blood clot and that might just have protected the bone. Dr Lind made his decision. 'I want hot water, boiled linen cloths, bed sheets will do, and some more rum'. Perhaps he was one of those doctors who took a liberal swig of that alcoholic libation before embarking on his work. Many did, and it was reputed that naval surgeons made a common practice of the habit. That was not James Lind's way. When the hot water and cloths arrived, he gently cleaned away the blood clots and blood stains to obtain and even better view of the wound. Then he cleaned the area again, this time with a rum soaked cloth and applied pressure until any bleeding had stopped.

Brampton was given more rum and then a pad of leather and told to bite on it. Dr. Lind then pulled on his patient's foot until with a little twist of his wrist, the broken bone end clicked back into place under the skin. He applied more rum and pressure, then tied a bandage over the wound. He then took two pieces of wood from his bag and fixed them on either side of the broken leg with more bandages. It was all he could do.

Next he ordered for Brampton to be carried into the house and put to bed. His instructions were also clear. 'He, Brampton, must take no alcohol, but be fed beef broth and bread four times a day. He must have fresh fruit each day also and he must rest.' He also needed to say his prayers that his leg would heal.

That completed, Mr Neal invited Dr. Lind to join him for a glass of wine in his study. The two men entered the room shortly followed by the butler, Reid. 'Is there anything you require sir?'

'Thank you Reid. Would you find us some of my best port.'

Reid disappeared and returned a short while later with a tray, two glasses and a decanter full of a dark red liquid, the best port. He poured out the wine and handed a glass to each of the gentlemen, then left them.

Mr Neal's first words were 'will he lose his leg?'

'Maybe, but I hope not. Only time will tell.'

'How long will it be before we know that?'

'If things go badly only three or four days, if things go well over a week, but I have no way to predict what will happen in any one case.'

'Will you see him again?'

'The day after tomorrow, then daily until we know if I will have to amputate his leg.'

'Thank you Dr. Lind.' With that Mr Neal walked to his desk and opened a drawer and found what he wanted. When he came back to his seat he handed Dr. Lind a little leather pouch with the top tied. It contained ten golden guineas. 'For your services Doctor.'

'Thank you Mr Neal. Then sir, I will bid you goodnight and I'll see your man in two days.'

Reid was called and the doctor shown out of the front door and into his carriage. On the way home he opened the little pouch to find what it contained. He was surprised by the contents. The footman Matthew who had called at his home had spoken correctly. Mr Neal the banker would be generous.

* * *

On the next day William became coachman to Mr Neal, although this was only in an acting capacity, until Brampton recovered. He found the triple yoked cloak of a coachman and put it on. He was dressed for the part and undertook his duties to take Mr Neal to his bank and then back home, and the ladies wherever they wished to go during the day. He had learned well and knew what to do.

* * *

On the second day after Brampton's accident Dr. Lind returned as promised, removed the dressing and re-examined the wound. There was no sign of pus or the development of gangrene yet. His treatment may have worked but it was too early to say for sure. Time would tell. He planned to return in five days unless Brampton developed a fever when he would need to be called back urgently. He repeated his advice about the diet his patient was to follow, especially that of no alcohol. Before leaving he redressed the wound.

* * *

Five days later, in the evening, Dr. Lind returned and repeated his examination. Again there was no sign of pus or gangrene and the skin had started to scab over. Both he and Brampton had been lucky so far, but there was always the risk with such injuries that a gangrene could begin later deep in the wound.

When Mr Neal heard that the doctor was in attendance again he asked to see him.

'How are things going Dr. Lind?'

'As well as can be expected so far. I am pleased that gangrene has not set in and hope your coachman will be able to keep his leg, but he will always walk with a limp.'

'How long before he will be able to resume his duties?'

'I will remove the splints holding his bones together in about ten weeks' time. We will see how he stands and if the bones have knitted together as they should. All being well he should be able to resume his duties again by March next year.'

'Thank you doctor, that's good news. He has been a faithful servant for many years and I should like to see him back at work. Fortunately we have his assistant William who can take over his duties for the time being.'

With that Mr Neal rang for his butler who entered this time carrying a tray, two glasses and more of the best port. 'I thought you might require this sir.'

They did and enjoyed their drinks together. Before the doctor left Mr Neal went to his desk drawer and pulled out another little leather bag. 'For you doctor.' This time it contained five guineas.

The banker was pleased he had found work for William as his reward for his honesty in returning the watch. He had made a good decision and would not lose his preferred method of travel to and from his bank.

* * *

Ten weeks later Dr. Lind returned to see Brampton again. He was pleased he had not been called out in the intervening period to carry out an amputation. His work today was to remove the splints and see if the bones had healed sufficiently for Brampton to stand up. He needed help to support the man and so young Reid was called for this task.

To their delight, Brampton could stand but needed a firm helping hand when he tried to take his first step. As predicted by Dr. Lind, Brampton would always have a limp. The bones had knitted together but his right leg was now shorter than his left by about half an inch. That would not matter. With time, he would learn how to compensate and be able to resume his duties as a coachman. He was fortunate that he had an assistant to help him.

Dr. Lind's final advice to Brampton contained the warning that if he wished his leg to continue to heal and prevent gangrene developing years later he must not consume alcohol again. Dr. Lind knew, but had never said, that his patient's fall was due to inebriation and that his facial features suggested he was well on the way to becoming an alcoholic.

All Brampton could do was agree and say' thank you doctor.' His secret was still safe, but only thanks to the Hippocratic Oath that required doctors to keep their patient's illnesses confidential and speak to no man about another.

Once again Dr. Lind joined Mr Neal to give him the news. The men shared more port wine together and there was another leather pouch handed over. This one contained another ten guineas.

Dr. Lind was delighted with his reward. He had another reward, this time his own professional pride. He must write up the methods he had used to treat this compound fracture and save a man's leg. Perhaps it might save unnecessary amputations and disabilities in the future.

William received the news about Brampton's recovery with mixed feelings. He enjoyed being in charge of the coach and responsible for its upkeep. It is what he had done for several years and he did not relish the thought of being treated as an underling, a mere nothing, on the coachman's return. Perhaps Brampton might not be able to work again, and he would take over. Time would tell, and meanwhile he enjoyed a further five shillings a week more wages and his freedom.

There were the winter months to come when he would need all his strength against the weather.

PART 4 – THE PRINTER

24

The year changed and William started to count down the days when he would become just the assistant coachman again. January turned to February and then March, and then it happened.

Exactly nine days before William was due to hand over the reins to Brampton, he had returned from the city only to find Mrs Neal and her daughter Charlotte dressed in their finery ready to go out for the day.

'Where have you been William' called out Mrs Neal.

'It has taken me longer than usual to return home Ma'am, a wagon had lost a wheel and was blocking the road.'

'We are already late, hurry up with the chaise.'

William ran. He did not change the horses' harnesses from the coach to that for the chaise, which he connected up faster than he had ever done before, then, he collected his cloak and drove to the front door of the house.

As usual he helped the ladies into their carriage, and as usual there was a scowl from Mrs Neal and a little smile and a nod of thank you from Charlotte, her daughter. William drove as fast as he dare to their destination, an even grander house than theirs at the far north eastern edge of Mayfair. Why had it been so far when he was late? He helped the ladies alight. They walked the short way along the drive, then up a few steps to the front door of the mansion and were admitted immediately.

There was a cold wind as William huddled into his cloak. It would not be his for much longer. He had been told the ladies would be at their social gathering for most of the day. Once he had placed feeding bags of hay on his horses' noses, what could he do while he waited? He did not smoke, as many other coachmen did, or drink secretly from hidden bottles. He decided to read his bible and huddled down into his cloak as far out of the wind as he could.

William had not noticed the passage of time that day until he was startled and jumped when he was poked in the ribs with her stick to the cry of 'wake up, you lazy scoundrel' from an irate Mrs Neal. She poked him again and cried 'wake up' to be sure he had her attention.

All William could do was say sorry, as he jumped down from his seat to open the door for the ladies. Their party had not been a success and they had left early, although William was not to know that.

He drove them home in silence, then returned to the stables to change to the carriage ready to collect Mr Neal from his bank. His rib was quite sore where he had been poked twice.

* * *

When Mr Neal entered his from door to the words of his butler 'welcome home sir' he knew something had to be badly wrong. His wife was waiting in the hallway accompanied by her maid. Just what was the problem? He had had a very trying day at his bank including refusing further credit to one of his long standing clients. He needed peace and quiet not a clearly irate wife standing in front of him. Just what did the woman want? It soon became clear.

'I demand that you dismiss William the coachmen this instant. He was late taking us to our party, and then afterwards, when he should have been attending to his duties I found him asleep. I had to wake him up.' With that outburst an angry mistress of the house turned away and walked to the stairs followed about a foot behind by her maid. As she reached the stairs to her rooms she turned and yelled out again 'I demand that you dismiss William now', then ascended to her rooms. Her maid dutifully followed her.

A bad day had just become worse for Mr Neal. As he turned towards his study to ponder just what to do, his daughter ran up to him.

'Papa, I heard what my mother just said, it's not true, William wasn't asleep.'

'Not now, I must deal with this matter.'

'But Papa, it is about this matter, I know what happened. I beg you to let me speak.'

Like many fathers before him and since William Neal had a very soft spot for his daughter. She was level headed and turning into a beautiful, capable young woman. With her inheritance she would be a fine catch indeed for some lucky young man. He decided he could not ignore he pleas. 'Come into the study with me and tell me what happened.'

Charlotte followed her father into his inner sanctum. She had rarely been allowed to enter and then only at times when her father gave her a dressing down for some misdemeanour or other.

'Very well Charlotte, tell me what happened.'

Charlotte told her father that they were late to their party because William's journey home from the bank had taken longer than expected. Her mother was angry and they had left the party earlier than planned only to find William huddled into his cloak against the wind. 'He was not asleep as mother claimed. Her eyesight is not as good as she thinks it is. William was reading.'

'Reading.'

'Yes Papa.'

'Reading what?'

'I don't know Papa. Perhaps we should ask him. And you need to know that since he joined us William has done all the work on our carriages and the harnesses. I have watched how hard he works. Brampton has not done much, and I think he was inebriated when he fell and broke his leg.'

This was all William Neal needed. Two conflicting accounts of what had happened that day. He was a fair-minded man who would not condemn anyone without hearing what they had to say. He would know if they were lying. He rang the bell and his butler Reid entered the room.

'You called sir.'

'Yes Reid, please find William Neal and bring him to me now.'

'Yes sir.' Reid had overheard the commotion in the hallway as soon as his master had returned home. He expected William Neal, the assistant coachman, would be shown the door before the day was over. He found William in his shirt sleeves washing down the coach, with warm water supplied by Cook, as was his habit on returning from the bank.

'William, put that down and come with me.'

'But I haven't finished washing the coach. Can't it wait?'

'No William, put down that pail and follow me now.'

William did as he was told and followed the butler into Mr Neal's study. He had never been in such a magnificent room before. The walls were lined with shelves, heavy with books, there was a large desk and two easy chairs beside a roaring fire. It was a gentleman's hideaway of which to be proud.

'William, tell me, and I want the truth, what were you doing when my wife poked you in the ribs?'

'I was reading sir. I'm sorry, but I did not see them leave the house. They were earlier than I expected.'

'And what were you reading?'

'My bible, sir.'

The man could read. He did not know that. What other talents did he have?

'Very well William, go and fetch your bible and bring it to me.'

Those words frightened William. His bible was his most precious possession. It had been given to him by Mrs Robertson all those years ago and he had kept it safe since. He decided that if Mr Neal tried to take it from him he would not succeed. William was younger and stronger and knew how to fight for himself if need be. He had already proved that in London. He might have to fight again.

William went to his room on the top floor of the house, the male servants quarters, and found his green coat, hidden in which was his bible. He put the coat on and returned to the study, then handed the bible to Mr Neal, watched by his daughter Charlotte.

Mr Neal took the proffered book, and noticed that it was both well-made and well worn. He opened the front page and saw in beautiful copperplate handwriting the inscription *'The Word of God for you.'* Now who had written that? He decided to test William and opened the bible at a passage he knew well, the gospel according to St John. He pointed to the page and told William *'read that to me.'*

William spoke in a loud clear voice. He knew the passage well. *'In the beginning was the Word, and the Word was with God and the Word was God.'*

Mr Neal was surprised, but then William could have learned that by rote.

'Very well William, open your bible at any page you like and read to me again.'

William knew his scriptures. He had been well taught and had spent many hours alone with his Holy book. He took and opened his bible at one of the most significant passages that had helped shape his life. The gospel according to Saint Matthew, chapter 7, verse 12. Again in a clear voice he read *'Therefore all things whatsoever ye would that men should do to you, do you even so to them: for this is the law and the prophets.'*

So he could read. Could he write too? Mr Neal found paper, quill and ink and gave them to William. 'Write your name.'

William did as he was instructed, then passed the paper back to his master.

Mr Neal looked and was amazed. Here was his own name written in the identical copperplate to the inscription in that bible. By comparison, his own signature was a scrawl. He handed William back his bible.

'Can you count?'

'Yes sir.'

Then came a series of arithmetical questions that William answered correctly without hesitation much to the surprise of the banker. This young man had hidden talents. Why had he not found them earlier. He knew the answer. He had found William looking like a vagabond, an honest one, and had assumed he had received no education. What should he do? He needed time to think so he said 'Thank you William and thank you Charlotte. Could you leave me please?'

They both left the study together, and once through the door Charlotte put her hand on William's arm. She had saved him or so she hoped from her mother's wrath.

* * *

Mr Neal now faced a significant dilemma. He had no doubt that William had spoken the truth when he said he had been reading his bible. His daughter had been correct in her judgment. William was educated, he could read and write well, but what was he to do with him. His wife had demanded his dismissal and would never be satisfied with less. She had a fiery temper. Why ever had he married her? He knew the answer to that question too. She was well connected and had brought a substantial dowry to the marriage that had enabled this William to grow his bank into the highly respected City institution it had now become. He had gained professional happiness at the expense of marital happiness.

He also remembered William's chosen text from Saint Matthew's gospel. Had that been a chance opening of a page or a deliberate attempt to sway his opinion? He did not know, but the words were quite clear about how he should behave towards his fellow man, and this was a man who had returned his watch. He could not put him out into the street that evening. He would not. He could not, that would be unchristian.

By the time he had climbed the stairs to his wife's rooms he had made up his mind. He knocked on her door and waited for her to bid him enter. How could he start the conversation?

'Thank you my dear for bringing this matter to my attention. I have seen William and he tells me that he was reading his bible and not asleep as you thought.' He made no mention of his daughter's input into the proceedings. 'I have checked and he does own a bible and can read, but he must go if you will not change your mind.'

'I want him dismissed this instant. I will not have him driving me again. I much preferred Brampton when he was well.'

'If you will not change your mind then he will have to go, but I will not dismiss him tonight.'

'I want him dismissed now.'

'No I have just said I will not dismiss him tonight. He once did me a great service, and I will not, in fact I refuse, to put him out onto the streets this evening or until I decide where he will go.'

'I will not change my mind.'

'Neither will I. This is my plan. I need a coachman to drive me to me to my bank each day, and Brampton is not yet fit to do so. Dr. Lind thinks he will be fit in about a week's time. When Brampton is able to drive William will go and not a day before.'

'I am not having that man drive me to my engagements ever again, so how can I fulfil them without my coachman to take me.'

'When is your next social engagement?'

'Tomorrow.'

'Then you will have to go without. William will be driving me to my bank tomorrow as usual. You will either have to stay at home or invite your friends to attend here. You have told me you do not want William to drive you again. So be it. He won't.'

'But, but, but.'

'You have had your say madam, and I have had mine. You promised to obey me when we married and obey me you shall. I will hear no more from you on this subject ever again. And, I shall be dining on my own this evening too.'

William Neal left his wife to consider his words. He would make sure that he found something else for William.

* * *

On the next morning Mr Neal informed William that he would be driving him to his bank and he wanted him to wait and not return to drive the ladies as usual. He decided not to mention that his wife had refused to be driven ever again by William and that he would have to find alternative employment for him in the next few days or dismiss him. He did not want to dismiss a young man with William's potential, but he had a wife to appease. What would he decide to do?

The next week, William drove Mr Neal to his bank and waited for him to be ready to leave for the journey back to Kensington. William wondered what would happen. Since the accusation by Mrs Neal he had been ostracised by most of the servants. Young Matthew Reid still greeted him as a friend and colleague which was supportive, but he expected to be shown the door anytime soon. He prayed that Brampton would never be well enough to drive a coach again, but his prayers were not answered.

On the first day of Brampton's return to duty William had prepared the coach and horses to his usual high standards. He had no intention of giving that man any cause to criticize his work. For once Brampton remained silent as he struggled, just a little, to climb onto the driver's seat at the front of the coach. Once he had helped Mr Neal aboard, William climbed up and sat next to Brampton. Again, the coach did not return to the Neal's house that day or the next when the arrangements were just the same.

Mr Neal now knew that Brampton could return to his duties following his accident, but would need to be watched more carefully if his daughter's accusations about his laziness and his possible drunkenness were true, and he had little doubt the Charlotte had spoken the truth.

On the third morning, there had been a change of plan. When William had opened the coach door ready for his master Mr Neal to climb aboard for his daily journey to his bank, he was called to enter the house by the front door, of all places by Reid. 'The master wishes to see you in his study.'

William started to shake with fear. What would happen to him? Was he being dismissed as the below stairs staff has predicted by their attitude towards him? It was even worse. On the floor in front of Mr Neal was a trunk. 'Here you are William. I want you to pack your things and come with me.'

The hammer blow had struck. In a daze, William went to his room and gathered together his meagre possessions. All the clothes he wore had been provided by Miss G, including the green coat of which he had become so proud to wear. It meant he belonged. He packed, then, carried the trunk down the back stairs and through the servants' quarters to the front hall. Other servants saw what was happening and gave knowing nods and winks to each other. William had got what he deserved, dismissal for falling foul of Mrs Annabel Neal.

William waited in the hall and took off his green coat ready to hand it back while continuing to wear his other clothes provided from the household supply. He had no others. He hung his head.

After a few minutes, Mr Neal joined him in the hall. William handed back his coat only to be told, 'no William, put our coat on, it's quite cold outside I think. Pick up your trunk and follow me.'

Both men left through the front door that was closed with a definite bang by Reid the butler. That's was another one who would not be coming back.

When they reached the coach, William went to put his trunk on the roof and join Brampton. 'No William, put your trunk in the coach and join me here'. William did as he had been instructed, while Brampton gave him the worst glare he could ever produce. What was the world coming to? This young upstart of his assistant, an underling, was invited and sitting in the coach with a gentleman. He hoped he would be told to drive the pair to where William could be made to join the Army. That would sort him out. William had a similar fear until Mr Neal called out to Brampton 'to the bank, if you please.'

* * *

The coach stooped at the door of the bank, when William alighted and assisted Mr Neal in the same task. 'Bring your trunk.'

William again followed his instructions and followed his master to the door of the bank where they were greeted by a flunkey wearing a long overcoat and a top hat, which he raised with the words 'good morning sir'. Here was the bank's doorman, and if need be, guard. He noticed William following his lord and master into those hallowed banking halls. Who was he? At least he was wearing the uniform green coat sported by Mr Neal's staff. He must belong somewhere, but where?

William followed Mr Neal into the great vaulted hall of the bank where the main transactions took place. There were desks with men wearing green coats sitting behind them, and on the other side sturdy oak doors to partitioned off rooms. On the doors were names of men written in gold lettering. What had they done to achieve such exalted positions. This must be the bank.

Mr Neal beckoned to William to follow him up a grand staircase to the first floor, where he turned to the right walked a few steps to another grand door with the name Mr William Neal written on it, this time in bigger letters than those on the doors on the ground floor rooms. William was bade to enter too. Here was an even bigger desk that that in Mr Neal's study in his Kensington house piled with a neat stack of papers. Mr Neal sat in a very large chair behind the desk then leaned forward until he found, hidden behind the papers, a hand bell which he rang several times.

A balding man wearing wire rimmed spectacles came rushing up, knocked on the door and was told 'enter.' He walked to the front of the desk and said 'you called for me sir?'

'Yes Jenkins. I want you to meet my namesake, William Neal. He will be joining us at my bank as from today. I want you to look after him, and teaching him all you know about banking. After all you are my Chief Cashier.'

Jenkins merely replied 'yes sir.' He had been told only two days before that there would be a new arrival on the bank's staff. He was really too busy with all his duties to teach a newcomer, but he would have to find a way. He had been told that William was literate and had a fine copperplate handwriting and could count. That was a start, but whether he had the aptitude to become a banker was another matter. Time would tell.

'William, put down your trunk, it will be perfectly safe in my room and go with Jenkins. Do as he says.'

But sir, where shall I sleep tonight?'

'Wait and see, now off to work with you.'

William followed Jenkins out of the room and gently closed the door behind him.

25

The men descended the staircase and turned towards one of the partitioned off room on the door of which was the name R Jenkins, Chief Cashier and into which they went. Jenkins sat William down and asked him 'what do you know about banking?'

'Nothing sir.'

Well at least that was a start and it meant that Jenkins had an unpainted canvas from which to teach this new recruit. 'I am told that you can read and write and count.'

'Yes sir.'

'Let me explain how a bank works. People lend their money to our bank for which we pay them some money in addition. We call that interest. Then when we have several people's money we can lend the greater sum to another customer and charge them a greater rate of interest and tell them how they must pay back their loan. It's this difference in the interest rates, our margin, that earns the bank money to pay us and keep our building in good order. You see we have to be careful to whom we lend money, and be sure they can pay it back, so there is a lot of checking to do. We also have to keep very careful records of where the money comes in and goes out each day. We record this in big books we call ledgers. Now come with me and I will introduce you to the other people who work here. You will soon get to know them all, but I must warn you the hours are long and your records must be perfect.'

Jenkins then took William to meet each member of staff, and explained what they did in the bank. They were all wearing green coats with a yellow cord sewn around the lapels and dark grey trousers. Where should he put his new recruit for his first experience in the bank? He knew. He would test how well he could read or write by getting William to copy records. William surprised yet another man by this carefully crafted copperplate handwriting all thanks to the Minister's wife, Elizabeth Robertson. William thought about writing to her, but soon dismissed the idea. He could not reveal his origins in case he was forced back to being a ploughboy.

That evening, at the close of the banking day Mr William Neal called for his protégé again and bade him pick up his trunk and carry it down stairs to the front door. As usual Brampton was waiting with the coach at the front door and expected William to be ordered to join him on his driver's box. He was both disappointed and disgusted when William was invited to join Mr Neal inside the carriage. Just what were things coming to?

Brampton expected to be told to drive back to Kensington. Instead he was handed a piece of paper by Mr Neal. 'Can you find this address Brampton'? It was in Shoreditch, an area to the east of the banking quarter in the City of London. Brampton knew it quite well: he had been born near there.

Off they set until the coach stopped outside a double fronted house that was far less grand than the Kensington house.

'Here we are Sir.'

'Thank you Brampton.'

William and Mr Neal alighted from the coach, and at the banker's signal William followed him to the front door where he rapped on the door using a big brass knocker. After a few minutes the door was opened by a lady wearing a pinafore.

'Hello again Mrs Fenwick, this is the young man I told you about. I want you to look after him for me, as we agreed.'

William wondered just what had been agreed between the two of them. Was he to be a coachman again, or worse. He shivered with fear.

'William, I have arranged for you to stay here with Mrs Fenwick while you are working for my bank. She will give you your own room, prepare your meals, and do all your washing for you. The bank will pay for this for you, because I did not want to lose your services after all is said and done. You can thank Mrs Neal for suggesting that you should have been moved to my bank.' That of course was a blatant lie. Mrs Neal had demanded William's removal from her house. Her daughter Charlotte had saved William, and Mr Neal was giving him the chance to make the most of his talents by offering this work at the bank. He expected William to succeed. He was a very bright young man, who through no fault of his own, only an accident of birthplace, had not been given the opportunities his intelligence deserved. Mr Neal thought he was a good judge of character and that his new banking protégé would do well for him and increase his bank's profits with time.

As he turned to leave Mr Neal handed William a book. 'I want you to read this.'

It was a handsome leather-bound volume entitled *An Inquiry into the Nature and causes of The Wealth of Nations* written by Adam Smith. The book was dated 1776. William was later to learn that this was a first edition of this book, and therefore just as valuable as his bible. William learned later that most people in banking referred to the book simply as *The Wealth of Nations*.

Mr Neal left William with Mrs Fenwick, and as he exited through the front door called out to Brampton the single word 'home.'

Mrs Fenwick closed the door and asked William to follow her to his room. He did so, and left his trunk there, then retraced his steps downstairs where his new landlady showed him to a warm kitchen, asked him to sit down, then she produced the evening meal. It was hot, plentiful and delicious. He would like it here if this was how he would be looked after. He went to bed very satisfied, only to find his bed was not made of straw as in the servant's quarters but of a much softer material, and there were two thick, woollen blankets to cover and keep him warm. He had a small desk and chair and there was a candle in a holder and a flint which by striking he could obtain light to read. He sat down and opened Mr Neal's gift and read until the candle guttered out having been used up. Only then did he lie down on his bed and sleep, dreaming of the free trade philosophy of the author.

* * *

It seemed to William that he had only had his eyes closed for a few minutes when there was a loud knock on his door. 'William, William, it's six of the morning and time for you to arise' called out Mrs Fenwick.

William rubbed his eyes and somewhat reluctantly given the comfortable bed he now found himself sleeping in, got up and walked to the door which he opened. Outside there was a basin and a large jug of cold and a small jug of hot water with which to wash. He took this into his room and placed them on his desk. He realised what he should use this for in addition. He needed to purchase a cut-throat razor and learn how to shave, rather than presenting himself at the bank with the ragged, wispy, beard that had started to grow on his face. That would be something else he had to learn.

He dressed in his clothes of yesterday including the green coat that he had been allowed to keep and which he wore with pride. He had been correct when he decided that the place he should flee to was London. He said a little prayer of thank you to Mrs Robertson again.

After a hearty breakfast with freshly baked bread and a jam, Mrs Fenwick took him to the front door and pointed out the way he would have to walk to reach Mr Neal's Bank. Fortunately it was not raining so he set of at a merry pace, past little shops and street vendors until about twenty minutes later he reached the front door of the bank. His bank, and was admitted by the doorman. He made his way to Jenkins office, but the Head Cashier had not yet arrived, although there was hustle and bustle around him from other bank employees.

A few minutes later Jenkins arrived and looked William up and down and did not like what he saw. The man had not shaved, then the thought struck him, perhaps he had not been told to, and his coat was that of a servant of Mr Neal, not of a member of his bank. He had overlooked that too with all that had happened the day before. It was time to put that right.

'William, you will remember when I introduced you to your new colleagues yesterday, that I used their surnames not their given names. This is how we address each other here. You will be called young Mr Neal, that is until Our Mr Neal's son Jonathan joins the bank when we may have to use that name for him'

'Yes Mr Jenkins.'

'There is another matter. You are wearing the jacket of one of Mr Neal's servants. That is not the uniform we wear here in his bank. You will notice that we still have green coats, which have tails down the back, piping round the collar and two brass buttons to hold the coat together at the front. We must get that for you. I shall send you to our tailor's, they are the best in London and are called Ede and Ravenscroft with an order for them to make your coat and send their account to me at the bank.' He pulled out a piece of paper, found a quill and wrote for a few minutes before signing the bottom of the letter with a flourish, then sanded it dry and sealed it closed. He took another paper and wrote again. 'These are the directions to the tailors. Take this letter with you. One more thing, while you are out you will pass one or two barber shops. They have a striped red and white pole outside so you cannot miss them. Get yourself shaved, buy a razor, and learn to shave yourself each day for the rest of your life. Here are a few shillings to pay the barber. I shall deduct the cost from your salary.'

William followed the directions he had been given until he reached the shop with the gold lettering on the black background declaring that this was the premises of Ede and Ravenscroft. He knocked on the door and walked in to the sound of a bell, that was attached to the door, ringing away.

An older man, wearing wire rimmed spectacles came out from a rear room and asked 'can I help you sir?'

'Thank you, yes please. I have been ordered to give you this.' This, was the letter from Mr Jenkins ordering William's banker's coat, and, unknown to William, a heavy top coat too.

160

The order had said 'please make for Mr William Neal the following items.' The tailor assumed that, although he spoke with a Scot's accent, Mr Neal had to be a member of a different branch of the banking family. He reacted accordingly, and with much more deference than if he had known that William was a mere employee.

'Yes sir, we can make these garments for you, but it will take a few days. We do have the special cloth that is reserved for Mr Neal and his family to hand. Let me measure you.'

Measure you. What was that, and why was he being assumed to be a member of Mr Neal's family. Then he knew, it was the same surname, and the name that had captivated Mr Neal at the public hanging those years ago, and the one that, surely, had given him his chance in life. Here was another lesson, always allow servants to serve you as they think fit, especially when it means that you will receive a better standard of care.

'If you please.' William intended to watch what was going to happen and follow the tailor's instructions as if he had been born into the gentry. There was no harm in that.

The tailor called out for a colleague to help him. This time a much younger man emerged from the rear of the shop clutching a sheet of paper and a pen. William could not read the printing on the paper, but it had to be related to his new clothes. The last time he had been given clothes by Miss G she had altered them to fit. Perhaps that would happen here?

The tailor took a tape measure and started to place it various parts of William's anatomy, each time calling out however many inches. He asked William to move his arm here, bend his elbow, hold out his arm, stand with his feet apart, and all manner of positions that William had never imagined were required just to make his coat. Eventually the tailor had all he required and dismissed his assistant.

'Thank you sir. We have your measurements and can cut out your coat and begin to put it together. If you would call back on this Friday afternoon we will have your trial fitting and can make any adjustments we might require to do. We are bespoke tailors and pride ourselves on giving our clients perfectly fitting clothes to wear.'

This was another learning experience for William, find a good tailor and always wear smart clothes. He gave a nod of acknowledgement to his tailor and said 'thank you sir, until Friday then.' With that he turned and left the shop to the tinkle of the bell as he opened the door to leave. He had found the tailors who would supply him with his clothes for the rest of his life.

On his way back to the bank he came across the red and white striped pole outside another small establishment and walked in to find two chairs, one of which was occupied by an older gentlemen who had cloths around his face and a man standing behind him. The other chair was empty. Another man walked forwards and asked William 'how might I help you sir?'

'I would like to be shaved, then to purchase a razor so I can shave myself in future if you would be so good as to teach me what to do.'

'Yes sir, please take a seat.'

William sat down, a large white cloth was placed around his neck and upper body, then the barber found a dish, soap, water and a brush then, worked a lather and applied it to William's face. The brush tickled William's skin, but he sat still when he saw the razor approaching and let the barber place it on his face. With a few rapid movements of his hand all the lather was removed, and of course with it, the straggly beard of youth. Next the barber wiped his face then applied a hot cloth, like the man in the next chair. After a few minutes, when the cloth had cooled, it was removed. William's face felt smoother and cleaner than he had ever experienced in his life before. He decided that he would shave every day from now on. His next task was to buy a razor and the accessories the barber had used and pay the man.

'I would like to buy a razor, bowl, brush and soap and pay you for your work. How much will that be?'

'Now let me see sir,' as the barber added up the money in his head. 'That will be three shillings and eleven pence ha'penny please.'

William found the coins that Mr Jenkins had given him and handed over four of the five shillings he had in his pocket and was given one half penny in change. He thanked the man who wrapped up his purchases and handed the small parcel to him. 'Thank you sir.'

William left and walked back to the bank. He felt good after the barber's attention and even better when he thought about the care the tailor had taken over his banker's uniform.

* * *

When he reached his place of work he sought out Mr Jenkins and handed over the change of one shilling and a ha'penny.

'So William, you have spent three shillings and eleven pence ha'penny then. That will be deducted from your salary. Let me show you how that works.'

Mr Jenkins proceeded to explain that William would not be paid each week, as he had when he had been the assistant coachman to Mr Neal, but only once per month, and that money would be paid into an account in his name at the bank.' You can then draw out any money that you might need and we will have a record of what is left. Now, as you will not be paid until the end of the month, I have an important question for you. Do you have enough money from your previous employment to cover your needs for the next few weeks?'

'I have a little sir.'

'Good, now do you have any money saved from your other work?'

'I have just a little sir.'

'Well, if you wish, you can place that money on deposit here in your account, and we will pay you interest on it. Say at three per centum per annum. Would you like to do that?'

For some reason William was a little wary of that idea. Yes he did have substantial savings from working for Mr Neal for all those years, but he was not going to tell Mr Jenkins about that. He decided on a very cautious answer.

'Well sir, I have so little that I think I ought to keep it just in case, for my needs for the next few weeks, until my salary is paid. If I have any remaining at the end of the month, then perhaps I could put it into my account.'

'Very well, now let me show you how your account will work.'

Mr Jenkins then went to his desk drawer, opened it, and pulled out a key. He then turned towards a large iron safe, placed the key in the lock and opened the door. He then took out a large ledger, opened it at a fresh page and at the top wrote '*William Neal*'. Underneath in one of the columns he wrote down the three shillings and eleven pence ha'penny that William had just spent.

He then explained 'this is the ledger containing all the salary records of the bank's employees for one year. I update it each month and let each member of staff know how much is there. We encourage our staff to save with us you know.'

He then turned the page towards William who saw columns marked for income, expenditure, interest and balance. It was a simple but effective system.

As Mr Jenkins returned the ledger to the safe, William saw that there was another book there. He wondered what that was for. Mr Jenkins had made no mention of that.

* * *

163

For the remainder of the day William was set to work copying figures from small ledgers into a much bigger volume. He was required to check the additions of monies in each of the several columns and make sure that they were correct, and that there was an accurate balance of money in and out. It was his introduction to double entry book keeping, and his task for the remainder of the week, except of course for Friday afternoon when he left the bank for a return visit to his tailors, as he now saw the firm of Ede and Ravenscroft.

* * *

As he entered his tailor's premises there was the usual tinkling of the bell on the door, soon followed by the appearance of the man who had measured his body from the rear of the shop.

'Good afternoon Mr Neal, sir, I'll just get your clothes.' With that the tailor, and William never knew if it was Mr Ede or Mr Ravenscroft or another Mr, went to the rear of the shop and returned with an armful of clothes.

'If you would be so kind as to remove your coat, we can try on your new one sir.'

William did as he was asked and put on the new coat. His tailor looked him up and down, then took out a chalk and proceeded to make little tick marks in various places. What were they for? William was then asked to step behind a curtain and remove his trousers and try the new ones. Again, the chalk marking process was repeated the same again when he tried on the overcoat. He waited for his tailor's explanation.

'Well sir, I am quite pleased with the fit we have, but we will have to make some final small alterations. Are you able to visit us again on Monday afternoon next when all will be complete for you to take away.

'Thank you sir, until Monday afternoon then.'

William left the shop to the sound of the little bell and thought someone would be working very hard for the next three days to complete the sewing together of his clothes. At least now that he was working at Mr Neal's bank, he had the Sabbath as he still thought of that day rather than the English Sunday, as a day of rest. He would read his bible and think which of the nearby churches he should attend to worship God. Mrs Robertson would expect that of him.

* * *

164

On the Sunday morning when William went downstairs at a time he thought would be convenient for his breakfast, there was a man sitting at the kitchen table talking to his landlady. That must be Mr Fenwick. William wondered why he had not met the man before, then realised that he had left his home for his work well before William and had not returned until late at night after William had retired to his room to read by candlelight.

'Good morning sir, Mr Fenwick, and thank you for taking me into your home. Your wife has made me very comfortable.'

'We are pleased to do. You see we have no children of our own.' With that Mr Fenwick gave a wistful, longing look in the direction of his wife, then said 'I had better be going.'

'But George dear, why don't you stay a little longer and talk to William'

'Sorry dear, but I must go back to the works. I have accounts to prepare.'

'Then why don't you wait a little longer and let William walk there with you. He can find out more about Shoreditch and walk back here when he is ready. We can all eat together tonight. You will be back home by then won't you?'

'I'm not sure. I have so much to do and am the only person who can prepare my accounts and invoices.'

'Sir, that is some of the work I do at Mr Neal's bank. Would you like me to help you today?'

Now that was something new. Not only had the Fenwick's income improved substantially by their letting of a room to William, but here was someone who was willing to help him. It was an offer he could refuse, but for some inner reason his mind told George Fenwick to accept.

'Yes please William. Now eat up your breakfast and off we will go. We must be back by suppertime you know.' He turned and gave a knowing wink to his surprised wife.

The two men set off together and chatted away as they followed the streets this way and that until they reached a building with a faded, painted sign saying *G Fenwick, Printer*. So that was what Mr Fenwick did.

George Fenwick unlocked a small door set into a much larger one and both men went in. The building was light and airy, but there was a peculiar odour, one that William had not smelt before – the smell of printer's ink. There was machinery with large handles on top set around the room and on one walk a large desk with multiples shelves and partitions above filled with box after box. What did they contain?

In one corner there was a desk piled high with pieces of paper. That had to be George's. He would never have been allowed to be so untidy at Neal's bank where documents were kept strictly in order. No wonder he spent so long on his invoices.

George decided to show William around his little works and described the different types of printing press that were needed for different jobs, the different types of paper that were used and showed the contents of some of the boxes from the area of shelves. They contained different type faces and different sizes. Some were made of metal and some of wood with exquisitely carved letters. These reminded William of some of the letters he had read at the beginning of chapters in his bible. George also showed how words and sentences were made up using letters placed in a holder, but put in upside down and back to front otherwise the printing from them would not work. This was known as compositing and it was a job that William thought he would never be able to do. It had been hard enough to learn to read and write the proper way up.

George and William returned to the mass of paperwork on the former's desk. He could see bills that had been sent out for printing done and bills received for the supply of goods such as paper and ink. It was a jumble. He asked George what he did

'I start at the top and work down. If I have not been paid then I have to keep my suppliers waiting you know.'

William did not know. He had seen daily transactions settled and recorded at the Bank. After a moment's thought he asked 'how long might you wait to be paid for your work?'

'Oh it usually takes months, and some people never pay me. I have to accept that as part of my work.'

William did not accept that as a normal way of conducting business. He had always been paid on time when he was in service with Mr Neal, and assumed that was how matters ought to be. He thought for a moment and then said 'Mr Fenwick, George if I may call you that, why don't I look through this pile of papers and find any bill that has been sent to you first.'

'Could you do that for me?'

'Yes.' And with that William started to look through the pile for bills that had been sent to Fenwick, Printers. He collected a pile of over 20 pieces of paper, then, scanned through looking at the date the bill had been sent. Some were months old. William wondered why other men of business were continuing to supply when they were not paid within a reasonable period of time. He shuffled the pile so the oldest by date was on the top, and the newest at the bottom and they were all in date order. As he did so William was adding up how much Mr Fenwick owed. It was nearly two hundred guineas.

While William was busy with his task, George was writing letters to the many people who owed him money for his services. No wonder he took all of what should have been the day of rest.

Each reminded the intended recipient how much was owed and for how long and ended with a plea when payment might be made. In some cases bills had been outstanding for nearly a year, and even more surprising, George had continued to print more items for these debtors. Some would never pay. In all William reckoned that George was owed over five hundred guineas, an enormous sum of money for the time. How had he kept working? William decided that he would have to give some thought to how he could help. At least he had written some of the letters and the two were able to return home in time for supper.

* * *

The next morning William practised shaving before breakfast and leaving for the bank. His efforts were not to the standard of the barber, but he thought that, with practice he would be able to get better. At least he had not cut himself yet.

At the bank he worked on copying details from customer's ledgers into the bank's ledgers. The totals were eye-watering, making the five hundred guineas for George look like a pittance.

When afternoon came he walked to his tailors. As expected his new clothes were ready, and under the supervision of the tailor who had taken all his measurements he tried the garments on. The fit did seem to please the man, and he did not make any suggestions for further changes and yet another appointment for the fitting.

As all was well, William changed back into what he now regarded as his old clothes. His new clothes were wrapped up in a large brown paper parcel and tied with string in such a manner that he could carry them back to the bank. Bearing in mind what he had learned the previous day at George's printing works he asked 'do you have an account for my clothes for me to take to the bank?'

'No sir, that is not what we do.'

'What do you do?'

At the end of the month we prepare an account for Neal's Bank, our messenger boy takes it then and we wait for payment.'

How long it take before you receive payment?'

167

'In confidence I can tell you that Neal's Bank are very good at settling their account. We usually only have to wait about three months.'

'Three months!'

'Yes sir, that is very good for our trade. We sometimes have to wait over a year for some of our gentlemen customers to settle their account.'

This was further evidence that the wealthiest members of society, who should have money to settle their tradesmen's accounts, were withholding payments. They could claim privilege in not paying on time, their suppliers could not. This was another lesson for William and a hard one, always make sure you are paid on time. He would have to think how best he could achieve that. He owed it to George and others of his class.

As he left he said 'thank you for all your help. I shall look out for your account and do all I can to see that it is paid promptly.'

'Thank you sir, it has been our pleasure looking after Mr William Neal of Neal's Bank.'

As William left the shop the little bell rang out again. He was now sure that his tailors thought he was a member of the banking family. He decided to remain silent on that matter.

When he returned to the bank with his parcel Mr Jenkins put him back to work with the heavy ledgers. It was to be another two weeks before he was asked to undertake another task. During that time the account from Ede and Ravenscroft for his clothes arrived on Mr Jenkins desk. He checked it, then, wrote it was agreed for payment, and put it to the bottom of the pile of other accounts that required payment. William saw what he had done. Perhaps that was why some people were paid early and others kept waiting for so very long. When Mr Jenkins had left the room, William found his tailor's account at the bottom of the pile and moved it to the second place, hidden under another piece of paper. The pile would be taken elsewhere and another bank employee was charged with making payments. His tailors would be paid in record time. He had fulfilled his promise.

* * *

At the end of the month William was given a slip of paper with the details of how much money had been paid into his account with the bank. Twelve pounds thirteen shillings and two pence, riches, particularly as the bank were paying for his lodging and food. William could do what he wanted with that money. He chose to save most, but to spend too. What could he spend his money on?

Later that day Mr Jenkins asked William if he had any other money left over to pay into his account and would have been surprised to hear just how much William had saved from his time as coachman to Mr Neal. That was his secret, and he was not going to share that with anyone. His reply was simply 'I have but four shillings and tuppence for that.' Jenkins was satisfied he had persuaded William to put what he believed to be all he had into the bank.

26

For the first time in his life William had money he could spare for himself, and more importantly each evening, after he had eaten the meal prepared for him by Mrs Fenwick he had time, and a time when he was not physically exhausted by his day's labours. In the first few days at the bank, after he had read Mr Neal's gift twice and his bible again he remembered how impressed he had been when he was taken into Mr Neal's study and saw it was lined with books. He enjoyed reading and while most of his reading had been from his bible, he had read novels with Mrs Robertson and *The Wealth of Nations*. Reading gave the knowledge he craved, and a library was the hallmark of a gentleman. He would buy books and candles so he could read into the night. Reading would give him the education he had never had. He would read any books he could find or buy whatever its title and so it proved. He read Shakespeare's plays, *Pilgrim's Progress* and then he found the works of classical literature such as the *Aeneid* by Virgil. He became an avid reader devouring books and craving to read more. It was to be a love of his life.

He would also visit his tailor and buy more clothes. He was welcomed as an honoured customer at Ede and Ravenscroft. Clearly, arranging for their account to be paid more promptly than they usually experienced had placed him in good stead. He chose two shirts, a pair of trousers and a very fashionable frock coat. Although his tailor had his measurements from the recent purchases of his banker's uniform, he was checked again. There were no changes despite the healthy and generous diet he now ate daily. He was surprised by the next question.

'Excuse me sir, what colour cloth would you like for your new coat. I have many colours available from which you can choose.'

In truth William did not know which colour to choose, so he fell back on a simple device, he chose the same green of his banker's and servant's uniforms. He liked the colour and decided there and then that it had brought him so much fortune that he would always choose that colour. His reply was 'I rather like this green.'

'An excellent choice if I may say so sir.'

It was a ritual that would be followed for the remainder of William's life as he bought other garments from his tailors until the colour became known as Mr Neal's green.

* * *

William kept Sundays for helping George with his accounts. At least the piles were more organised, but still the printer preferred to hand write his accounts to his customers. It was the way he had been taught when he was a young apprentice all those years ago, and it is always difficult to persuade people to change the habits of a lifetime. William could see that there was an easier way. He had a very quick mind and was able to see solutions to problems. It was his God given talent. How could he persuade George to make his life easier. That was the challenge that would require careful thought. If he made a mistake then George would not invite him to his works, and he liked what he saw there. If truth be known, the whole process of printing fascinated him.

* * *

William was kept working on the bank's ledgers for the following months. He found the work tedious but learned another lesson about the need for accuracy. Eventually, and it may have been due to Mr Neal senior's prodding, William was told he would have to learn how to be a bank teller and meet the customers and learn who they all were. First he stood behind one of the older tellers and watched what happened. Each teller had their own place behind a counter. As each customer came into the bank they were greeted by name and asked what they wished to do on that day. Sometimes it was to pay money into the bank, at other times money was taken out, and sometimes both transactions were required. The procedure was always the same. The teller left their counter and turned towards a long series of shelves behind them. These shelves were filled, almost to capacity, with more ledgers on the spines of which were written in gold letters the name of each account holder. The teller found the correct book, then returned to the counter and carried out the transactions required. When money was paid in they added up the new balance, and the same when money was taken out making sure that the figures were correct. It was easy if a customer paid in or took out money in pounds or guineas, but if they wanted to pay in or withdraw pounds, shillings and pence, it took longer, and sometimes much longer. Occasionally a queue of customers built up but they just had to wait their turn. After the transaction for each customer had been completed the teller placed the ledger on a shelf next to where they sat. At the end of each day's banking, when the doors had closed, it was their responsibility to add up all the money paid in and given out and achieve a balance down to the last penny. William could now see why he had spent so much time adding and subtracting for Mr Jenkins.

After another four weeks of watching and learning William was given the chance to be a teller himself. His teacher stood behind him and watched every move he made, and occasionally whispered the odd word of guidance in his ear. Few were needed, but the best guidance of all was introducing each customer. Gradually William began to recognise the regulars and not so regulars and become a competent and useful member of the bank's staff. The longest time was balancing the books at the end of the day. No one could leave the bank until all the books had balanced.

For six weeks William's every move was watched until the great day came when he was told he had earned the right to be one of the bank's tellers. It was a day to celebrate. Some of his fellow tellers might have found an alehouse and drunk their fill to celebrate. That was not his way. He had seen the effects of drunkenness and debauchery at first hand when he had been forced to live in the St Giles rookery. That was not for him. No more slums. He had his books. He was becoming a very widely read and therefore educated young man thanks to that chance event at the public hanging when he had met Mr Neal senior, the banker.

27

The contacts with the customers William could now meet had another useful outcome. While they were waiting to be served, and even better if two partners were standing side-by-side while their business was being transacted, they gossiped. There was money to be made here or there. These shares were a sure fire winner and would rise in value quickly when it would be a good time to sell, or even more valuably, do not buy those shares. It sounded as if money could be made easily by those in the know, and despite his frugal upbringing William found himself tempted to try to make some money this way for himself. His bible had warned him about the money makers at the gates of the Temple and usury. For once in his life temptation took over. On the next occasion that hear heard a nearly whispered conversation about a sure-fire share bet he decided to invest some of his money. He decided that if he lost he would never tempt fate or Mammon again, but perhaps he would be lucky. He heard two men discussing that the Corporation of the City of London intended to give a contract for new buildings to this company. It had been decided that very day, and the unsuccessful bidders would not be told for a week. Buy into the winning company was the tip and their shares will rise. William did to the tune of twenty pounds. Within a week of the announcement about their winning the contract the shares had nearly doubled in value. Now was the time to sell which William did. He also decided that he would take his money in Bank of England promissory notes, paper money, that he believed he could trust. There was no way he would put that windfall into his account at Neal's. Questions would be asked about its origin, questions he would find difficult to answer. As predicted, the shares fell back in price but were always more valuable than their initial purchase price. William had sold at the top of the market. He planned to do that again.

So he listened to his customer's small talk. If he thought that a man was not being totally honest, and there were plenty of crooks about, he declined to invest. He soon found which men were accurate in their predictions about which shares would do well. He listened and learned, only investing if he thought that the insider information was plausible. He decided also that when any share he had bought had increased in value by one half, he would sell them. It reduced the risk and kept his wealth growing. Soon he had amassed over one thousand pounds, a princely sum by any standards. He kept his methods to himself.

* * *

Within a further ten months he had doubled his money to two thousand pounds but he had made at least one mistake. On this occasion the shares he had purchased had not risen as predicted and stayed at the same price for three months. That would not do, so he had sold them only to find about a month later that they did indeed rise in value albeit by less than he had hoped. He had learned another lesson. There were some shares that could be sold quickly to make a profit while others needed to be kept for a longer time. He would have to determine which shares to keep for longer if that were possible. He needed to find out more about the companies to which he was trusting his money rather than trusting overheard gossip in the bank. That was another lesson.

* * *

Meanwhile his life continued with its routine, working in the bank during the day and reading to educate himself at night.

He noticed that some days there were relatively few customers in the bank, but every three months, on those days that were called quarter days, it was chaotic. These were the days when traditionally bills were settled. The tellers could not keep up with their customer's demands, queues formed and tempers frayed and there was even talk of changing banks. Eventually everything was sorted out, but there had to be a better way to organise the bank's work to prevent this happening. He did not want to see the bank lose longstanding customers, so he thought about the problem and came up with a solution. Who should he tell?

He decided that the person he should approach was Mr Jenkins, the Chief Cashier. It was a mistake.

He knocked on Mr Jenkins' door and waited to be invited in. 'May I speak with you sir?'

'Yes, William.'

'I have noticed that on some days and especially the quarter days we are unable to keep up with our customer's demands as quickly as they would like. I have an idea how we could improve our service and reduce the delays.'

'Well have you now. You have been working in this bank for just a short while and you are here telling me that the methods we have used for many years are incorrect. How dare you! I will have none of your nonsense in my bank, now get back to your till and learn how to work harder. Get out of my room and do not ever come back again with your half-baked ideas. I will not have them.'

William had unwittingly made an enemy of Mr Jenkins. He could not understand why. He had only wanted to make his bank better. He would have to watch his back from now on.

28

Fortunately his relationship with George Fenwick was very different, George was grateful for the help that William provided with his accounts and bills. He had some free time on Sundays now but never enough to go to church as he thought he should. At least now the law did not require every man, woman and child to attend. There was an air of freedom both in speech, the written word and personal lives.

For some months William had been pondering how he could speed up the accounting process even more, and how he could persuade George to give his ideas a try. The man was a traditionalist, doing what he had always done. It reminded him of his father, '*It's God's Will.*' Well, it shouldn't be so. The country was prospering as never before, industry was making lives easier and he wanted to help the man who had become a second father to him. He dare not upset him and have the reaction he had received from Mr Jenkins. The answer was not just to tell him but to show him how his life could be easier. He had his plan.

On the next Sunday the two men sorted out the paperwork that needed attention into the usual piles after which William begged to be excused, suggesting it was a call of nature. It wasn't. William walked over to one of the desks where George's men set up the type from all the separate letters. What had George said, the letters went upside down and back to front. He found one of the blocks into which the letters were placed, then carefully chose the type he wanted for a name he had remembered. It was one of their major customers who always wanted items of print, usually at short notice. He set up their name and address and hoped he had not made any mistakes then fixed the letters in place so they could not move. He then found on a bench the carrier the printers used to coat the letters he had set up with ink, then, he pressed a piece of paper on top. When he inspected the sheet of paper there was a name and address he knew well, Neal's Bank. He had his prize and something to show George. He now understood why Mr Neal senior had been able to find his lodgings.

When he returned to see George, he kept the sheet he had just printed behind his back. 'Mr Fenwick sir, I have something to show you', and with a flourish brought out his first ever printing. 'I have had an idea to save time. You have about twenty regular customers and many occasional ones. What if we print the major customers name onto your letterhead. It would save a great deal of time writing their names and addresses, something like this.' He showed George the result of his labours.

The reply surprised him. 'Well bless my soul, that would save me time. Now why didn't I think of that.' William had passed his first test. Would it be so easy for his next idea?

William decided to strike while the iron was hot and put forward his next idea. He asked George 'by how much could you reduce your prices and still make a decent profit.'

'I can't, I won't, I expect to be paid properly for my work.'

It was time for William to change tack. 'Tell me George, when you borrow money from the bank they charge interest don't they.'

'Yes, its usurious, four per centum, but I have no choice do I.'

''You do. What if you gave a discount of say two or even three per cent if your customers paid you as they collect their printing. You would both be better off.'

'Maybe.'

'You would be.'

'I'm not sure I want to do that, and my customers might not agree, but I am not reducing my prices.'

And there the matter remained. At least George would have a lot to tell his wife about when he got home. It had been their lucky day when Mr Neal senior had asked them to take in William. That young man had hidden talents and would go far, or so he hoped.

29

The year of our Lord 1815 proved to be a turning point for all concerned. In September of that year William Neal senior's daughter Charlotte reached her majority and there was a great family celebration of her coming of age. She was a tall, dark haired striking woman who had been well educated at home by a governess, and had joined her mother on the social circuit she had for the last three years. In short, she was a catch for any man, and a wealthy catch too.

On that day her father had told her that there was the sum of five thousand pounds in her account at his bank, and there would be a generous dowry to follow when she married. He did not say how she could access her newly found riches, merely implying that he could bring back from his bank any money she might require.

In the evening there was a sumptuous party and dance at the Neal's home. Charlotte's mother had spent several weeks preparing her guest list and made sure that there were several very eligible men in attendance. There were army officers and the sons of minor aristocrats invited. She made sure that a few daughters of the ladies of her social group were present to ensure that there were sufficient partners for dancing. Her Cook had been given an even harder time than usual, especially when she changed her mind about some of the food she intended to serve. It was to be a very special occasion. It was time her daughter was married, and here was an occasion to ensure she met the men of her own class that her mother thought would make a good husband for her. She had chosen carefully and had a particular favourite.

As expected the meal was a perfection of seven courses. Not too many as there was dancing afterwards. Mrs Neal even found time to compliment her butler, Reid, on the choice of wines and how well he had organised the servants for the occasion. For Reid that was a rare praise indeed, his mistress had a sharp temper and was usually quick to criticise even the slightest mistake. He knew why the evening had gone well. His staff had made a huge effort not for the mother but for Charlotte who they liked for her quiet good manners. Reid sensed that there was a degree of friction between mother and daughter, but when had it started? Perhaps it was there before the altercation he had witnessed at the time that second coachman had been dismissed from the house? Reid expected that one day there would be a real breakdown in relations between the two ladies. It came far sooner than he anticipated.

Following the usual convention of the times, Mrs Neal had arranged her daughter's dance partners and their names were written on a little card against each dance. She had written the name of a Captain Rogers of the Royal Artillery against the first and last dances. Here was the man she would like to have for a son-in-law. He was tall, ramrod backed, of a good family with money and had distinguished himself in the field at the recent battle of Waterloo. She had learned that he would soon buy his promotion to Major, and it was expected that he would rise rapidly through the other officer's ranks and be a General. She rather liked the thought of having a General Officer as a son-in-law, and intended to help him advance any suit that he might have for her daughter.

The sound of the musicians hired for the evening tuning up gave the signal to the guests that now was the time to walk to the ballroom. Mr Neal led the way with Charlotte on his arm. As the first dance was announced Captain Rogers walked over to Charlotte, bowed and asked 'may I have the pleasure of this dance Miss Neal?'

'Yes sir.' Charlotte took his outstretched hand and walked the few steps on the dance floor. She liked what she saw. He was an officer proud to wear his best uniform. There were other uniformed men in the room, but theirs were different. Charlotte did not understand why there were so many differences, but she intended to find out. 'Tell me Captain, why are there so many different uniforms in the army?'

'Each regiment, that is a group of soldiers, wear the same so that we can find each other during a battle. It is source of pride that we have different uniforms you know.'

'Thank you Captain.' They took the floor and danced together. Captain Rogers could dance well and was light on his feet. She wondered which dancing-master had instructed him in these skills. At the end of the dance as she was being escorted back to her seat Charlotte said 'they tell me Captain that you fought in the recent great battle at Waterloo.'

'Yes ma'am. I had the honour to lead a battery of eight cannon. It was hard work but we shot those damned Frenchies to bits. It was great sport.'

Sport. Killing men like that. Charlotte was horrified. Those last four words had just lost a certain Captain of Artillery any chance of seeing her again. She noted his name as the last dance partner on her card and knew full well the social conventions that this was the man her mother hoped she would marry. Well she would not marry any man who had so little regard for human life. She also decided how she would handle the tricky problem of that last dance.

Charlotte danced with the men on her card as expected, but with one exception all were army officers. If they all behaved as the Captain had, she would reject all of them. As the last dance was announced, Charlotte slipped away. She was not there when the Captain came looking for her, and he was left to kick his heels in a foul temper. Where was Miss Neal?

Charlotte had slipped away as she had planned not only to avoid the Captain. She walked through the house and down the stairs to the servant's quarters. She was not supposed to do that, but she did not care. As she opened the door she saw the whole household busy clearing up after their meal. There were piles of plates and pans in the sinks and lots of heads down working supervised by Cook and Reid.

Reid saw here immediately and called out 'Miss Charlotte, you're not supposed to come down here.'

'I know Reid, but here I am. Would you ask everyone to stop work please.'

Reid did so, and all eyes turned expectantly towards Charlotte. Their mistress had thought the party had gone well, but what had displeased the guest of honour?

'I should just like to say thank you to you all, for the work you have done and for making my twenty-first birthday party such an occasion. I shall remember it for a very long time. Thank you.'

Now that was praise indeed. It would be worth working for a lady like that who appreciated her servants, rather than her martinet of a mother who made excessive demands on them.

Charlotte's final act was to whisper into the ear of the most junior maid, the one who would have to get up at the crack of dawn, however tired she was or late to bed this night. Whatever was said there was a smile on the maid's face.

Charlotte climbed back up the stairs and re-entered the ballroom just as the last notes of the last dance were fading away. Her mother rushed up with a face like thunder and demanded to know 'where have you been?'

'I've been...' The implication was obvious even to her mother.

As expected Charlotte joined the line with her parents to bid goodbye to their guests. As Captain Rogers reached her he said 'I missed being able to have the last dance with you. May I call on you again?'

'No sir.'

Mrs Neal heard that emphatic reply. Just what had gone wrong with her plan to introduce the good Captain and let him seek her daughter's hand in marriage? She would never find out the real reason.

Later, when they had retired upstairs she called at Charlotte's room and demanded to know what was wrong.

'I decided I didn't like him.'

'But I thought he would make a splendid husband for you.'

'No he won't. I would refuse to marry him, and I will choose who I will marry not you.'

Mrs Neal left the room. Just what kind of daughter had she raised? Such behaviour would never have been allowed in her social circle when she was that age. The rift between mother and daughter would widen further in the months ahead.

30

Early the next morning there was a gentle knock on Charlotte's door. The maid walked in and gave Charlotte, who was still asleep, a gentle shake. Her eyes opened, was it that time already for her to put the next part of her plan into action. She rose, said thank you and dressed in what was for that time, casual clothes. She would not be wearing the silks and laces and joining her mother at another ladies gathering where the gossip was about men and who might marry whom. Her mother would just have to explain her absence to all her friends. She was twenty-one years old, she was of age, and she would make up her own mind what she did. Her parents could no longer direct her life, and she had her own money that they no longer controlled. It was heady thought.

As she descended the stairs to the hallway the house was quiet. As she had done on the previous night, she made her way to the servant's quarters and found Cook. 'Excuse me Cook, but could you make me a simple breakfast please?'

'I can't do that Miss. You shouldn't be here. If anyone finds out I will be dismissed.

'No you won't Cook, mother could never manage without you, and anyway I will say you were following my orders.'

'Thank you Miss. I'll get you some bread and cheese.' Cook found Charlotte just that, the same food that all the servants ate for their first meal of the day. It was basic, and quite unlike the food her mother would be served upstairs for her breakfast.

Charlotte ate slowly until she heard the sound she had been waiting for. There it was, the sound of horses being led out and her father's coach being prepared. She looked through the window, and there was Brampton at work. He was moving quite slowly and still had his limp. She wondered what had happened to William his former assistant who had just disappeared. As Brampton was ready to climb up to his coachman's seat Charlotte ran out of the servant's door and climbed into the coach much to Brampton's surprise.

'You can't do that Miss Neal. This is your father's coach for the bank and you shouldn't be here.

'I am here.'

'Please Miss, get out of the coach so I can drive to the front door of your father's house to collect him for the journey to his bank. I don't want to be late.'

'You won't be late Brampton, just drive me to the front door, and that is a request.'

Brampton knew better than to disobey. While it was a request and not an order he wondered what Mr Neal would have to say when he found his daughter in his coach. He drove to the front door.

As always as the coach arrived, Reid was there to open the door for his master to leave his home for work. On this morning Mr Neal was not in a good mood. He was tired after his daughter's party and more tired following his wife's tirade about their daughter's behaviour and how she had spurned the man who would have made a good husband. The only saving grace from that conversation was when his wife had told him that his daughter had said she would choose her own husband. In an odd way he approved of that. His marriage had been arranged, although it was never put like that, and it was not a happy arrangement.

Mr Neal climbed into his coach only to find his daughter sitting there, waiting for him, bold as brass. 'What are you doing here? You should be going with your mother to one of your ladies meetings.'

'I'm not going with her to one of those meetings ever again. They are boring. All they do is sit and gossip, and I have to sit at the back in silence even when I know they are talking about me. I am twenty-one now, of age, and neither you nor she can make me go with her. I refuse.'

'You really ought to go out with your mother you know.'

'No, I refuse, I will not go with her ever again.'

'Then tell me Charlotte why you are sitting in my coach?'

'I'm going to the bank with you.'

'No you're not. My bank is a place for men not young ladies.'

'I'm going to the bank with you whatever you say.'

'Why?'

'You told me last night that I now have my own money. I want to see how it is looked after, and how I can take money out.'

'I can bring back any money that you might need you know.'

'No Papa, I want to see how it all works for myself. What would we do if, heaven forbid, anything happened to you and my brother Jonathan. I have accepted that Jonathan will take over from you, but what if anything happened to him? Who would look after my interests then?'

There was no answer to that last argument. She was quite right. She could be cheated out of her rightful inheritance if both he and her brother were dead. It had happened before and no doubt it would happen again. Reluctantly he agreed to her request and called out to Brampton 'to the bank.' Secretly he admired his daughter's thinking, but in this man's world he could not say so.

* * *

On this September morning the doorman of Neal's Bank was surprised to see two people alight from his Master's coach, the Master himself and a young lady. What did that mean? Surely Mr Neal did not have a young mistress and even if he did, he would not want to bring her to his bank. Then as Charlotte turned her head towards him, he noted the facial likenesses. It had to be Mr Neal's daughter, and so it was. The two entered the bank and went up the stairs to Mr Neal's office. Downstairs there was a little buzz of excitement amongst the staff, Mr Neal had brought his daughter with him.

Mr Neal led Charlotte into his office and bade her sit down. It was still the grand room William had entered those years ago, except that there were more papers piled on the desk all waiting the attention of the Head of the bank.

'Charlotte my dear, I have all this work waiting for my attention.' He pointed to the pile on the desk. 'I do not have much time for you today, but I will ask our Chief Cashier, Mr Jenkins, to show you around my modest place of work and start your instruction in banking. There is a lot to learn.'

With that, he rang a little bell on his desk and an elderly man entered. 'You called for me sir.'

'Yes Roberts, can I introduce you to my daughter Charlotte.' The two exchanged glances, smiled and nodded their heads. The introduction had been made. 'Can you find Jenkins and ask him to come to my office please?'

'Yes sir' and with that Roberts left to carry out his instruction.

* * *

Roberts knocked on the door of Mr Jenkins' office and walked in. 'Excuse me Chief Cashier (because Mr Jenkins preferred to be addressed by his bank title rather than by name) Mr Neal would like to see you in his office now.'

'Doesn't he know I'm busy.'

'I know Chief Cashier, but those are my instructions.'

Jenkins put down his pen, left his office and followed Roberts to Mr Neal's office. He was announced as 'the Chief Cashier to see you sir.' With that Roberts withdrew to his own office, another panelled place next to Mr Neal's office. There was also a secret door in the panelling giving Roberts direct access to Mr Neal, and that was something Jenkins must never find.

184

The truth was that Jenkins rather looked down on Roberts, who was described as Mr Neal's Clerk. He should not have done, and had he thought about it, which he hadn't, Roberts was privy to far more banking secrets than Jenkins ever would be. Roberts saw every document that passed over his master's desk and was often able to make careful suggestions that over the years had proved valuable. Roberts' discretion was absolute, and that was why he held his post at the bank. He was also paid more than Jenkins, although that was another secret.

* * *

'Good morning Jenkins, thank you for coming to see me. I should like to introduce you to my daughter Charlotte' as the Chief Cashier and Charlotte turned and nodded a greeting to each other. 'I have set up an account in her name, and I want you to be personally responsible for it. If she wants to draw any money for herself she will come to you and not to the tellers, do you understand.'

'Yes sir.'

'Good. I also want you to teach her how the bank works if you please, but of course she will not be working here.'

'Yes sir.'

Jenkins and Charlotte left Mr Neal to his paperwork.

Perhaps, thought Mr Neal senior, I should have asked Roberts instead of Jenkins to show Charlotte how the bank worked, but on that morning, he required the services of his Clerk. It was a decision that was to have unforeseen consequences.

* * *

Jenkins and Charlotte walked down the stairs to the banking hall. The Chief Cashier showed her to his room, sat her down comfortably and then found her ledger. Her showed her an open page with yesterday's date and a balance totally five thousand pounds, her money. 'Now Miss Neal, if you do not spend any money, on each quarter day, and I'll explain what they are later, the bank will add interest to your account at the rate of three per centum per year. That figure can change if the Bank of England changes interest rates. It could go up or go down and that would affect how much money you had gained just by leaving it with your father's bank. You may choose to spend some of your money when we would write it down there', he pointed to a column, 'calculate

185

the balance' when he pointed to another column. 'In this way we can keep track of your money. Now, there is another point to remember. We only pay interest on the balance in your account on the quarter day.

'Tell me Mr Jenkins, if I were to settle my accounts on the quarter day I would earn interest from the bank on my balance at the end of that day when money might have been paid out for me, but if I were to settle on the next day after the quarter day I would earn more.'

'Yes miss.'

That was food for thought.

Here was a bright woman. She had seen through one of the bank's tricks to make money immediately. What could Jenkins say? He thought for a moment then said 'but Miss Neal, that is precisely how our bank makes some of its money. We also borrow money at a low rate of interest and lend at a higher rate of interest, but only to those people we are sure will be able to pay us back.'

So that was how her father had become so wealthy. She did not like the trickery that Jenkins had implied. She would always make sure that if she wanted to withdraw her money, it would always be on a day after a quarter day, but when were they?

'Mr Jenkins, when are the quarter days?

'Why Miss, they are Lady Day, Midsummer Day, Michaelmas Day and Christmas Day.'

Charlotte knew when those days fell in the calendar, a product of her very Christian upbringing.

Jenkins continued 'we have books like the one I have just shown you for every customer, we call then ledgers, and they are brought up to date every day, so we always know what money has been placed in our care, and what has been lent out. Shall I show you the other parts of the bank?'

They left Jenkins' office and walked into a large hall. On one side were a row of counters with men in green jackets looking after customers who came into the bank, saw one of the men, then left though the imposing oak front door.

'We call these men tellers. They take in and pay out customer's money and record it in the ledgers. It is a most responsible job requiring absolute accuracy in their calculations. They are not allowed to go home at night until every penny is accounted for.'

What a task thought Charlotte, being kept at work for all hours. She was very glad it would not be her job. As she looked along the line of tellers sitting behind their counters, she thought she recognised one of the faces but could not be quite sure. The face she saw was clean shaven, his hair had been cut and he was wearing a smart green jacket with the yellow piping that all the tellers wore. It looked like her father's former assistant coachman, but it could not be him, could it? As she walked on across the banking hall floor, following Jenkins, she managed to have a closer look at that teller. She was sure now. That was William Neal as large as life. So that is where her father had put him when he had been dismissed from the house to satisfy her mother. Whatever had happened to him, he looked very well. She thought about going up to William and saying good morning, but decided now was not the time. She walked on behind Jenkins until they came to another door that had a very large, heavily built man wearing the bank's uniform standing guard.

'Now, Miss, this is the entrance to our strong room and safe where we keep all our money and where all the money is put at the end of each day. It is kept locked, and there are two keys. I have one, and the guard has the other. We both have to agree to open the door and then go down to what we call our vault deep in the basement. Would you like me to take you there?

Charlotte would not. She thought Jenkins was a somewhat creepy and obsequious man. She did not like the thought of being alone in the vault with him. She would like to see down there some day, but would make sure she brought her maid, or another lady, with her as a chaperone.

She had seen enough for one day, and asked to be taken back to her father's office. However her presence in the bank had been noticed out of the corner of his eye by a certain teller.

31

On their way home Charlotte and her father discussed her day at the bank. It was quite clear that she had enjoyed herself and learned a great deal already about banking and had made some shrewd insights into how customers who paid their bills promptly on quarter days were placed at a disadvantage in earning interest. She thought that was wrong, but who was she to argue with her father. The family were very wealthy as a result of owning the bank and her lifestyle depended on her father's business skills. She kept silent on the matter, but, if ever there was an opportunity to change the system in the future, she would want to do that. Perhaps the time would be when her brother, Jonathan, took over running the bank from their father. Perhaps he might listen to her views, but then again he might not. Men could be such stubborn creatures at times.

'Papa, I learned so much today, but there is so much more to learn. I should like to come with you to your bank each week if I may.' She hoped her father would not deny her request, he could if he chose, but fortune smiled on her.

'Yes, if that is what you would like to do.'

Charlotte had then to think about what she might do during the remainder of the week. She would not be going with her mother that was certain, the words they would have that evening, when she reached home, were going to be challenging. She expected that Brampton, the coachman, would already have told her mother what she had done. He had. The stage was set for confrontation over the supper table, and so it proved.

On that September evening, only Charlotte and her father and mother were dining. As usual there were several courses to savour, but Charlotte could only pick at her food. She would have to find time to see Cook later and explain that her appetite had not been its usual self. The meal was consumed in silence. Mr Neal sensed the atmosphere between his wife and daughter and sensibly decided it was for the two ladies in his life to sort out their differences. He asked to be excused on the grounds that he had work to attend to in his study.

As soon as he had left the room Charlotte's mother started shouting at her. 'How dare you embarrass me by your absence today. Brampton told me what you had done. Banking is not for ladies. If you come with me tomorrow I shall say nothing more about your impertinence.'

'I shall not be coming with you tomorrow Mama, I shall not be coming with you ever again. You so-called friends are a bunch of gossipy old women. You are boring, boring, boring and I have other things I intend to do with my life.'

'How dare you speak to your mother like that. You will come with me tomorrow and that is the end of the matter.'

'No I will not. I am of age now and I will decide what I do not you, do you hear me.'

'How dare you...'

'Enough of that Mama. I will not be going with you tomorrow or any other day ever again, and you are wasting your time trying to make me change my mind. That is something you will never do.'

'But, but.'

'I will never discuss this with you again. And, never again try to find me a husband. I have decided that I will not marry a soldier, and especially one who kills people for sport.'

With that Charlotte left the dining room, and although she had been told she should not do so, walked down the stairs to the kitchen to find Cook.

'I'm sorry Cook, your food as always was delicious, but I was not in the mood for so much.'

'That's all right Miss Neal, you may feel better tomorrow.'

Along with the whole household she had heard the shouted encounter between mother and daughter. She knew who's side she wanted to take. She expected an even harder time from the mistress of the house when it came to planning future menus, but that would have to wait for another day. She sighed and started the process to clear up. At least, with all the food that had been returned, she and the servants would eat well that night. Perhaps that was what Miss Charlotte had intended after all.

* * *

Mr Neal had heard the commotion in the dining room between his wife and his daughter, but what should he do? He decided that he would not nor could take sides between the two women in his life. They would just have to learn to respect each other's point of view more. He closed his eyes and let his head fall onto his chest as if in sleep. He was deep in thought when his wife came bursting into his study to confront him.

'Did you hear what your daughter said to me?'

189

'Pardon, I've been asleep I think.'

'I said did you hear what your daughter just said to me, and why did you take her to your bank today. She was due to come out with me?'

This was a time for diplomacy for Mr Neal or he would be in trouble with both his wife and his daughter. 'I'm sorry my dear, but I fell asleep and have not heard a word. What did Charlotte say to you?'

'She told me she would never join with me in visiting our lady friends ever again.'

'Perhaps she just meant for today?'

'I don't think so, and you haven't answered my question about taking her to your bank either.'

'Charlotte was already sitting in my coach before it reached our front door. Ask Brampton. She said she wanted to see how the bank worked in case she ever wanted to withdraw money from her account, a reasonable request I thought.'

'Did you ask her where she should have been today?'

'No my dear I had no reason to, and anyway she is now of age. I thought she was being very sensible asking about her money.'

'Sensible my foot! She wanted to avoid my friends and you let her.'

'How was I to know that she was meant to join you with your friends today? You hadn't told me.'

'But we go out together nearly every day.'

'From what you have said it may be a few days before she joins you again. I suspect it is just a passing phase of being twenty-one.'

'That's nonsense. That young lady needs to do as she is told. Will you talk to her?'

'If that is what you want my dear, I'll send for her now.'

With that, Mrs Neal left her husband's study. Her temper had hardly mollified. She hoped her husband could make his daughter do what she was told to do, but she had lingering doubts.

* * *

Mr Neal rang the little bell on his desk, His study door opened almost immediately and there was Reid, his butler, ready to meet his master's call. 'Yes sir.'

'I should like you to find my daughter and bring her here please Reid.'

'Yes sir.' Reid left the study. He had heard the altercation between mother and daughter and had seen Mrs Neal enter he husband's study, although when she left she still had a face like thunder. What would happen to the daughter?

Reid decided that the most appropriate member of his staff to go looking for Miss Neal was Miss G, the housekeeper. He found her and gave her his instructions, but he did not know exactly where Charlotte was to be found. Miss G's instinct was to look for Charlotte in her own rooms. She was right. She found the young woman sitting upright in a chair looking into space.

'Excuse me Miss Charlotte, you father wishes to see you in his study now.'

'What for?'

I don't know Miss, but I think you should come with me. It's always better to get these matters dealt with as soon as possible, don't you agree?'

Charlotte did not agree, but she had a great respect for her father. It was better not to keep him waiting. She followed Miss G to her father's study, knocked on the door and walked in. She made towards a chair and started to sit down until her father interrupted her action.

'You are to stand in front of me Charlotte. I want to know what has been happening between you and your mother. The pair of you disturbed my whole household after dinner. What will our servants think?'

Charlotte did not care what the servants thought, that was for them. She stood in front of her father and remained silent.

'Well, I want to know what was said.'

Charlotte took a deep breath and started to speak. Her frustrations at being made to sit at the back of a room without speaking while he mother gossiped away with her cronies was too much. She told her father what happened at the ladies' get-togethers. 'It's boring, I'm not going again, I want to do something with my life, so there!'

William Neal had not been spoken to like that for a very long time. He appreciated his daughter's frustrations with her mother's social life. He had no idea what the ladies did. How could he, when his life was spent at his bank. However, he now knew without doubt that his daughter would never change he mind. He secretly admired that, but he had to maintain order in his house.

'I want you to say sorry to your mother.'

'I can't and I won't.'

'And if I order you to say sorry.'

'I shall disobey you Papa.'

Oh dear, this interview was not going well. He had to decide what to do. 'If you will not say sorry to your mother then you will eat your meals alone in your room, until you du decide to say sorry. There will be one exception when

191

your mother and I are entertaining guests at our table. You will join us when asked and behave like the lady we brought you up to be.

'Yes Papa.' The outcome was better than she had feared. She had considered running away from her home, but who could she run away with and run away to? A wicked thought crossed her mind and she gave a little smile.

At least William Neal could tell his wife that he had dismissed their daughter from the supper table until she learned some manners towards her mother. Her mother would expect more, his daughter would not relent. It was the best he could achieve despite his skills in diplomacy.

'Very well Charlotte, that is agreed. Now tell me what you plan to do to fill your days.'

I should like to come with you to your bank on one day a week. There is so much more I should like to learn. I should also like to borrow books from your library and read them all.'

'And what else will you do?'

'I don't know yet Papa, but something will turn up. It usually does.'

It did, and sooner than she expected.

32

Despite her mother's further requests to change her mind and join her and her friends, Charlotte continued to refuse. She had to decide what to do with her time. The days seemed long and the only time she knew she had planned would be her weekly visit to her father's bank, unless he changed his mind too. She had asked to borrow books from her father's library, and that filled part of the day. She had her embroidery to practice, and again, this filled another few hours. It was not her favourite task. She read the three new novels by Jane Austen, *Sense and Sensibility*, *Pride and Prejudice*, and *Mansfield Park* to seek guidance about what an eligible heiress in the early years of the nineteenth century might do. She was not inspired. The stories were all about how to marry for social standing or for financial security. She had both. Perhaps marriage was not for her and she would have to arrange her own social circle and be like her mother. She did not relish that thought either. She then had another idea. If a woman, Jane Austen could write books, perhaps she could too, although most of the author's names in the library were men. She had been well-educated at home by a nanny and then a governess. She picked up pen and paper and thought about what to write, but the words would not come. She did not know just what to write about. Perhaps being an authoress was not for her after all.

As part of her coming of age arrangements, she now had her own maidservant, Mary. This was someone she could talk to, and share experiences despite the very considerable differences in their social standing. What might they talk about? Perhaps it would be more women's gossip again?

As September moved towards October the weather showed that late burst of sunshine so typical of the British autumn. Charlotte was bored indoors and thought about enjoying the last of the sunshine before the chill of winter arrived. She decided that she would like to go for a walk in the nearby Hyde Park, but protocol and the etiquette of the times demanded that she should not walk out alone. She would need a chaperone, and who else to accompany her but Mary. She rang for her maid and when Mary arrived, she gave a little curtsy of respect and asked 'Yes mistress?'

'Mary it is a very nice autumn day outside and I am bored staying indoors. Would you like to come out with me for a short walk?'

'Yes mistress, but I do not think you should wear your indoor silk dress for that. Do you have other clothes that you could go out walking in?'

'No Mary, this is all I have. I have never been allowed to go for a walk on my own before. Mother is out with her friends and has been taken by Brampton in the carriage, Papa is at his bank, Cook is busy and I must have a chaperone.'

'Well Mistress, I do have some spare ordinary outdoor clothes that should fit you. We are about the same build. Would you like to use them?'

Yes Charlotte would like that very much. The plot was laid and Charlotte eventually changed into clothes that made her look like a servant girl too.

* * *

The ladies walked out of the carriage entrance so no one would see them as they set out on their adventure. They crossed a road that was deeply rutted on both the side nearest and farthest from them. The occasional carriage or cart passed them, but once they had crossed that road, the open space of the park beckoned. Mary had been there before and knew the way so she led Charlotte along a well-worn path. There were other people walking in the park enjoying the autumn sunshine.

They passed a man and his wife, arm in arm, and looking lovingly into each other's eyes, a nanny with her young charge held firmly in check by a determined hand lest he run away, and then they saw in the distance a group of men moving slowly in their direction. Should they turn back? There was a whispered conversation between the two, and they decided to walk on. As they got closer to the men they could see just four of them. They were in rags and looked like beggars, but something told Charlotte that they should not turn back. They walked forward, and this time Mary clutched at Charlotte's arm, she was quite afraid.

As they came a few steps away, one of the men, who had a wooden leg, removed his cap and asked 'alms for the poor miss.' They had no money with them and all they could respond with was a shake of their heads.

The request was repeated but this time the man said 'alms for old soldiers miss.' So that was what they were. Another man in the group had lost an arm and two others had bandages over their eyes. They were blind. Their coats were a dirty red colour and on one Charlotte saw a brass button with an insignia pressed into it. Now where had she seen that before, and then she remembered her twenty-first birthday party and a certain captain who had failed to impress her. Where had these men been?

Charlotte decided that these men would not harm them and boldly asked 'did you fight at the battle of Waterloo?'

194

The man with the wooden leg, who seemed to be the leader of this ragtag group replied 'yes miss.'

'And which regiment were you?' Hannah already knew, or thought she knew the answer, so to a certain extent the question she had posed was a test.

The group's leader called out 'ten'shun' and all four men stood rigidly as they had been taught in their parade drills when they had first joined the army. 'Royal Artillery, miss.'

That was the answer Charlotte was hoping for. Her next question was 'what has happened to you?'

'Well miss, we were the smartest and best set of men ever to shoot a cannon against the King's enemies. There were ten of us for our gun. We practised and drilled until we could shoot in our sleep if we had to. We fought Napoleon at Waterloo. We were just behind the ridge on the reverse slope with the infantry behind us. We fired and we fired at the Frenchie's columns that day as they came up the hill. It was murder Miss. We fired until our barrel was red hot, and then it happened.'

'What happened?'

'One of those damned Frenchie cannon balls hit us and our gun blew up. Six of my friends, my men, were killed that day, and look at us now. I lost a leg, John here an arm, and Sam and Ed are blind. We have stayed together because no one wants us.'

'But haven't the Government given you a pension for all you have done?'

'No miss. They have told us to go back to our own parishes to be fed, and walk there. We want to stay together. It's all we have left, our friendship. We fought those Frenchies together, we'll die together.'

Charlotte was moved to tears by this story. How could the King and the Government allow this to happen? Every fibre in her just twenty-one year old body told her it was wrong. 'And how do you eat?'

'We beg what we can miss, but sometimes we go hungry. People don't want to see cripples like us.'

'Have you eaten today?'

'No Miss.'

Charlotte had eaten that day. Her breakfast, and that of the entire Neal household, had been plentiful to the extent that food had been returned to the kitchen. That could not be right, that the men who had fought to keep the country safe were starving and discarded by society. She made her decision. She pointed back in the direction from which she and Mary had walked and asked 'can you all walk to that corner of the park and wait there for me?'

'Yes miss, but it will take us quite a time. Why?'

'Will you just do as I ask?'

The man with the wooden leg had been the sergeant of the gunnery team and was used to taking orders. He recognised the voice of authority, nodded his head and said 'yes miss.'

'Come on Mary, we have work to do.' Charlotte turned and pulled Mary's arm quite firmly and set off back to the Neal house as quickly as she could. The Sergeant watched her go and wondered if she would meet them again as she had said. There was nothing to lose in following her instruction. His little band had lost so much, but not their dignity and pride in their regiment. He would have like to call out quick march to his men, but that was an order he could never give. It would have been too cruel, when none could obey.

* * *

Charlotte and Mary reached the Neal house and returned by the servant's entrance and went into the kitchen to find Cook. Charlotte called out to her 'do you have food to spare? I want bread, cheese, meat and some of those apples that were put out this morning.'

'Why Miss Charlotte, I can't do that, I have to account to your mother for every penny I spend.'

'Cook, I want you to prepare a basket of food, just as I have described and I want it now. As for my mother, I do not care what she thinks anymore.'

That indeed was the proof that the servants had been expecting that the rift between mother and daughter was almost beyond repair.

Cook repeated her warning 'But I have to account to your mother for every penny I spend.'

The reply surprised her even more than Charlotte's comments about her mother '...and if I pay for the food?'

'Well yes Miss Charlotte, but do you have any money for this?'

Charlotte did. She had a considerable fortune sitting in her father's bank gathering interest. She had no intention of divulging to any servant just how much she had thanks to her father's gift when she reached her majority and decided that her answer needed to be quite simple 'I will pay.' That was the end of the matter, so Cook set to the task of filling a basket with food as ordered. Just what did Miss Charlotte want this for?' Cook knew she would never be given an answer.

* * *

As soon as the basket was full to Charlotte's satisfaction, she and Mary, who carried the basket, retraced their steps to the park. They were both pleased to find that the little band of soldiers, who Charlotte now thought of, unpatronisingly, as her troops were waiting exactly where she had told them to be. She offered them the basket and removed the cloth cover. 'This is for you.'

'But Miss, where did you get this? Is it stolen? We can't have stolen food even if we are hungry. How did you buy all this?'

'That is my secret. The food is not stolen, it is fresh, and I want you all to have it. Your country has need of brave men like you and this is my gift to you for your courage.'

The Sergeant drew himself up to the full height his bent body and wooden leg allowed and saluted. 'Thank you miss, God bless you.'

'What was your rank?'

'I was the Gunnery Sergeant for my men miss.'

'Now Sergeant, if you and your men are here tomorrow at this time, there will be some more food for you.'

'God bless you miss.'

'Tell me Sergeant, did you know a Captain Rogers in the artillery?'

'Oh him.'

That was all Charlotte wanted to hear. She had been quite right in rejecting that man's suit. Her mother had been wrong again.

As they walked back home Charlotte turned to Mary and said 'this must be our secret. You are never to tell a soul what we have just done. Tomorrow, I want you to take them their food as I must join my father at his bank.'

33

On the next morning Charlotte joined her father for the journey to his bank. She intended to learn more about how the bank worked from Mr Jenkins and then ask him to withdraw money from her account. She should have asked Cook how much money she should give her, but in the rush to get food to the hungry gunnery sergeant and his men she had forgotten. She decided that she would ask for five guineas. She also realised that she had much to learn about how to keep a household when, and if, the time ever came for her to have her own home. She was aware that when her parents had died then, their house would pass to her brother Jonathan who, no doubt would wish to keep most, or even all, of the servants to look after him. She would be allowed to stay in her own rooms, but when her brother married that lady would take charge of the household, and rightly so. Depending on whom Jonathan married, she might stay, but the relationship between the two might not work. She said a prayer that she could marry and have her own home before that dreadful day arose. Meanwhile, when her mother was out of the house visiting her friends, she would ask both Cook and the housekeeper, Miss G, to teach her what to do. It would fill some of her time usefully.

Meanwhile she turned her attention towards Mr Jenkins' office and wondered what he would teach her about banking today. It proved to be about bookkeeping and the need for accuracy, not the most exciting subject in the world, but a necessary one.

As the day wore on towards the time that the bank closed its doors, Charlotte asked Jenkins 'I should like to withdraw five guineas from my account. Could you do that for me please.'

'Yes Miss Neal.' Jenkins thought how clever Miss Neal really was. They had talked about keeping proper records for most of the day, and here she was asking for a practical demonstration of how her account, and its records would work in practice. He walked over to a shelf and pulled down her ledger and opened it at the first page showing the sum of five thousand pounds. 'Now miss, you want to withdraw five guineas, that is five pounds and five shillings and no pence, so we put that figure in this column. We then take away that from the money you started with, we call it an opening balance, so that you now have four thousand nine hundred and ninety-four pounds fifteen shillings left. Each time you take out your money we will keep this record for you.'

'And what about interest on my money?'

She had remembered that. 'It will be added on each quarter day as we said last week. You can ask to see the balance at any time you know.'

That was more interesting information, for now Charlotte just wanted her money. Jenkins left his office, collected the five guineas from the nearest teller and told him how to keep his own records correct, then returned and handed the money to Charlotte. 'There you are Miss, five guineas.'

As soon as she returned home, Charlotte would give that to Cook. She hoped it would be enough.

* * *

During the day Mary had collected another basket of food from Cook and walked to the rendezvous place she had agreed with the Gunnery Sergeant. When she reached there she expected to find the four men she and her mistress had met on the previous day. This time she counted five men.

'Good morning Sergeant, I have brought you some food as we agreed, but I have only brought enough for four, not five.' She looked at the extra man, who also was wearing a ragged green coat with a different pattern of buttons to the other four. He had an arm in a sling of dirty cloth.

'Never mind miss, we will share what you have brought for us, thank you.'

'I would have brought more if I had known. Who is the other man and why is he wearing a green coat.'

'That's George, we met him yesterday and agreed to let him join us. His jacket is green because he was a rifleman, and that's their uniform colour.'

Mary clearly had a lot to learn about the different uniforms worn by soldiers in the British Army, but now was not the time. She made an arrangement to meet the five men in the same place and at the same time tomorrow.

* * *

As soon as she returned home Charlotte slipped down the stairs to the servant's quarters and found Cook. 'Here you are Cook, five guineas, will that be enough?'

'Only just Miss Charlotte, Mary tells me that your little group now has five men not four, so I will put out food for five tomorrow.'

'Thank you Cook.'

Charlotte returned to her rooms in the elegant family home. How could she eat when men who had fought to keep her safe from a French invasion of England were abandoned and starving. At least she had been dismissed to eat in her own rooms following her argument with her mother. She would save some of that food to add to tomorrow's basket.

* * *

On the next day Charlotte and Mary collected their basket of food after both her mother and father had left the house. Thank goodness they did not know what she was doing. Her mother would most definitely disapprove, and her father might stop her withdrawing her money to support these men. Thank goodness too that, unlike her mother who treated the servants as beneath her, she had made a friend of Cook.

When they reached the rendezvous the Sergeant's band had grown from five on the previous day to eight men today. They would have to share again.

Charlotte asked the Sergeant what was happening.

'Well miss, there are a lot of us. We are supposed to return to our own parish to be looked after, but most of us can't get there. They don't want to look after us. I would have to walk over two hundred miles to Yorkshire, and how would the lads who are blind make their way. We stay here and do the best we can.'

'And how many more of you are there in London?'

'I don't know miss, but we need your help. You have been kind to us, most people turn away. Perhaps there are hundreds like us, old soldiers on the scrapheap.'

Charlotte was moved to tears again. She could not understand how the Army and Government could be so cruel to these men. The problem was more than she could solve with a daily basket of food, but what could she do? She had to think. Meanwhile all she could offer was to meet the eight men tomorrow.

'Sergeant, I'll see the eight of you tomorrow, but no more please. I need time to think how we can look after you and perhaps more.'

* * *

After she and Mary returned home, Charlotte saw Cook again and asked for food for eight men for the next day.

Cook replied 'you have spent all your five guineas Miss Charlotte. What do you want me to do?'

'Make a basket of food for eight men tomorrow, and I will find more money for you.'

'Yes Miss, but I can't keep hiding all this extra food in my accounts. Someone, and it will probably be your mother, will find out what we have been doing and then I shall be dismissed. I'm sorry, but I just can't keep hiding things for you.'

Charlotte left the kitchen. How could Cook be so unfeeling to not want to help old soldiers who were hungry? Then she thought about Cook's accounts and what she had learned from Jenkins about keeping records. She, Mary and Cook would be found out. She had to find another way.

* * *

Charlotte had been taught by her Governess that, when she had difficult problems, she should pray for guidance. She sank to her knees and prayed harder than she had ever done in her life. What would God want her to do? Could she do what God might tell her to do?

Suddenly, and unexpectedly she heard a voice in her head 'use my Church.' Of course, that was the answer, use the Church to help, after all it preached about Christian charity. The parable of the Good Samaritan came to mind. He had not passed onto the other side. The question was, which Church to use? There were so many. Her own church was St James's, Piccadilly. This was a high Anglican church chosen by her mother, Charlotte now realised, because it was close to the wealthy south of Mayfair. She had seen members of her own class arrive by coach, as she and her mother and father did. They sat at the front in pews marked with their own names and reserved for them. She had seen servants sitting at the back of the church. Perhaps they had been ordered to attend? Her dear father was more enlightened. He believed that his servants should be free to worship in their own way, although he was always pleased to see his own staff in St James's. She could not see this church helping what she now regarded as her soldiers.

The other nearby established church was that of St Mary Abbot, but she had never worshipped there and thought it would be very unlikely that they would want to help. But the voice had said very clearly 'use my church' and that voice had to be obeyed. She decided that she would discuss the matter with her maid, Mary, and rang the bell to call for her.

Mary arrived promptly, did a little bob of respect and said 'yes Miss Charlotte.'

'Mary, I've been thinking, perhaps a church could help us and our soldiers.' She made no mention of her prayers; prayers were a private matter.

'I go to St James's in Piccadilly and there is St Mary Abbot's down the road, but somehow I don't suppose they would help. What do you think?'

'I agree Miss, but perhaps my chapel might help us.'

'I didn't know you went to chapel Mary, which one?'

'Well Miss, I don't hold with those churches anyway. I was brought up as a Wesleyan to have a belief in God, but to praise him in a simple way. I go to the chapel in Clarence Place.'

Charlotte had not heard about this chapel but wanted to encourage Mary to tell her more. 'Tell me about it please Mary.'

'Well Miss there are just a few of us at present. Our Minister, Mr Trevelyan, he's from Cornwall, has set up a meeting place in his house. I like it there. He makes us all feel we belong to God's Kingdom.'

'And where did your Minister train to be a priest?'

'I don't know Miss. In our chapel anyone who can read is allowed to preach. I think it's just something he did. He's a very good man, you will like him. He came here to save us sinners.'

Maybe Mr Trevelyan was a good man, Charlotte would decide for herself. 'When can we meet your Mr Trevelyan?'

'We could walk there now. He should be there. His door is always open.

The pair left the Neal's house again by the servant's entrance and started to walk into the village that called itself Kensington. As they did so the houses were less grand, then little more than hovels until they reached a small grassy square with houses built round it. Mary led the way to one of the houses, then said 'this is our chapel', and walked through the open door into what should have been the front room. There were chairs of various ages and descriptions arranged in lines and at the opposite end a small table adorned with a simple wooden cross, beside which a slightly stooped man wearing a threadbare coat was standing. That must be Mr Trevelyan.

He turned around to meet the two women and said 'Hello Mary, this is a surprise, and who is your friend?'

After a pause for thought Mary replied 'This is Charlotte.'

'And have you come to join our little congregation Charlotte?'

'Probably not Mr Trevelyan, but I, sorry, we, do need your help on another matter.'

'And what might that be?'

Charlotte explained what had happened, how they had been feeding starving, wounded old soldiers and how they needed to make better arrangements for each day. 'We thought of you.'

Yes Mr Trevelyan would like to help if he could but 'I have no money to buy their food and I will need help. I live her alone while I am trying to build up my chapel. One day I will have a proper place of worship.'

Charlotte believed him. Mary had guided her to the right place. Her answer was clear and left no room for doubt. 'I will find money for you'. She did not say how. 'Shall we say ten guineas each week to begin with? As for help, Mary will come and help you each day if she agrees. Would you do that Mary?'

'Yes Miss Charlotte, but what will I say if I go out every day.'

'You will say you are following my orders. No one will question you if you say that, and no one will dare question me, not even my mother.'

Mary understood. She had heard the recent argument between Charlotte and her mother. She knew who had won.

* * *

On the next day at the rendezvous with the Sergeant and his men there was no basket of food for them. The disappointment on the Sergeant's face was obvious for all to see, but hunger was part of their lives. They had been fortunate for a few days. Perhaps their luck had run out?

'Sergeant may I have a word with you' asked Charlotte.

'Yes Miss.'

'We want to help you and your men, but our present arrangements need to be better. Do you agree?'

'Yes Miss.'

'We have arranged for you all to be fed at a little chapel. Mary will take you there. It's not far, and there will be food for you every day.'

'If it's a chapel, will we have to go for prayers and sermons?'

'Only if you choose to. But you will have to help with the meals. You may be able to find more of your colleagues too. Trust me, I know this will be better for you.'

The Sergeant did trust this lady. He knew she would never let them down. How she had done it he did not know, but he did know how to say thank you. He called his men to attention and saluted. For Charlotte that was thanks enough.

* * *

Charlotte watched as Mary led her men towards the chapel and safety. There were tears in her eyes. She walked home, the first time she had done that without a chaperone, and despite her simple dress marched up to the front door to be let in by a surprised Reid, the butler. She went to her room and fell to her knees again. Her prayers had been answered.

34

The next time Charlotte visited the bank she withdrew the sum of ten guineas. This was the amount she drew each week for the remainder of 1815. She was working harder than she had ever done. Mary's absences while she was at the chapel took up a significant part of each day and someone had to work to cover up for her. In doing so, Charlotte learned a great deal about running a household. She also met with Cook and took with her paper and pen in order to write down the recipes. Some were very grand with many stages to achieve the finished dish and these were the ones that Charlotte chose not to write down. Having seen men starve for want of basics, she could no longer eat the many courses prepared for her parent's meals, especially if they were entertaining guests, a frequent occurrence in the Neal household. She chose to eat alone. If she had been allowed, she would have eaten with the servants, although that would have been a step too far down the social ladder.

* * *

Each visit to the bank was seen by William. He would have liked to speak to Charlotte, if only to say good morning. Their lives continued apart.

William continued to collect books and read as much as he could. His Sundays were spent helping Mr Fenwick rather than attending church, but even that was much quicker thanks to the methods he had introduced. It rarely took longer than the morning. The two men could return home by midday when Mrs Fenwick had prepared a hot meal for them. Afterwards William was invited to join the Fenwick's in their sitting room, a welcome break from the loneliness he otherwise endured.

* * *

As the year came to a close, a certain Scottish Earl contemplated his lot in life. He had made the correct decision to move to London. That was where life was. Dr Johnson had spoken the truth. Money from his estate continued to accrue, and he continued to spend to support the hedonistic lifestyle he now enjoyed. He would wait a while yet before looking for a wife. There was only one problem to mar his enjoyment. Recently he had had a touch of the agues and developed a rash, but it had not lasted long and he had had no need to see one of the many doctors practising their trade. He was looking forward to 1816 and all that the New Year would bring.

* * *

As the church bells rang out their peal to welcome 1816 several other people wondered what the year would bring. Mary wondered how she could tell Miss Charlotte that the little band at the chapel had grown, word had spread and there were more men to feed. She would have to ask for more money. She was pleased that some of the soldiers had joined their congregation. She prayed that they would and that one day they would be able to build a proper chapel, maybe for two hundred or more. Dr Wesley would approve of that. Charlotte wondered how long her money would last and when her parents would find out what she had been doing. Mrs Neal wondered if her daughter would ever apologise and join her social circle again. Mr Neal wondered if his daughter would tire of visiting the bank and when she would rejoin the family at his supper table. William wondered if he would ever be able to speak to Miss Neal. Mr and Mrs Fenwick wondered when would be the time to tell William of the decision they had reached. Reid the butler, who knew what was happening, wondered if he would be asked how Miss Charlotte spent her days. Cook wondered if her creative accounting to cover the food Charlotte had bought, would ever be discovered.

* * *

On the day before Charlotte was due to visit the bank in the first week of January, Mary asked to speak with her. 'Miss Charlotte, I'm sorry to have to ask, but can you spare any more money for our soldiers? Word had spread and we now have more mouths to feed than we can buy food for. Some of the men have joined our congregation, praise the Lord'

'I think I might be able to help a little more.'

'Thank you Miss.' A discussion followed and Charlotte agreed to double her investment, as she thought of her spending, to twenty guineas each week. What would her father say? Then again, he never asked Jenkins to show him her ledger.

* * *

206

The weeks followed their established pattern through the remains of winter, spring, summer, and into autumn. The last Sunday in November proved to be a day when all fortunes turned.

* * *

When Mary returned from Sunday chapel she asked to see Charlotte and said 'I have some news for you Miss.'

'Is it about our soldiers?'

'No Miss, it's about me. Mr Trevelyan has asked me to marry him and I have said yes.'

'And what has your father said?'

'He's not here Miss. He went to Australia to seek his fortune for me.'

Charlotte could read between the lines. Her father had been convicted of some petty crime and sentenced to deportation, a common occurrence.

'So who will give you away?'

'I've asked the Sergeant Miss, and he has said yes, but he will need to get his peg leg repaired. He says it will be the longest and best walk of his life.'

'And do you have a dowry?'

'No Miss.'

'Leave that to me.'

One her next visit to the bank Charlotte made two withdrawals, twenty guineas for her soldier's investment fund and a hundred guineas for Mary. She had been a loyal servant and friend. She had her dowry.

* * *

On the other side of London in Shoreditch, William went with George Fenwick as usual to his printing works. The man seemed troubled by something, although the accounts were in order and soon completed. They returned for their meal, and Mrs Fenwick also seemed on edge. Afterwards, as they sat together in the drawing room, George looked at his wife, cleared his throat and said 'William, there is something important I have to say to you.'

William could not stop himself putting his hand to his mouth in shock. Surely they were not going to ask him to leave.

George cleared his throat again and said 'William, Mrs Fenwick and I are getting on in years and have never been blessed with children. You have become like a son to us, and your ideas for my accounts have made us think.

207

We should like to offer you a partnership in the printing works, and when we have passed away it and this house will all be yours. What do you say?'

William was at a loss for words. There were tears in his eyes as he mumbled his reply, 'thank you both, yes please.' But how would he leave the bank and Mr Neal?

35

William had much to think about. How and when should he leave the bank? How would he help George Fenwick grow the printing business that would become Fenwick and Neal? Should he invest his considerable savings from his share dealings into the business? He decided that time would give him the answers. Time, that precious gift from God, that should never be wasted. But he had no means to tell the time other than the striking of church clocks. He remembered back to his first encounter with his mentor, Mr Neal, and that watch. That is what he ought to have, a pocket watch, the mark of a man of affairs. He had the money. He had read in the newspapers about the new shops at Burlington Arcade in Piccadilly, that every luxury man could desire were sold there. He resolved to find out for himself as soon as possible. Surely there would be a watchmaker's shop? What about the following Saturday. He would have to ask to be excused working in the bank. That could be difficult; he knew he had to try.

On the following day, Monday, he approached Mr Jenkins with his request to be absent from his counter on the following Saturday. He cited personal matters that he had to attend to that could not wait.

'I should say no' replied Jenkins 'but if matters are as urgent as you say, then I will agree but only this once.'

William looked forward all week to his adventure on the Saturday. Before he left Shoreditch he placed a quantity of bank notes in his pocket. He would not spend more and he hoped he would be able to spend less. He set out for the long walk to Piccadilly. Fortunately the weather was dry but it was also cold, and he was glad of the overcoat he had been so kindly provided by the bank. He reached the Arcade. What a wonder to behold, many small shops selling clothes, furniture, jewellery and there were two shops selling clocks and watches. He looked in the window of the first shop and then started to walk across the way to its rival. As he did so he looked and saw a familiar face.

'Why, Miss Neal, good morning to you' said William as he touched his forehead in respect to one of his betters.

'Why, William, good morning, and what are you doing here?'

'I would like to buy a pocket watch Miss, and I was told that this was the best place in London for that.'

'I think it may be, would you like me to look with you?'

William's heart jumped at that thought, 'yes please Miss.'

The two entered the second shop and examined the wares on offer. Should the watch be in gold or silver? William decided it had to be gold, but the prices being charged were more than the money he had brought with him. He could not say that to Miss Neal so suggested gently that they might look at the first shop before he made up his mind. They crossed the Arcade again.

At the first shop there were more pocket watches for sale than clocks and a choice of several designs. This was better and the prices were more reasonable. William's eye was drawn to one watch with a white face and larger hands than the others. It was the one he liked.

'Miss Neal, do you like this watch?'

'Yes William I do, it's the one would have chosen too.'

'Then that's the one I'll buy.'

William removed his Bank of England notes to pay for his watch and received some guineas in return. The exchange had not gone unnoticed by Charlotte Neal. Where had William earned that much cash?

'Would sir like me to wrap the watch for you?' asked the salesman.

'No thank you, sir would like to wear his purchase.'

William started to attach the watch and its chain to his waistcoat, but was struggling with the unfamiliar process.

'William, would you like me to help you fix your watch in place?'

'Yes please Miss Neal.' As he did so their eyes met. William was instantly smitten.

As they left the watchmaker's shop William asked what Miss Neal would like to do next.

'I think I should like to go home.'

William knew where that was and asked if Miss Neal would allow him to walk home with her.

'That would be nice William, but Brampton brought me here in our carriage. I must tell him what we are going to do.' They walked over to where Brampton was waiting.

'Brampton, I have decided that I will walk home. You may go.'

Brampton looked at the man his mistress was standing next to. He thought he recognised that face. It was that upstart of his former assistant, dressed like a gentleman, and with Miss Charlotte. He would not be dismissed. He would follow behind them both with his whip in his hand. If that William laid a finger on Miss Charlotte he would whip him hard. It is what he richly deserved.

As they walked Miss Neal decided she could trust William and said 'if you like William, you can call me Charlotte.'

William did like that and murmured his thanks. As they parted at her home he contemplated the long walk back to Shoreditch. He wondered what more life had in store for him.

36

As non-conformists Mary and her husband to be, John Trevelyan, would have to be married in an Anglican church. They arranged to see the vicar of St Mary Abbot's with their request as technically they both resided in his parish. Once he heard who John was and what he was doing the vicar said he thought it would be better if they found another church for the ceremony.

They returned to the chapel. Mary was in tears and told the Sergeant, who had agreed to give her away, what had happened.

'Did he now?'

'Yes, but I do so want to marry John, he's such a good man.'

'And so you shall.'

The Sergeant knew what he would do. He called for three of his old comrades and together set out for St Mary's Vicarage. They walked up to the front door, not the servant's entrance, the Sergeant rang the bell and they all sat down.

'We are all old soldiers from this parish and we have come to claim parish relief.'

'I don't recognise you from among my flock.'

'We're non-conformists and the law says you have to take us in.'

'We are but a poor parish, and I can't take you in.' The parish was not poor.

'Then I will call for the other twenty of my men I have left behind and we'll wait until you do take us in.'

That was blackmail. What did the man really want? The vicar invited the Sergeant into his house but only as far as the hallway where a heated discussion took place. An agreement was struck between the two men. John and Mary were married on Epiphany 1817 and Charlotte was a bridesmaid. How did she manage that she never told a soul. The Sergeant and his men much preferred the chapel than anything a certain parish might have been able to offer, and to it is where they returned.

* * *

As the New Year began, Charlotte continued to visit her father's bank to withdraw funds for the soldiers at the chapel. She began another practice that, when she thought no one was looking and she could catch William's eye, she gave him a little wave. It was enough.

* * *

January turned into February. It was still cold, and most of the population of London hoped that there would be no more snow. William still had to decide the date when he might leave the bank and just what he would say to Mr Neal, the man who had given him his chance in life. The routine at the bank continued its familiar pattern until, on Wednesday the 26th an event that had never occurred before took place. Mr Jenkins was absent from the bank. He was absent on the Thursday and when the Friday came and he still had not arrived he had presented Mr Neal and Roberts with a major problem. The staff had to be paid on the last day of the month and that was Jenkins' responsibility. He kept the books in his safe and he had the key. There was a buzz of excitement around those hallowed halls as men wondered what might happen. The buzz reached Roberts' ears and he knew action was required. Then he remembered. Hadn't Jenkins shown young Neal how the salary ledgers worked as part of his training before he was sent to be a teller? Roberts walked downstairs and walked up to William.

'Young Neal, do I remember correctly that Jenkins taught you about the salaries book when he trained you?'

'Yes Sir.'

'Could you do that work today in Jenkins' absence?'

'Yes sir.'

'And how will you open his safe?'

'I know where he hides his key.'

Did he now? That was one smart young man. There was one further obstacle, he required Mr Neal's agreement, and asked William to follow him to Mr Neal's office, where he knocked on the door.

'Come in.'

Roberts and William entered and stood before Mr Neal while the Clerk explained both the problem and the solution he proposed.

There was a simple question from Mr Neal. 'Can you do that for us William?'

'Yes Sir.'

'Then off you go and I will see you later when you have finished.

William found the key and opened the safe then took out the ledger and started to work his way through the list of names and their salaries. Not all

213

were the same and he wondered why some men earned more than others. He also noticed that Mr Neal's and Roberts' names did not appear in the book. As he worked through he saw that sums of interest has been added where balances had been held on the relevant quarter days. That was odd, the interest was a few pennies short of what it should be here, and as he looked through there, and there, and there, and more going back over a year. Surely Mr Jenkins would have made sure his calculations were correct. He had been so demanding for accuracy from his tellers and here he was, with inaccuracies in his records. What should William do? He looked back in the safe and there, tucked at the back, was another small book, that he thought he might have seen when he first received his training. He opened that book and knew what had been happening.

Before he could take any action the door opened and a certain young lady walked in.

'Why William, what are you doing here, I was looking for Mr Jenkins as I should like to withdraw some money from my account.'

'He's not here today Miss Charlotte, and I have been asked by your father to do his work. How can I help you?'

'As I said, I should like to withdraw some of my own money. My book is over there.' She pointed to a shelf and a book which William took down and opened to the current day's page. He saw she had been making regular withdrawals.

'How much would you like today?'

'Twenty guineas please.'

William made the entry then left her while he collected he money from the nearest teller and asked him to make his own record of the transaction. He returned and handed Charlotte her money, then looked at her account again. For some reason Jenkins had never applied interest to her account. He looked at Jenkins little book and saw why. He had his evidence.

'Miss Charlotte, will you wait here please as I have some work I must do now.'

Charlotte sat down. How long would she have to wait?

* * *

William ran upstairs with three books under his arm, knocked on Mr Roberts' door and ran in.

'I must see Mr Neal now on a matter of urgency.'

214

'He's very busy right now but he did say he would see you at the end of the day. Can you come back then?'

'No Mr Roberts, I really must insist on seeing him as soon as possible.'

That was so unlike young Neal. Roberts had always thought he was a very level-headed young man, and if he said it was urgent then, he trusted his judgment. He walked to his master's office and interrupted him. 'Excuse me sir, Young Neal is here and has asked to see you on a matter of urgency. He said it could not wait.'

'Very well, bring him in, but I want you to stay too.'

William was brought into that room he had first seen so many months ago when he did not know what his fate might be. He brought the three books, and showed Mr Neal the evidence. If he had been a witness in a trial what he said could not have been clearer, Jenkins was an embezzler.

'Well bless my soul, who would have thought it. This is a very serious matter and must, for the time being, remain just between the three of us. Do we all agree?' They did. How could they put matters to rights?

William spoke first, 'well sir, individually these are quite small amounts and we could always claim that Jenkins had made a miscalculation. I can work out what has gone and we can put the money back gradually so, if we are lucky, no one will notice.' That was agreed. But what about Jenkins.

Mr Neal was quite firm 'when and if he returns you will leave him to me. I have the bank's reputation to consider'. That was agreed.

'Now William, you have done me another great service, and I wish to reward you. I'll promote you to be my Chief Cashier, what do you say?'

'No thank you sir. I think you should promote, and he gave the name of the man who had taught him how to be a teller.'

'But William, I should like to give you a reward?'

'Thank you sir. I should like your permission to ask your daughter Charlotte to be my wife.'

'Pardon?'

'I should like your permission to ask your daughter Charlotte to be my wife.'

'But you are a near penniless bank teller and my daughter has a fortune of five thousand pounds.

'No sir, your daughter has been drawing money every week from her fortune which is three thousand five hundred and eighty-seven pounds and six shillings, plus, of course, the interest that Jenkins took. 'And, no sir, I am not penniless. I have saved every penny from my wages at your home and here. I do not drink and would never spend my money on some of the women who loiter around our streets. I have three thousand two hundred and twelve pounds, fourteen shillings and seven pence to my name.'

'And how did you get that? You haven't been stealing from my bank too have you?'

'No sir, I used the knowledge I had gained from working here to buy and sell stocks and shares for profit. And, Mr Fenwick has offered me a partnership in his printing works. I think the time has come for me to join him.'

'Have you asked my daughter to marry you?'

'No sir.'

'And what if she says no?'

'Then, sir, I shall never marry another, and spend my life printing books.

'Why books?'

'Sir, there is a great thirst for knowledge, and as more people learn to read and write that is how they and society will grow. I want to help them.'

'Not bibles.'

'No sir, Mr Guy has that monopoly.'

Now those were clever answers. Young Neal would go far, but what would his daughter say? 'Is Charlotte still in the bank?'

'Yes in Jenkins office.'

'Roberts, would you be so kind as to ask her to come here?' Roberts departed to his task and came back with that certain young lady to her father's office.

'Charlotte, young William here has something to ask you.'

'Miss Neal, Charlotte, will you do me the honour of being my wife?'

There was a pause during which William's heart sank and he thought she would say no.

Her voice came through the fog of his brain 'yes William, I will.'

37

'Thank you, Charlotte. I want you to wait downstairs.'

'But Papa.' Then she saw the furrowed brow and steely look of determination in her father's eyes and knew he had given her an order. She left the room, but what would happen now?

* * *

'Well William, my daughter may have said that she will marry you but I have not given my permission. I have to be satisfied that you look after her properly once you have left the bank. You have said that you want to print books, so where will you start?'

This was William's opportunity. He remembered how Jenkins had refused to listen to his ideas about improving the bank's efficiency and service to its customers. Now was his chance. He replied in a strong clear voice 'with your bank sir.'

'What do you mean, my bank? I grant you Mr Fenwick does our general printing but not books. We do not need them.'

'You do sir, let me explain.' So William explained how inefficient it was that the tellers had to find each customer's ledger when they came in, even if it was just to check how much money they had in their account. Queues built up especially on quarter days and tempers were easily frayed. William's proposal was radical. 'I should like to change what we do. I think each customer should have his own book into which our tellers can enter how much is taken in and paid out and what their balance is. That would eliminate one reason for them to call here. Then each teller will have a sheet on which they can write each day's transactions. It will be much quicker for them to balance their money each day as they will not have to look at every ledger. Then we will have other tellers who, on the next day will write up the ledgers and check there have been no mistakes or stealing.'

Mr Neal senior thought for a moment then turned to Rogers. 'Would that work?'

'Oh yes sir it would, but I do have a one question. What would happen if one of our tellers lost one of his sheets with part of his day's work?'

That was an interesting question, but William had the answer. 'We will number each sheet so that it will be obvious if any have been lost.'

217

'And what if a customer writes in his book that he has paid in money when he hasn't?'

'We will have all the teller's sheets and his ledger, and if we have our own colour ink that should deter forgeries.'

'Perhaps.'

'William then asked for pen and paper and drew out the various columns for both the customer's personal books and the tellers day sheets and showed then to Mr Neal and Rogers. There was a long pause before Rogers gave an almost imperceptible nod of his head to Mr Neal senior who returned the nod.

'There was an even longer wait while Mr Neal senior looked again at the two draft documents William had prepared. For William, it seemed like an eternity before he had his answer, 'Yes William, I think we should try that, but your scheme must be in place and working before you leave my bank, what was it for, to print books.'

'Now William, let me explain some other matters for you. On her marriage my daughter Charlotte will receive a dowry of ten thousand pounds so you had better find somewhere appropriate for her live. That is all she will receive, as her brother, my son Jonathan, will inherit the bank when I am gone. Do you understand?'

'Yes sir, I promise to look after and cherish her as the good book says I should.'

'Very well William, then I will give you my blessing. I think you had better find your fiancée now don't you.

William left the office. He had his bride, a contract to print books and the teller's record sheets, his monopoly. How he would be able to print all those numbers easily, or make the special ink he had thought of on the spur of the moment, he did not know. He hoped George Fenwick had those answers.

* * *

As William left his office, Mr Neal senior scratched his head. What a day it had been. Then a dark thought crossed his mind and his brow furrowed deeply again. Just how would he tell his wife who Charlotte had chosen to marry?

38

At the end of a day that had changed his life forever, William Neal senior left his office, collected his daughter and entered their coach that Brampton had already brought to the front door of the bank.

'Charlotte my dear, there are some things we must discuss before we reach home. Please tell me when you decided you wanted to marry my namesake, the other William.'

'Papa, I have always liked him. He was very polite when he drove Mama and I. I liked him more when we found he could read and you believed me when I said he had not been asleep. Then he went away and I thought I would never see him again, until I came to your bank, and there he was, but we never spoke. We met by accident in Burlington Arcade when I was shopping and William was buying his own pocket watch. I helped him choose, and then I fixed it to his waistcoat pocket. Our eyes met. I knew than that he had fallen for me, and I think that is when I fell for him.'

'Very well Charlotte, do you want to change your mind about marrying William? You can you know.'

'No Papa, I am quite certain I have made the right choice.'

'Then we will have much to arrange. The first matter when we reach home is that you, and not me, will tell your mother you are now betrothed and to whom.'

'Will you come with me when I tell Mama?'

'No I will not. You have made your choice, and as an adult, over the age of consent, you must be responsible for your own actions. Now we know William is entirely honest and god fearing and he came from Scotland. Have you been able to find out more?'

'No Papa. When I asked him he would not say, but I think something terrible has happened in his life. All he would say was I owe everything to Mrs Robertson and your father. I don't think he will ever say more even to me when I am his wife.'

Charlotte's opinion about William's silence proved to be correct. How could William tell her that he was just a little ploughboy.

* * *

As soon as their coach had arrived home and William senior and Charlotte had entered into the hall through the front door held open by Reid, the butler,

Charlotte was ordered to find her mother and tell her the news. Reid overheard the conversation and wondered what that news might be.

Charlotte climbed the stairs up to her mother's rooms as slowly as she could and knocked on the door, then waited until an imperious call of 'enter' rang out. Charlotte entered and stood in front of her mother.

'Mama, I have some important news for you. I have just accepted a proposal of marriage.'

'Darling, that is good news, who is he, a soldier, an aristocrat? I would so love to have a title in the family.'

'No Mama, he's a printer.'

'How could you do this to me? A printer? That is trade and therefore beneath your station in life. I don't think I know of any printers other than Mr Guy who prints bibles. Is he from that family?'

'No Mama.'

'Well I don't want to meet him.'

'You already have.'

'I don't think so.'

'You have. His name is William Neal, and he is the man you chased away from here those years ago. He has done well since then. 'She decided she had better not tell her mother that the very same William Neal had been working in her father's bank. That must remain their secret.

'He's trade and I don't want you to marry him. I want you to write to him tonight saying you have made a mistake and regret you cannot marry him.'

'No.'

'But what will I tell my friends? My daughter has married a former servant who is now in trade. How could you do this to me?'

Charlotte thought she could do so easily. It would serve her mother right to have to go and tell those gossips she met daily what she had done.

'Mama, I have one question for you. What happens in the marital bed?'

'You lie back and let your husband do what he wants to your body when you want to have children. At all other times you make sure he has his own bedroom.'

Charlotte was appalled by this answer. So that's what her mother had done to her father and perhaps that was why he appeared so melancholy at times. Then she understood more. Her father was a banker who lived by the rule that his word was his bond. He had entered into a marriage contract, as the prayer book said, till death us do part, and he would never break a promise.

* * *

Charlotte left her mother's room. How could she be so cruel? She found her father sitting at his study desk looking at various pieces of paper.

'Have you told your mother Charlotte?'

'Yes Papa.'

'And.'

'She wants me to write to William and call off our engagement and marriage.'

'Will you?'

'No Papa. I have given my word and will never go back on it.'

What a good reply. She was her father's daughter after all, and spoken like a banker. It was a pity that women were not allowed to enter that profession. She may even have been the equal, or better, than his son Jonathan at his bank.

'Very well Charlotte, now we have some other matters to discuss. When you marry William you will receive a dowry of ten thousand pounds, and that is because your brother will inherit both the bank and this house. I think you should use it wisely to buy your own home so where will that be?'

'William's printing works are in Shoreditch, and I think he would like to live near there. I am sure we can find something suitable.'

'Very well, now tell me on what you have been spending your inheritance.'

'May I show you tomorrow?'

'As you wish.'

'You will have much to do to set up your new home. I will arrange for Brampton to take you where you will need to go.'

'Thank you Papa.' Charlotte then walked behind her father's desk and gave him a huge embrace and kissed his forehead. He understood.

'Now Charlotte I think you ought to go to your room.'

Charlotte obeyed her father's instruction. At least he had accepted William as her future husband.

* * *

William Neal senior wearily climbed the stairs up to his wife's room. He knew what he would say. This was a time for diplomacy.

'My dear, Charlotte tells me that you have asked her to change her mind about who her future husband will be. I have tried too, but she will not change. I think we have to accept her decision with as good a grace as we can muster.'

'How dare she marry beneath her station in life. What will I say to my friends? You must stop her marrying trade and a servant. It's undignified.'

'I don't think I can. If we try there is a risk she will elope. It is my wish that we see her properly married.'

'How could she do this to me? I think I have a headache coming on with all this strain.'

William withdrew and left his wife to her low spirits. He would be dining alone again.

39

That very same evening William rushed home to the Fenwick's from the bank. He had much to tell them. His life, and theirs, had changed on this day too, and he wanted to share the pleasures of the day with the two people who had become second parents to him. As luck would have it, George was already home.

He was excited and wondered where to begin. He took a deep breath and said 'I have some very important news that I must share with you. It has been quite a day.'

'Do tell us William.'

'I have decided that I will leave the bank and join your printing works. It may be quite soon, but I do have work to finish first at the bank.' He decided that, having been sworn to secrecy, he could not mention the financial discrepancies he had uncovered or his temporary promotion.

'I have also had my proposal of marriage accepted by Charlotte and I want George to be my best man. I also need to know where the best place to live in Shoreditch is.'

'William, who is Charlotte?'

'The love of my life, oh, and she's Mr Neal's daughter.'

'Which Mr Neal?'

'Didn't I say? Mr Neal the banker.'

The Fenwick's looked at each other and nodded sagely. He had done well for himself, but they always believed he would. They would have to find the very best house for them they could.

'And there's more. I have got a printing contract for books and sheets of paper from the bank. It will give us regular work.' He explained his scheme. 'And I said we could print serial numbers on the books and the paper, and find a special ink too. I knew you would have the answer as to how we do that George.'

George didn't. It had not been done before except by laboriously hand stamping, and there would be no profit in that. George chose not to dampen William's enthusiasm by saying no. His reply was another essence of tact 'we'll have to work that one out won't we.'

40

On the next morning, Saturday, Charlotte dressed in the clothes that Mary had let her borrow. As she came downstairs, intent on going to the servant's quarters for her breakfast, she noticed that the door to her father's study was open and he was already sitting behind his desk. He had a pen in his hand and paper, on which some words had already been written, sitting in front of him. He seemed at a loss for words. Charlotte knocked on the door and went into her father's inner sanctum.

'Good morning Papa, what are you doing?'

'I'm writing to your brother to tell him what has happened, unless, of course, you tell me that you have changed your mind about marrying William.'

'No Papa, I have not changed my mind. I am more certain than ever that he is the man I want to marry.'

'I have also been thinking about what to do. Your fiancé, if I may call William that now, has turned into a fine young man who will do very well, but we have to convince your mother that he is the man for you. Incidentally, I do agree with you and will not stand in the way of your marriage, but your mother may. I intend to invite William to dine with us when we can discuss the wedding arrangements. I should like your brother to be here too and that means he will have to be given permission for a special *exeat* if I can persuade the Head Master of Eton College to agree. This is his final year and I want to see him go up to Oxford University before he joins me in the bank. That may have to change, but I hope not.'

'Papa, please let Jonathan go to Oxford. William and I will manage somehow.'

'Very well, but why are you wearing servant's clothing? '

'I am taking you somewhere I regard as very special and important to me. These are the clothes I wear when I go there.'

'And Reid lets you go out dressed like that?'

'He doesn't know. I leave by the servant's entrance and walk.'

'The streets aren't always safe for wealthy young women.'

'No one has ever harmed me.'

What Charlotte did not know was that her safety had been guaranteed by the Sergeant and his men. They had let it be known to all the ne'er-do-wells, cut purses and the like, that if any harm ever befell Charlotte they knew to whom they would have to answer and what their fate would be. Their description of that fate had made public hanging sound merciful.

'Then we will walk together later.'

* * *

After Mr Neal had breakfasted, he and Charlotte left by the front door and walked through the back streets of Kensington to the chapel. There were signs of life, bustle, and when they went through the front door the place was spick and span. They were greeted by Mr Trevelyan.

'Good morning Charlotte and welcome, but who is this with you?'

'My father.'

'Good morning sir, and welcome too. We cannot manage without your daughter's help.'

'And what help is that?'

Charlotte provided the answer by pulling out a little leather bag from her apron pocket. It contained her usual weekly contribution of twenty guineas. The action was not lost on her father.

Before he could question what his daughter was doing, a man in the worn uniform of a Sergeant of Artillery hobbled up, stood as upright as his injuries would allow and saluted. 'Good morning Miss Charlotte, God bless you.'

'Thank you Sergeant, how are you all today?'

'All present and correct Miss.'

That was the reply Charlotte wanted to hear, although it was the same reply each week.

The reverie of the moment was broken by a sharp demand from Mr Neal senior 'just what is going on here?'

Charlotte took him to one side and explained. It was not a short explanation about how she had found destitute soldiers wounded in the Battle of Waterloo, how she had fed them, she omitted the deception she had made with Cook, and how that had found refuge here at the chapel with Mr Trevelyan and his wife Mary, 'who used to be my maid' and how they needed her help each week.

'We cannot let them starve Papa.'

'No we can't. But I want you to keep your money for yourself now and leave things to me.'

'I can't agree unless I know that they will all be looked after.'

'Charlotte my dear, I have asked you to leave things for me now, and yes you have that promise.'

'Thank you Papa.'

Her father did not explain that amongst the customers of his bank were Ministers of the Crown, of whom he would be asking some searching questions. Meanwhile he would fund the chapel. He could well afford to.

'Charlotte, I think it's time we returned home. I do have to go to my bank today.'

'Yes Papa, but I would like to speak with Mary first.'

* * *

Charlotte turned to Mary and whispered that she would like to talk to her where they would not be overheard.

Her first question was 'what happens in the marital bed?'

Mary's answer was quite long, and it was the very opposite of her mother's. She described the pleasures husband and wife could have together.

Charlotte's second question was 'will you be my Maid of Honour? I do not want to have the offspring of some of my mother's friends as bridesmaids.'

'Yes please.'

* * *

The deals had been made so Charlotte and her father could return home and carry on with the business of the day.

41

William and George had also risen early and were at work on the bank books and forms William had devised and sketched out on the previous evening. Could George print them and how long would it take to have proofs for William to show Mr Neal senior?

'I shall work on them today. I can get the basics set up so that you will be able to show Mr Neal something on Monday morning if you like, but, we still have to work out how to obtain the special ink and how to print the numbers economically. Then what colour do you want to have for the covers of the bank books?'

William looked up, smiled and pointed to the colour of his jacket. George understood, dark green, and was surprised by William's next request.

'I want you to leave to cover of the books plain brown for now.'

What was he doing? George just nodded his agreement to the idea.

'George, I want you to be my best man when I marry Charlotte and I want us both to wear the same colour coats. We will go to my tailor, and I will pay, but we must go soon as there could be a long wait.'

'Yes William.'

'Next I shall need your advice about where to live in Shoreditch. I want to live near where I work. Charlotte will need a grand house too, she is entitled to that from her station in life, and it is my duty to give that to her. Where do you suggest?'

George had discussed that very question with his wife as they lay in bed the previous evening discussing that day's events. His wife had given him the answer where, if money was no object, she would like to live.

'That's easy William, Hoxton Square. They are building some very fine houses there. Let's agree to go there tomorrow and I can show you what I mean.'

Another deal had been struck.

* * *

Before William left for the bank he placed his gold watch and chain in his waistcoat pocket. He was the acting Chief Cashier now and, as he had learned in the past, it pays to look the part. He certainly did.

When he reached the bank he entered the Chief Cashier's office, his office now, opened the safe with the key that now had a new hiding place, and set to work to calculate how much Jenkins had stolen from both his fellow workers and Charlotte.

It took most of the day as he made his calculations then he checked them again for accuracy. Before he left to return to Shoreditch he was able to present Mr Neal senior with the true losses his bank had suffered.

42

The next day, Sunday was a busy day for both William and Charlotte. George took William to show him Hoxton Square and the nearby streets. There was a nice house, in the new regency style, number 15, at a corner with the adjoining street giving access to the rear with its stables and carriage yard. While it was smaller than Charlotte's father's house William hoped this would be their new home The building looked empty, it overlooked a pleasant green grass open space. If it had been left just to him, William would have bought the house on the spot, but he had to get his bride-to-be to agree because she would have to buy their furniture and decorations.

He and George made the short walk to the printing works where the prototype bank book and forms were ready for his inspection. William made one change with pen and ink and added the number '17' in front of the space reserved for the sequential numbering he had promised.

'Why have you done that William?'

'Well George, that is for this year and we will change as each new year arrives. We can then have fewer numbers that we have to change. I want to print thousands of these in the years ahead.'

'How are we going to get the numbers to change.'

'I have an idea. Do you remember that a Mr Brunel, an engineer, said he could tunnel under the River Thames?'

''I think so.'

'If he can tunnel under the river, something that other men say is impossible, then he should be able to design a machine to change numbers for us.'

'But what about the ink?'

'The reputed best chemist in England is a man called Sir Humphrey Davy and he is in London, so I should see him too.'

'But what about the cost of all this.'

'But what about the profit from the bank.'

They laughed at that thought.

* * *

Meanwhile Charlotte, her father and mother were attending divine service at St James's, Piccadilly. After the service, as the Vicar greeted his departing parishioners Mr Neal said 'I should like to talk to you Reverend as soon as possible if you please.'

'Yes of course Mr Neal, If you can wait a few minutes until my flock have left I can see you then.'

Mr Neal sent his wife and daughter to wait in their coach. This was man's work. Then he and the Vicar began their conversation.

'I am pleased to be able to tell you reverend that my daughter Charlotte will be getting married soon and I would like the service to be here.'

'And who is the lucky man?'

'By an odd coincidence he has the same name as me, William Neal.'

'Well, well, and which is his parish?'

'He lives in Shoreditch.'

'That would be St Leonard's. He will have to publish the banns there Mr Neal, while Charlotte's banns would be read here.'

'They discussed dates, and thought a late June or July date would be best, providing that their house was ready.

43

The next day, Monday, the two Williams and Rogers arrived early at the bank when the three went up to William senior's room. He has given instruction to the doorman that when Jenkins arrived, and if he did, he was to be shown upstairs immediately and not allowed to enter his own office.

Jenkins did arrive a short while later and looked quite flustered when shown up to Mr Neal's office.

William senior had decided how he would handle what could be an unpleasant experience. He had the bank's reputation to consider.

'Ah Jenkins, there you are, we all missed you last week.'

'I'm sorry sir, but my wife died and I wanted to see her buried. I did write a note and paid a boy sixpence to deliver it to you explaining my circumstances.'

'Unfortunately your note was not delivered. You wasted your money.'

'Never mind, but I can prepare the salaries now to make up for lost time.'

'In your unexplained absence on Friday last I asked William here to prepare the salaries. Now I have a question for you.' He turned to a page in the staff salary book and pointed to an entry. 'Could you have a look at the interest you calculated for that account?'

Jenkins did as asked, then licked his lips before replying 'I may have made a mistake.'

'And would you look at this page, and this page.'

Jenkins did so. His face grew pale and he was sweating. He did not reply.

'And Jenkins, see here, could you tell me why you have not added interest to my daughter's account?'

The man answered. 'I may have forgotten.'

'You Jenkins, forget. That is so unlike you. Now tell me what is this?' Mr Neal senior produced the little book that Jenkins had hidden at the back of his safe and which William junior had found.

There was no reply.

'You Jenkins, have been stealing from your fellow workers and from my daughter. I demand to know why.'

'I'm very sorry, my wife was ill and I had to find money to pay the doctors.'

'Which ones.'

The doctors who follow the ideas of Dr. Messmer.'

'You are a fool as well as a thief. There's charlatans, fly-by-nights, not proper doctors, they could never cure a soul, and you were taken in. And now I have to deal with this. You will be dismissed immediately, and I have considered sending you to jail. The evidence is here in these books, but I also have to consider the good name of the bank.'

'Where do you live?'

'Bloomsbury sir.'

'Do you own your own home?'

'No sir, I pay rent.'

'That's a pity, because if you had owned your own house I should have required you to sell it to pay back what you owe my daughter and your colleagues. However, I have decided to be lenient with you, but only if you follow, to the letter, what I say. You will never, ever say a word about what has happened here, and neither will I. However, there is a place for thieves and others of similar persuasion. They are transported to the penal colony of Australia. That is where you will go but not in chains yet, I shall pay your fare. Meanwhile we will explain your absence that you are looking after your wife. You are lucky that the note you say you wrote was never delivered. Then after a few weeks we will announce her passing, and that you have asked to go to Australia to set up a branch of my bank. That should suffice don't you think.'

'But I'm not sure if I want to go to the other side of the world.'

'Jenkins, I have given you a simple choice, prison, and I shall ask for the Marshalsea until you repay what you owe with interest, or Australia. What is it to be?'

'I don't know sir.'

'Well, you had better make up your mind quickly, I shall count to ten, and if you have not replied then it's the Marshalsea for you. One, two, three, four.'

'I'd better go to Australia sir.'

'That Jenkins, is a very wise choice. Now I should like you to wait in Rogers' office for the time being. Jenkins knew where that was and left the other three men to contemplate the outcome of the meeting.

'If I may say so sir, you handled that in a masterly fashion, better than a barrister could have done. We do need to keep him quiet at his home until we ship him out.'

'Thank you Rogers, that's an excellent idea. I agree. But we still have to get him home, and kept there until we can get him on a ship. Could you find someone to do that? We can't have him going around telling everyone what has happened can we.'

Rogers most certainly could. He knew the backstreets of his city and where to find just the men. He had another point to make. 'I'll have them hiding by the side of the bank ready to catch him. I think I should walk with him to the front door, all friendly like. It will make the story we tell sound more real.'

'I agree. Could you do that now please.'

Rogers could and left the room to the two Williams.

* * *

'And what else do you have for me today Chief Cashier?'

William produced the teller's from. 'Here sir. I have made one change. You will see that I have put the year before where I shall put the serial numbers, say 1 to 999. It will make it easier to find the record if we know under which year to look.'

'That's a good idea. I like that, but what if I need more than 999 forms?'

'Then sir, we add a letter of the alphabet.'

'Then when can you deliver the first 999 forms?'

'I shall accept your order on behalf of my partner, and put it in hand immediately.'

'And what else do you have?'

William brought out the customer's book in its bare brown cover and handed it over for inspection. It passed muster as there had been no changes from the drawing that William had prepared only three days before.

'I don't like the brown.'

'Well sir, we left the book like that for you to choose which colour you might like.'

'And what colour would you choose William?'

William pointed to the dark green colour of his coat, and was met by a roar of laughter from William senior. The clever young rascal had wanted that colour all along.

* * *

Their meeting continued.

'Tell me William, how am I to pay back the lost interest to my staff without telling them what Jenkins has done?'

'Well sir, why don't you pay them back what is due and a little more as a Christmas bonus. That would hide what we have agreed to hide would it not?'

William senior nodded his head. That was another clever idea.

'Now, William, as my future son-in-law. I should like to invite you to dine with my family on Saturday week. My son Jonathan is returning from school to join us. We have a wedding to plan. I shall send Brampton to collect you and he will drive you home afterwards.

'Thank you sir, I am delighted to accept. May I raise another matter with you?'

'Please do.'

'When is Charlotte coming to the bank again?'

'I think that may be tomorrow. Why?'

'Well sir, I think I may have found a suitable house for us and I should like her to see it before I make any purchase.'

'Knowing my daughter that would be very wise.'

'Thank you sir, and I should like to take a few days leave from the bank, say until Monday next as I have my arrangements to make for our wedding.'

'Agreed William, providing of course that they is no urgent banking business requiring your attention.'

44

On the very next morning William was waiting at the front door of the bank for Mr Neal to arrive. He hoped Charlotte was with him, and she was. Her father left his coach, and as Charlotte got up to leave too, William got in.

'I have something I want to show you.' He then gave Brampton instruction where to go, Hoxton Square.

With some reluctance Brampton drove off. How dare his former assistant give him orders, but he had been told that he was to drive Miss Charlotte anywhere she wanted to go, so he jangled the reins, gave the horses a quick flick of his whip and off they sped eastwards.

When they reached the square William turned to Charlotte and said 'George told me this is the best area of Shoreditch. I need to live close to the printing works as I aim to make as big a fortune from printing books as your father has from his bank.'

'William directed Brampton to the house he had thought would be ideal for his future bride and asked 'what do you think?'

'I like the square but not that house.'

'But why, I don't understand.'

'William, I said I like the square and yes I would like to live here, but in that house.' She pointed to another identical house on the far side of the square.

'I still don't understand why that house and not this. They are both the same.'

'No William they are not. This house faces to north and south. The house I want faces east and west, so we will have the rising morning sun on our front door, then the setting sun in our garden at the end of the day. Please.'

There was no answer to that. Charlotte had chosen and that was the house he would have to buy for her.

45

William put the days away from the bank to good use. On the Wednesday morning George and he both returned to Hoxton Square where they found the builder of the house Charlotte had chosen, and expressed their interest in its purchase. How much? When would it be complete? Could my fiancée visit to supervise the decorations? When would the other houses in the square be completed? And so it went on. When William was satisfied with the answers he had been given he made an offer of ten per cent less than the builder's asking price as he did not need to borrow money from a bank. Negotiations took place until eventually, after much haggling, a price was agreed. William had saved nearly six per cent providing the deal was completed by the March quarter day. That would depend on lawyers, contracts and banks.

* * *

There next port of call was William's tailor where again he was greeted as a highly valued customer.

'Good afternoon to you Mr Neal sir, and how can we help you today?'

'I should like to purchase the best set of clothes you can make for my wedding, and a like set for my best man here.' He turned and pointed to George.

'Congratulations if I may say so sir. Excuse me.'

He departed to the rear of the shop where he found the measurements he had taken for William's last set of clothes, then proceeded to check each one with his tape measure as before, noting down any changes if need be. There were none. He then turned to George and repeated the task, making notes as he did so, on his form to a tune of hmm, mmm as he wrote. What these sounds meant were lost on his customers.

'Now sir which colour cloth would you like for the coat?'

William gave him a quizzical look, pointed to his sleeve and said 'my usual.'

'And the style sir?'

Now that was a more important question. William had never been married before and did not know what would be the most suitable style for a prospective bridegroom. He would have to take his tailor's advice. He had to trust the man.

'And what would you suggest?'

236

'Well sir, this is the latest fashion' as he showed a drawing of a dandified man's outfit 'or this is the traditional design we have been making for the last twenty years.'

The choice was easy. William was a traditionalist.'

'And when is the day sir?'

'Probably in June or July.'

'Thank you for coming in so early sir. We shall have plenty of time for fittings and alterations as necessary. Shall we contact you at your bank?'

'For the time being, yes, but I do have a new business enterprise in Shoreditch that requires my attention. Here is our address.'

'George and William left the little shop to the tinkling sound of the doorbell. It hadn't changed in years.

* * *

William had found that the best engineer in the land, Mr Marc Brunel, was working on his tunnel plan down at Rotherhithe. That was too far to walk so he dressed in his best clothes and wore his gold watch. He looked the part of a successful business man, which was what he intended, as the carriage he had hired for the day set out eastwards from Shoreditch., eventually reaching the gates of a large worksite. The horses trotted through until William saw a workman and hailed him.

'Excuse me, could you tell me where to find Mr Brunel, the best engineer in England?'

The man pointed to a building about 100 yards ahead 'Mr Brunel is there sir, but he is mightily busy.'

William indicated to his driver to continue as instructed and stop at that building where he alighted from the carriage, then knocked on the door and walked in.

'Excuse me, but I am looking for Mr Marc Brunel, the best engineer in England.'

A small man wearing spectacles looked up from a drawing board 'I'm Brunel, and who sir are you and what do you want? I am very busy just now.'

William described what he wanted, a device to change numbers as each sheet of paper was printed up to 999. He finished by saying 'and of course sir, we will immediately pay your reasonable fee when the device has been shown to work.'

Now that aroused his interest. Fees paid on time. His tunnelling machine was proving to be ruinously expensive to make. He was borrowing heavily from the banks and here was an opportunity to make some money for a few day's work. He could not refuse.

'Well Mr Neal, that is an interesting challenge that you have set me. I should like to see your printing machine and how we might be able to solve your problem. I see that you have a carriage outside. If you will take me to your works now, and promise to have me driven back, I might be able to spare a little time for you now.'

'Thank you sir, I agree, shall we return to Shoreditch.'

* * *

The return journey was made in silence. When they reached the printing works Mr Brunel asked for two things, show me how your printer works, and please give me the type you wish to use for these numbers. His request was answered as he took out of his pocket a ruler and made some measurements. Crafty Mr Brunel. He had thought how to solve the problem during the journey.

'I think I can help you, but it will take two weeks to make my machine. My fee will be one hundred guineas. Can we agree?'

They could. Hands were shaken to confirm the arrangement, and as promised two weeks later a smiling Mr Brunel returned with a box with levers and wheels and rods which were fixed to the printer. It was as simple as that.

* * *

On Friday William again dressed in his best business clothes and ordered his carriage to drive to the Royal Society in Carlton House Terrace. As he entered that august building he was stopped by a flunkey who asked 'Can I help you sir?'

'Yes indeed my man, I should like to see your President Sir Humphrey Davy.'

'And do you have an appointment sir?'

'No, but I should like to make one if you could show me where to go.'

'Follow me sir.'

William was led up a grand staircase and shown into a small office. A young man looked up from behind his desk.

'This gentleman would like to make an appointment to see the President.' He then left William to make the arrangements.

'Tell me sir, why would you like to see Sir Humphrey?'

William explained that he was looking for a secret ingredient to add to ink to stop forgeries in books for his bank.

'I do not think anyone has asked for that before sir. I will ask Sir Humphrey if he is interested in your question.'

He departed and came back a few minutes later. 'You are in luck sir. Our President has a few moments to spare and will see you now. I think he is intrigued by your proposal.'

William was ushered into the presence of the great man.

'So you want a special foolproof ink do you?'

'Yes sir, and I am told you are the best chemist in England.'

Flattery would get him everywhere thought Sir Humphrey, then realised that he was the best chemist in England and this was an interesting, new intellectual challenge.

'Thank you for those kind words. I think I can help you. While I was in Paris in 1812, I was able to prove that a purple substance, iodine, was an element. I think we can add this to your ink, as there is a test we can use to show it is there. If you would like to leave this with me for the next week, I shall experiment and have the formula for you then.'

'Thank you Sir Humphrey, and your fee?'

'I don't want a fee. I shall relish this challenge, but if we are successful as I think we will be, I shall ask you to make a donation of fifty guineas to the Royal Society here. Are we agreed?'

They most certainly were. They shook hands on the deal.

46

Charlotte had also been very busy during the same week. She had spent many hours with Cook and the Housekeeper, Miss G, and had written pages and pages of all the items that she would require to establish her new home. She was relieved that her father had given permission for Miss G to accompany her when she made her purchases. She would make sure that she would not be cheated with low quality goods or excessive prices. They would have to find a place in her father's home to store all the items, and there would be cartloads, before they could be moved to her new home in Hoxton Square. She hoped William had been able to purchase for her the house that faced the morning sun. But, she had had no word from him during the week, not even a note. She worried what he had been doing and whether he could afford to buy her house even with the generous dowry her father had promised. She did not know about William's own fortune, he had forgotten to tell her.

* * *

Her father had also been busy at his bank following the revelations about Jenkins' embezzlements. He had agreed to take William's advice and new scheme into his bank and would want to know both when it could start and when William might choose to leave. He would want William to teach his staff about the new method of working. He also had to find space for the new class of workers he would have to recruit to carry out the next day checking system in the plan. He thought of them as the backroom boys and that is where they would have to work. He and Roberts had found a half empty store room that would have to do. He did not know how large his new department would become. In time the result would surprise him.

* * *

Mr Neal had made other decisions. He would personally fund the chapel for the time being, that was his promise to Charlotte until he found out more why wounded soldiers were left on the streets to fend for themselves. He called for his Clerk, Roberts and asked 'do we have any member of the government who banks with us, and better still anyone from the War Office?'

'Yes sir, Lord R is a junior minister there. I had been looking at his account with us recently, he does have quite a large outstanding loan.'

'Then Roberts I think we should write to him asking him to come and see me to discuss his financial affairs. You know the sort of thing to write, very friendly and hinting that we may be able to extend his loans further.'

Roberts knew precisely what to write. It would not be the first time that he had written such a letter, nor did he suppose that it would be the last. He left Mr Neal's office to follow his instructions.

* * *

A few days later Lord R arrived to discuss what he thought were his banking arrangements and how he could borrow more. Mr Neal began the interview.

'Lord R, I am just a little concerned, a little mark you, about how you plan to repay your debt to my bank.'

'Mr Neal, you know how it is, I am a Government Minister and must keep up appearances and entertain regularly. It is expected of me you know.'

'Quite Lord R. Now would fifty guineas help you today?'

It would. He had hoped for one hundred guineas at least, and he would have cut back a little on his lavish lifestyle. He was an aristocrat, a ruler of the country, and he expected lesser mortals, and he saw Mr Neal as just another servant, to fulfil his every need.

'Now my Lord, while you are here can I ask you another question?'

'Yes of course, but I may not know the answer.

'Could you tell me what the Secretary of State for War and the Colonies policy is towards wounded soldiers?'

'They are required to return to their own parishes which will look after them under our Poor Laws.'

'And if they are unable to return to their own parishes?'

'They must, that is the law.'

'So a Scotsman, for example (and he thought of one of the sergeant's men) blinded at Waterloo would be expected to walk back home.'

'Yes of course.'

'And how would he find his way?'

'That would be for him. There would likely be fellows from his own regiment who could help him.'

Not if he was an artilleryman and the only Scot in his battery thought Mr Neal, but did not say so.

'I understand, but do you grant these men pensions?'

'Rarely, you see the Government can't afford to do that.'

241

Now there was the truth. An uncaring, mean-spirited Government who encouraged men to give their lives for King and Country and who were then abandoned when it suited. Mr Neal did not like that answer and could see now why Charlotte had done what she had with her money. He said a little prayer of thanks for her generosity.

'Thank you Lord R for that explanation, I understand the Government position perfectly now.'

* * *

After Lord R had left with his fifty guineas William Neal took his own revenge on his arrogance and uncaring manner. He marked the account for no more loans, and when that man came for more of his money he would be told he had to repay all that was owed there and then or it would be the debtor's prison. He smiled at the thought of his Lordship in a filthy cell.

47

The next event in their lives was the dinner party for William. He was collected by Brampton and appeared at the front door of the Neal's house to be welcomed by Reid, the butler.

'Good evening sir, and welcome.'

'Thank you Reid, I am pleased to be here.

He was shown into the study where William and Jonathan Neal were waiting for him.

'William, let me introduce you to my son Jonathan.'

'Jonathan spoke first 'how do you do sir?'

'How do you do Jonathan? You father tells me that you are hoping to go to Oxford soon.

'Yes sir, I have set my heart on going to Magdalen College, but I must pass my exams first.'

'Then Jonathan, you have my best wishes for your success.'

'Thank you sir.'

Mr Neal intervened and rang the bell for Reid. 'Would you ask the ladies to join us for dinner?'

Reid departed as instructed and returned quite quickly with Charlotte, who immediately went up to William, put her arm in his and gave it a powerful squeeze, and looked adoringly into his eyes.

'I'm afraid sir that Mrs Neal asked to be excused, she has a severe headache again.

'Thank you Reid, we will go through to dinner now.'

William Neal the banker was furious at his wife's behaviour. How could she do this to her future son-in-law. Then he remembered her demands for his removal from the house all those years ago. She would never accept him. He had, and was secretly proud of the fine young man William had become. He had saved for his watch, and now his bank from disgrace and produced a revolutionary new scheme that would undoubtedly bring in new customers when the news got out. This evening was to plan the wedding. They would plan and his wife would just have to fall in with their arrangements. What other choice did he have?

Young William announced that he had agreed the purchase of the Hoxton Square house chosen by Charlotte and would complete the purchase on the March quarter day to allow time for decorations and furnishings to be in place in time.

'William dearest, that means our money will have to be in father's bank on that day doesn't it. I want you to pay on the next day.' She gave no explanation. He father knew why. She had just cost him and his bank more money.'

Discussions continued and decisions came thick and fast. Jonathan and three friends from Eton College would act as ushers and would wear their best school uniform (a cost saving0 and would be taken to St James's church, Piccadilly, where the wedding would be held first by Brampton in the coach. He would then return to collect Charlotte and her father, while he mother would be taken in a separate carriage to be hired for the day. That carriage would bring back the Neal's and the boys home for the wedding reception, while William and Charlotte would return in style in Brampton's coach.

William would join Charlotte and family when the wedding banns were read, as required by law, on three successive Sundays, and would have to start attending St Leonard's, Shoreditch, his parish, where the banns would also need to be read for him. And so all the planning continued until all the details had been finalised.

Mr Neal then spoke. 'William, I want you to make two promises, first that you will cherish my daughter and second that you will only bank with Neal's.'

'Yes sir, you have my solemn word.'

'Now William, you will need to employ your own household staff. Have you thought who you would like to have as your butler?'

'Yes sir, Reid.'

'You cheeky young puppy, you are taking my daughter and my butler, that is too much.'

'Yes to your daughter, but I want to take young Reid if I may. He has been well trained here and deserves promotion.'

'If it's young Reid then I will agree. Have you asked him yet?'

'No sir, I needed your permission first, but I am sure he will say yes.'

'Is there anything else we need to agree?'

'Yes sir. Fenwick and Neal will be pleased to print the wedding invitations without charge to you.' I should also like you to promise that your bank will only use Fenwick and Neal for all their printing requirements in the future.'

They all laughed. The plans were in place.

48

On the Monday morning following their family dinner, Charlotte rose early, dressed quickly, and met Miss G in the hallway. They climbed into Brampton's carriage together before the sun had even appeared. Today was the day she would begin shopping for furniture for her and William's new house in Hoxton Square. On the journey to the first destination, she chatted with Miss G excitedly about what they would buy and what her new home would look like. All the while, thoughts about the life that lay ahead of her filled her mind and she glowed with pride. She had escaped the controlling clutches of her mother, and was free to live how she wanted to.

Mr Neal had instructed Brampton to take Charlotte anywhere she wanted to go to purchase necessities for her home. The coach driver felt bitter that the low-life William had managed to secure Miss Neal's hand in marriage, and he did not exactly hide his anger. Regardless, he had to perform his duties, and so he had woken earlier than usual that morning to prepare the carriage for Charlotte.

'We're almost there, Miss Charlotte' Brampton hissed, as he turned the carriage down towards Pall Mall, heading for the Royal Opera Arcade.

'Thank you, Brampton' Charlotte replied brightly, pretending she had not noticed her coach driver's bad mood. Nothing could dampen her spirits today.

Brampton pulled up outside the shopping arcade and opened the door for Charlotte and Miss G. The two ladies stepped out and felt the sun hit them, the day was just beginning to warm up.

'Brampton, Miss G and I are likely to be here for most of the day so there is no point you sitting here for hours. We will be perfectly safe. Why don't you go off and busy yourself, then meet back here by 4 o'clock in the afternoon when the delivery carriages will arrive?'

'That is not protocol Miss Charlotte. I was instructed to take you where you need to go, and wait for you.'

'I am telling you to take these next hours off Brampton. Just be here by 4 o'clock to collect us, and you will have done your duty.'

Brampton nodded his head, got back into the carriage, and drove off. As he did so, the two ladies walked arm in arm into the Royal Opera Arcade, which was lined with a range of shops, some of which sold furniture and household items.

Charlotte pulled out the long list of furniture and household items she needed to purchase.

'There is one thing I have forgotten to mention Miss G' Charlotte piped up.

'Yes, Miss Charlotte?'

'I do not necessarily want to fill my new house with anything and everything. What is important is buying good quality furniture that will last a long time.'

Miss G smiled to herself. Despite being brought up surrounded by all kinds of riches, Charlotte was aware of getting value for her money. She was a smart and sensible girl.

'Well then, we had better get to work. It will take a long time to choose everything to fill up your whole house.'

The two ladies set to work choosing furnishings and decorations, ticking items off the list methodically. When the time came to meet Brampton, Charlotte had already chosen a sofa, armchairs, and coffee table for the living room, a table and chairs for the dining room, 3 beds for guest bedrooms, bookshelves for the library, and various pieces of decorative furniture, such as mirrors, vases, and paintings. Charlotte was a decisive and determined character. With Miss G's wise guidance to make sure she was paying the correct price for everything, they had had a very productive day.

Upon making her purchases, Charlotte had agreed that the items would be collected at 4 o'clock that day to be transported and stored at her current house. When Miss G and Charlotte walked out to the front of the Arcade, a row of carriages was there as expected. Charlotte handed details of the shops and furnishings to the men, and they began collecting everything she had bought. Charlotte insisted on staying to ensure everything was picked up. Finally, when the last mirror had been collected safely, Miss G and Charlotte climbed back into Brampton's carriage, and they followed the long line of vehicles back to the house.

The next days followed the same format. Brampton would take Charlotte to her chosen destination early in the morning, accompanied by Miss G, where the two would embark on a day of shopping. They travelled all around London, Charlotte grateful for once that she had been forced to attend those lunches with her mother, where the ladies had gossiped about the best and worst places to shop. Charlotte was careful yet quick in choosing her furnishings, ensuring that she always asked about the quality of the piece. By the following Saturday, everything had been crossed off her list and delivery of all items had been organised.

As she sat with Miss G, sipping tea at the end of their final shopping day she felt a sense of accomplishment. She loved putting her days to good use, as she had previously done at the bank and in helping the soldiers.

'Miss G?' she asked her friend.

'Yes, my dear?'

'Will William have to have a separate bedroom to me? My mother has told me he will, so I have bought furniture for his room, and for mine.'

'That is the general practice for your class, Charlotte, although it is becoming less so, Miss G said with a slight smile. 'It is up to you and your husband. You will have to decide what you want to do.'

Charlotte thought about her parents' loveless marriage, and how sorry she felt for her father. She did not want her marriage to be like that.

***

Mr Neal, much to the disapproval of his wife, had organised for Charlotte's new furniture to be stored in various rooms across the large house. Mrs Neal had suggested the barn, to which Mr Neal had replied, 'No, it will get damp or damaged out there'.

Now all they had to do was wait. Charlotte needed confirmation from William that, firstly, he had managed to purchase the house she had chosen and, secondly, when she would be able to start moving furniture in.

It came the very next day. Miss G handed Charlotte a thick envelope along with her breakfast. Charlotte opened it hastily and read a long letter from William, which included a confirmation that he had bought her the house she wanted, number 7 Hoxton Square finalising the purchase on the day after the March Quarter Day as she had asked. He also informed her that she could begin furnishing their home from the start of the next week. Charlotte felt excitement bubble inside her. There was much to do.

***

On the next Sunday evening, Charlotte told Brampton that she wanted to set off by 7 o'clock the next morning. The coach driver had to refrain from releasing a sigh of annoyance. She then found Miss G and asked if she would accompany her once more. She was not a requirement this time, but Charlotte had realised the woman had an extraordinary eye for detail and hoped she would be helpful in organising her house. Miss G agreed with a smile.

Charlotte awoke even earlier than necessary the following morning, feeling nervous and excited in equal measures. She had never executed a task like this, but she also relished the challenge of it.

On the way to Hoxton Square, the two ladies spoke occasionally, but the journey was mainly made in silence. Miss G felt quite tired to admit the truth, although she was happy to be helping Charlotte. Charlotte on the other hand was deep in thought. She was looking forward to seeing the inside of her new home and she was determined to make William proud in her task of furnishing it.

As the carriage pulled up outside number 7, Charlotte saw a woman standing outside observing the building. After a moment she realised who it was, let herself out of the carriage, and ran up to her.

'Mary!' she exclaimed, 'What are you doing here?'

'I received your letter saying you would be furnishing your house today, and I wanted to come and help you. Charlotte, this place is beautiful.'

'That is very kind of you to say, Mary, and even kinder to offer your help. With the three of us, I think we will make a wonderful job of this.'

The three ladies explored the empty shell of a house and the picturesque gardens which stretched out behind it, as they waited for the furniture carriages to begin arriving. They started to pull up mid-morning. Charlotte decided that the most efficient way to go about this would be to unpack one carriage at a time and deliver each piece of furniture to the desired spot. If Charlotte changed her mind at the end, she could just ask some of the men to do some moving around.

The team of people worked through the day, only stopping to eat the food that Cook had packed for all of them. The delivery men would carry each piece of furniture carefully out of the carriage and as they walked to the house, the three ladies would discuss the best position for it or which bed should go in which room. They would then place the furniture accordingly and move on to the next piece. By 9 o'clock that evening, the job was finally done. Charlotte waved all of the delivery men off, thanking them for their hard work.

The ladies walked around the house to observe the finished product. Charlotte had planned this perfectly. The house did not look too cluttered, nor too bare. The furnishings were tasteful and clearly good quality. She had even made one room into a library for William. There was just one job left to do.

* * *

William and Charlotte needed to hire some servants for their new house. Reid would be coming to work for them, but she still needed a cook, a footman, a couple of maids, and some gardeners. She approached her father to ask for advice.

'Father, I have now furnished my house completely but I still need to hire some servants. I have some money left over from furnishing the house which I can keep for my servants' wages. How shall I go about hiring them?'

'Leave that to me, Charlotte,' Mr Neal said. He wanted to ensure she had the best group of servants there was.

'That is very kind of you to help father. I would like a cook, footman, 2 maids, and 2 gardeners for now.'

'I will put some advertisements out or find suitable people myself,' Mr Neal said, thinking back to when he found William.

Within the next couple of days, Mr Neal found all of the servants Charlotte wanted. He called her to his office and explained this.

'These are all of their details, Charlotte,' Mr Neal handed her a long document, 'You will need to write to each of them and tell them when you would like them to start. You must agree with them their wages, duties, and any other benefits before they start working for you. You must tell them what you expect of them and what behaviour you will not tolerate. Is that clear?'

'Yes father. Thank you so much for your help. I will write to William now and tell him that I have organised the house and servants.'

Charlotte spent the rest of the day writing letters and finalising arrangements for number 7 Hoxton Square. It was not long until she would be married and living there now.

49

The counting machine, designed by Mr Brunel worked as expected. Fenwick and Neal printed five hundred numbered bank books and nine hundred and ninety-nine forms and delivered them to the bank for a handsome profit together with Sir Humphrey's new ink, although they kept secret from the staff why they had made that change. A subtle hint that it was cheaper and better sufficed.

As agreed, once he had trained the tellers in his new methods William left the bank in April to control the finances and find more customers for Fenwick and Neal, Printers.

Charlotte had created their new home from the shell of the house in Hoxton Square finalising their purchase on 26th March 1817, the day after the March Quarter Day. How she had done that convinced William he had chosen the best woman on earth to be his wife. She had even found space for William's own library.

Young Reid, Matthew, had agreed to be their butler, and had been busy with Cook and Miss G finding their domestic staff. He himself had moved to Shoreditch in June 'to make sure everything was as you would like it to be sir.' He had one other request for William.

'Sir, it was kind of you to invite me to your wedding, but I must decline. I wish to be here when you and Charlotte, sorry, Mrs Neal return home for the first time. It would be my duty and pleasure to open the front door for you and welcome you both to your new home.'

* * *

The great day, Saturday the fourth of July arrived. William set off early from Shoreditch wearing Ede and Ravenscroft's finest creation, accompanied by the Fenwicks.

Charlotte and her father left in Brampton's coach for St James's Church.

It was to be the happiest day of their lives.

Historical notes

The Earl of Brackenholm never existed. However there were large estates in the Scottish borders ruled over by generations of noble families. It was not unknown for one generation to be kind to their workers, an early form of socialism, while others could be very cruel and change policies when they succeeded to their titles.

Income tax began at a rate of 2 pennies (just less than 1 pence) in the pound and was introduced in 1792 by William Pitt, the Younger, to help pay for the Napoleonic Wars.

The names William, Robert and John were in common use in Scotland for boys at this time, while Annie and Elizabeth served the same function for girls. The names were often repeated for another child if the first born to carry that name had died. It was also common practice for Christian names to alternate between generations; William and Robert in this story. We know of at least one noble family in England that maintains this tradition.

Large families were common as was early death in childhood from measles, whooping cough, diphtheria tuberculosis and starvation.

Rudolf Virchow (1821-1902) working in Berlin, was one of the greatest and most influential physicians in medical history. He was the founding father of systematic autopsy with microscopy whose principals last to this day virtually unchanged. He established his own journal based on scientific method and understood aspects of public health. In 1848 he said 'wealth, education and liberty depend on one another and thus conversely do hunger, ignorance and servitude.

Similarly, puerperal or childbirth fever led to the death of many woman a few days after giving birth. The cause of this was not found until 1847 by Semmelweis working in the maternity department of the Lying in Hospital in Vienna.

The novel *Robinson Crusoe* was first published on 25th April 1719.

Black coats and armbands as a sign of mourning came into general use during the Regency from about 1770.

There was a drover's road from the borders to Carlisle where 300-400 of the prized black cattle could be moved and sold for a higher price in the English markets. William would have known about this. Other drover's trails existed in Lancashire, and it is quite possible that a handy lad would be passed from drovers group to drovers group as an unpaid assistant for his food only.

Drives of 10-12 miles per day were usually made. The usual number of drovers per group of cattle was 4-5 men. They lived rough while on the trail.

The Bridgewater Canal was opened in 1759 and ran from Worsley near what would become Manchester to Runcorn in Cheshire. Barges were horse drawn along a towpath.

The Press Gang was a group of navy sailors under the command of a junior officer who were given the legal right by the Crown under parliamentary authority dated 1703, 1705, 1740 and 1779 to size men for enforced compulsory service in the Royal Navy. Many merchant seamen were impressed. The practice was not used after 1815.

A further drover's road from Ynys Mon (modern Anglesey) went to London where again black cattle sold for high prices in Smithfield meat market. In 1794 more than 10,000 cattle a year made this journey, and numbers rose in subsequent years until the arrival of the railways. I have invented the route to the growing, and nearer, Birmingham conurbation.

The Grand Junction Canal opened from Birmingham to London in 1805. There were long tunnels at Braunston and Blisworth, the latter of which is said to be haunted. At the London end, one arm went to the river Thames at Brentford, the other to Paddington Basin. This arm had opened in 1801.

St Giles, a rookery, was an area of central London notorious as the haunt of criminals, prostitutes and the very poor.

The third Theatre Royal, Drury Lane opened in 1794 and lasted 15 years until it burned down in 1809. The fourth, and present theatre opened in 1812.

Up to the 19th century public hangings were a spectacle watched by thousands. The traditional place was Tyburn, what is now Speakers Corner at Hyde Park. The last hanging at Tyburn took place on the 3rd November 1783. Hanging then took place at Newgate Prison thus saving the unfortunate condemned the humiliation of being driven three miles across London in a cart. The practice of public hanging was abolished in 1868. Jack Jackson is fictitious.

William Neal the banker is an imaginary person, although there was a bank in London with a Mr Neal as one of the partners at the time in question.

Ede and Ravenscroft are London's oldest tailors having been founded in 1689. They are the leading suppliers of parliamentary, court and academic dress at the time in question and to the present day, when they hold three Royal Warrants.

Dr. James Lind was a brilliant naval surgeon who instituted the first medical clinical trial to show the benefits of fresh fruit to prevent scurvy, at a time when the Royal Navy were losing more men dying of that disease than killed in battle. He died in Gosport aged 78 years in 1794. For the purposes of this story he retired to London and was alive in 1815.

Adam Smith's *The Wealth of Nations* was first published in 1776.

Thomas Guy made his fortune printing and selling bibles. He founded the hospital in Southwark that bears his name to this day.

Shoreditch was a wealthy suburb to the east of the city of London. During the early 19th century many fine gentlemen's houses were built, some of which are still standing. There was a ready supply of workers for many trades from the poorer areas nearby. It would have been an ideal area for William Neal to take over a small printing works and build up a substantial business.

Burlington Arcade opened in March 1819. For the purposes of this story the opening has been moved back to 1816.

Weddings for non-conformists took place in Anglican churches well into the nineteenth century.

Traditional quarter days when accounts were settled are:

Lady Day	25th March
Midsummer Day	24th June
Michaelmas Day	29th September
Christmas Day	25th December

Other books in the *So Great A Man* trilogy

FORTUNE (release Sep 2018), *FINALE* (release spring 2019)

William Neal has married the banker's daughter and become wealthy printing books. His wife dies young, but they have a son, Robert. William wins the Brackenholm Estate from the conniving Earl in a game of cards and revives its fortunes. After his death, Robert sells his shares in the printing works and becomes a Member of Parliament. Robert's elder son William inherits the estate, while younger Robert decides on a career as a surgeon, marries a servant, and is disinherited.

CPSIA information can be obtained
at www.ICGtesting.com
Printed in the USA
LVOW10*1629040618
579518LV00006B/207/P